SHORT
MISSION

Book 2 in the McGregor and Moore Series

D.J. SCOTT

ACKNOWLEDGEMENTS

No book is the work of a single person. I want to recognize the enormous contributions of Dave King, my editor, and Alivia Kistler, my editorial assistant. Both made Short Mission a better book, and me a better writer.

Also, a special thanks to the people of Orkney, who welcomed and assisted me, and to whom I hope to return.

SHORT
MISSION

D.J. SCOTT

PROLOGUE

MARCH 5, 2019 0015 Z, 0215 LOCAL

USS *Theodore Roosevelt* (CVN 71) Eastern Mediterranean

COMMANDER JERRY "IRISH" O'Connor both heard and felt the satisfying 'clunk' as the tow bar of his F/A-18E Super Hornet engaged the catapult shuttle. The flight deck crew guided him through the check routine for his control surfaces. A quick inspection of his ordnance and he was ready for launch.

Tonight's ordnance load was the extended-range version of the reliable two-thousand-pound JDAM (joint direct attack munition), a weapon no one in O'Connor's squadron had ever delivered. This was why, as squadron commander, he had assigned himself to lead the four-aircraft strike. The usual JDAM was an ordinary bomb with a bolt-on guidance system that allowed weapon to direct its descent from altitude, then land within meters of its target. Its range of fifteen miles, however, was not quite enough for this mission. The JDAM-ER had small wings that would pop out after launch and—when launched from a high enough altitude—could add up to twenty additional miles to its range.

A quick salute to the catapult officer, and O'Connor was away. The mission profile called for approaching the Syrian coast at two hundred feet in order to stay below their radar. When his strike group was twenty miles out, the loitering EA-18G Growler electronic warfare aircraft began jamming the Syrian radar and the strike aircraft went to afterburner and climbed to 30,000 feet for weapons release. Timing was critical, as the Russians operating the Syrian's sophisticated S-300 air-defense system would respond quickly to the jamming and start to bring up additional radars.

O'Connor knew only that their target was a group of trucks moving Syrian weapons to the port of Latakia for shipment to Iranian allies in Yemen. According to an unnamed source, the convoy would spend the night in a secure location northwest of Homs. Once they stopped, the source would send a microsecond-burst transmission to a communications satellite, which would forward the location directly to the weapons systems of the four waiting Super Hornets.

Less than a minute after reaching altitude, a blinking light signaled that targeting information had been received and the weapons system indicated course and speed for weapons release.

When the computer-directed flight parameters were all within specs, O'Connor released the weapon. Freed of more than two thousand pounds, he was able to perform a snap roll and head for the deck. His squadron mates—visible in the moonlight—were doing the same.

It took almost five minutes for the JDAMs to reach their targets. Jamming was continued during this time, partly to reduce the already-low probability of an air-defense intercept, and partly to obscure their exact origin. The four impacts occurred within a second of each other and the acre occupied by the Syrian convoy, along with the millions of dollars' worth of weapons, was reduced to a field of smoking scrap metal.

Over the next few days, reports of mysterious deaths of civilians and livestock more than a mile from the attack trickled in from humanitarian agencies. Experienced observers thought these deaths sounded suspiciously like the effects of a nerve agent. But that made no sense.

Why would the Syrians use nerve gas on people allied with the Assad regime?

CIA analysts, however, who knew both the destination and the destruction of the convoy, wondered if Syria—and indirectly, Iran—had been shipping nerve gas to the Houthi fighters in Yemen. If so, the convoy represented a potentially alarming escalation.

MARCH 5
Patrick V. McNamara Federal Building; Detroit, Michigan

FBI SPECIAL AGENT Calvin DeSantos leaned back in his chair and gazed out the window of his office, across the calm water of the Detroit River. The ice was out early this year and maybe the weather on Lake St. Clair this weekend would be good enough for him and his brother to take out their twenty-four foot fishing boat.

His thoughts were interrupted by his desk phone. He forgot the weather for a moment, and picked up.

"Agent DeSantos? Gary at the front desk. There's a guy here says he has information about a suspicious Arab. Metal detector picked up something in his pocket."

Suddenly more alert, DeSantos asked, "A weapon?"

"No, just a piece of metal. Says he brought it to show you."

"Okay, I'll send Rick down to bring him up."

A few minutes later, Rick Willis, DeSantos's partner in the Counterterrorism Unit, showed a short fireplug of a man into their shared space on the twenty-sixth floor. DeSantos introduced himself.

"Joe Wozniak," said the man who extended a calloused hand. His grip was strong, and he gave the impression of being a man in charge.

"You have something to show us?"

Wozniak glanced at Willis, who removed a metal disc from his jacket pocket. He handed it to DeSantos, who examined it carefully. It was about six inches in diameter with a rounded flange around the edge, a round depression about the size of a quarter in the center, and a shallow channel going from the center depression to the edge. Judging from its weight...steel, maybe? It looked like a part from some gadget sold on cable for $19.95.

"What is it?" asked DeSantos.

"Damned if I know," replied Wozniak. We made five hundred for some outfit called Alliance Fabricating. They set up the deal with my boss, sent CAD specs. Then we did the tooling and stamped out all five hundred in a day. Pretty simple two-stage process."

"So what makes it suspicious?" asked DeSantos.

"For one thing, I've never heard of Alliance Fabricating, and I've been stamping metal for more than twenty years. Second, they sent a young Arab kid around to pick them up. He gave me an envelope with twenty-five hundred-dollar bills to give to the boss."

"That's unusual?"

"Sure it is. For big orders from our regular customers we usually invoice. Sometimes on a small one-time order like this, they pay with a credit card. Never with cash."

"What about this Arab kid? Was he local?"

"Don't know. Could be—no accent."

DeSantos turned to his computer and searched Alliance Fabricating on several public and internal FBI databases. Nothing.

"Well, it isn't illegal to buy stamped metal with cash, but I agree it is unusual. We'll look into it. Special Agent Willis will take a formal statement. Here's my card if something more comes up. Thanks for stopping by."

Wozniak seemed pleased to be taken seriously—blue-collar guys seldom were. DeSantos spent a few minutes examining the disc, trying to get some idea what it might be used for. He decided to let the lab guys take a look, bagged the disc, and then promptly forgot about it.

March 5

Aurora, Nebraska

JEANINE SANCHEZ WAS close to being late for work at McDonalds. The noon lunch rush would start soon, and she could not afford to be late again. But what could she do? Her class at Central Community College in nearby Grand Island had ended at 10:30, but her worn-out old Nissan wouldn't start—again—and it had taken twenty minutes to get a jump.

As she rushed towards the entrance, a young man in a grey hoodie pulled open the door and with his left hand lobbed what looked like a green ball, about the size of a softball, into the restaurant. He quickly turned and walked away.

He had just rounded the corner of the building when an explosion blew out all the front windows. Sanchez was showered with glass fragments and thrown to the pavement by the force of the blast. From inside, she began to hear screams.

The man in the hoodie jumped into a small silver SUV that pulled up just after the blast. In minutes, he and the driver were traveling west on I-80, where they watched emergency vehicles—lights flashing and sirens blaring—streaming east.

MARCH 19

Arkansas Technical University; Russellville, Arkansas

WITNESSES SAID HE looked like a student: windbreaker, ball cap, and a backpack. Several were sure he was a white guy. A few thought he could have been Hispanic and one was pretty sure he was an Arab, though he had to admit he didn't think that until after the explosion.

Everyone agreed that as he walked out of the library, he turned and rolled a ball—most said it was green—back down the entryway. The ball rolled against the wall, bounced off, and rolled a few more feet before hitting the foot of Jimmie Cook, a third-year engineering student.

Jimmie died instantly when the ball exploded.

Unlike the weapon used at Aurora, which had contained carpet tacks, pieces of glass, and some steel shrapnel, this one was filled with a mixture of buckshot and a powder that created a dense cloud of white smoke.

First responders were told they had to don gas masks before entering, which took time—especially because, unlike the firefighters, the ambulance crews didn't carry gas masks. The delay in care, combined with the more deadly buckshot, resulted in eleven deaths, compared to only five at Aurora.

The white powder was ultimately determined to be ammonium chloride, a relatively harmless industrial chemical used in some types of fertilizer. Though not very toxic, the high concentration released by the bomb induced a severe asthma attack in library employee Jessica Walsh, who died before first responders could get to her.

A witness saw the terrorist getting into a rusty and dented old SUV, confirmed later on a surveillance camera to be a 2001 Chevy Blazer. A few days after the attack it was found, completely burned out, in the nearby Ouachita National Forest.

Two terrorist attacks in small towns within two weeks, with sixteen dead and thirty wounded. Nobody claimed responsibility and there were no demands. And aside from the composition of the bombs, there was little forensic evidence.

CHAPTER 1

PRESIDENT BRENDAN WALLACE surveyed the faces of the people gathered in the Situation Room. He preferred small groups and specified that only people with something useful to say should be there. Unfortunately, he still had to deal with the inescapable needs of politics and bureaucracy. There was, for example, Harvey Lyon from Homeland Security, a capable administrator who had given long-overdue attention to the needs of the Coast Guard—something Wallace strongly endorsed . But despite aggressive briefings by his staff, Lyon was usually clueless and often deferred to one of his junior colleagues, now lined up against the wall. This was fine with Wallace, but why couldn't he just send the guy with the answers while staying in his office doing his job?

Alexander Clarkson from CIA, on the other hand, had an encyclopedic knowledge of relevant details. A Princeton grad from old New York banking money—both qualities Wallace usually disliked—Clarkson was weeding out some of the old curmudgeons at Langley and getting real results. He also had the capacity to admit ignorance on the rare occasions he had nothing to add.

To Wallace's immediate right was his National Security Advisor, Richardson "Sonny" Baker. Baker, an old friend and fellow Citadel grad, had come aboard just over a year ago when the war that Wallace, on the

1

advice of Baker's predecessor, had started with Iran over the latter's testing of a nuclear weapon began to go sideways. After thousands of American casualties and aircraft losses numbering in the hundreds, Baker was finally making progress in negotiations and was on the verge of getting a ceasefire. Nonetheless, an entire Army division still occupied Queshm Island in the Strait of Hormuz and almost half of all deployed naval vessels were still in the area. Baker was also at the center of last year's recovery of stolen Russian nukes from a regional warlord in Yemen. Though the operation lasted but twenty-four hours, US casualties numbered in the hundreds and it was only by luck and the courage of a few Navy and Marine Corps officers that dozens of wounded were not left behind and captured—or massacred. Despite the political peril still surrounding the war, he was the president's closest advisor and Wallace owed him a huge debt.

Finally, there was the new FBI Director, Frank Branigan. He had not been the president's first choice, but being politically weakened, Wallace was saddled with the favorite of the new Senate Majority Leader. So far, Branigan had proven competent and well-liked in the Bureau, but this would be his first genuine test

Standing behind Wallace was Karen Hiller, his Chief of Staff. The former South Carolina basketball player was smart, ambitious, and totally devoted to him—often defending the president to the point of undermining the rest of his advisors.

The president usually let his National Security Advisor run these meetings. In most administrations this job would fall to the Director of National Intelligence, but the DNI was undergoing complex treatment for an abdominal cancer. Wallace, with a background in intelligence himself, found this convenient as he could do the DNI's job himself while getting points for compassion by not replacing him. He trusted Sonny to prioritize the issues he knew Wallace would find most important.

"Go ahead, Sonny, let's get started. I hear there have been developments."

"Yes sir, several, and they may be related. Let's start with Frank."

"Mr. President," Branigan began, "you may have seen the report put together by our forensics people about the explosive devices used in these attacks."

"Read every word, Frank."

"Good, good. Several things struck us as odd. First, the design of each was essentially the same, but the explosive used was different. Ordinary dynamite in the first, but in the second they used RDX—a military explosive, much more powerful. Also, the first device was filled with carpet tacks and broken glass, while the second was a combination of buckshot—a lot more deadly—and ammonium chloride powder. The powder produced a dense cloud of white smoke, apparently designed to delay the first responders until they knew it wasn't some kind of WMD."

"Escalation, then," said Wallace. "The second was a step up in terms of lethality."

"Exactly. And now we may have a clue as to where they might be heading. We recovered pieces of shrapnel consisting of stamped sheet steel at both sites. The lab at Quantico put together a composite of what they looked like before detonation and one of the techs recognized it as probably the same as a metal disc sent in by an agent at the Detroit Field Office. Nobody had been able to identify it, but after linking it to a terrorist attack, details were disseminated to all field offices. An agent in Denver who had served in the Army identified it as being almost identical to a part from the M-139 bomblet, a 1960s-era device for delivering sarin with a short-range missile."

The mention of the word "sarin" brought an audible intake of breath around the table. Branigan put up several photographs on a large flat-screen monitor. They showed the metal disc from Detroit, a digital reconstruction of the recovered fragments, and finally, the part from an actual M-139 bomblet. There was no escaping the similarity.

"Mr. President," Sonny added, "the fact that they escalated to use of a chemical payload, albeit a benign one, and the fact that they have a device obviously capable of disseminating a nerve agent is of grave concern."

"Grave?" exclaimed the president. "For Christ's sake, Sonny, we've got a terrorist or team of terrorists bombing multiple targets with the potential to move up to nerve gas. Could this get any worse?"

"Yes, sir. I'm afraid it can," Brannigan said. "The sample our people got came from a manufacturer who made them to order. They made five hundred."

"Oh, dear God."

Karen Hiller injected, "We need to think about the publicity."

Wallace spun around. "God damn it, Karen, we've got better things to worry about than the press."

"No, sir," she said. "The press is the point. They're already making connections between the two attacks, and people are already nervous enough. What do you think is going to happen when the media gets hold of the sarin angle?"

Wallace was about to say something, but he paused. She was right. The reason they were starting slow, the reason the bombs were so distinctive, was to create panic. That was the battle they were fighting. "Right. What do you recommend?"

"Well naturally, there must be a news blackout on this information. Highest priority national security classification."

He might have guessed. Hiller's style rarely included transparency where the public was involved.

"Right, look how well that worked with those Russian nukes in Yemen." Wallace laid his hands flat on the table. "We have to get this under control, and now!"

"Totally agree, sir," Sonny said. "I think Alex has something that might be useful in that regard." Sonny Baker looked at Alexander Clarkson with eyebrows raised, a look that screamed, "This better be good."

"Sir," Clarkson began, "two days ago our Station Chief in London was handed an envelope by a messenger while having dinner at a restaurant across the Thames from our embassy." A single piece of paper was displayed on the flat-screen. It read:

You are the CIA Chief of Station for the United Kingdom. Please pass along this offer to your superiors.

I am Maxim Korshkin. I came to your attention last year regarding that unfortunate incident in Yemen. Don't think me disingenuous when I say that I profoundly regret the loss of American lives associated with the recovery of those warheads.

It may be possible for me to compensate you for your losses. First, you may or may not know that I am, in reality, not simply the small dealer in arms information that I pretended to be. I am, in fact, Janos, the man who arranged the sale. In my own defense, I am sure you know by now that those warheads had been modified to make them unusable and the plans for the permissive action link encoder that I provided were likewise useless.

Let me provide you with a bit of context. First, the British security services have learned of my true identity. They are determined to prosecute me, and no doubt wish to imprison this old man for many years. Second, my former masters in the Kremlin, likely through leaks from the British, are apparently seeking to spare me the indignity of prison by simply ending my life in as violent a manner as possible. As if this weren't bad enough, my health has failed dramatically, and I am unable to flee—or I surely would.

Now to your troubles. A few days ago, a former customer rang me up and, apparently unaware of my current diminished status, was eager to obtain about a hundred kilos of sarin or a similar nerve agent for delivery in North America. He did not identify himself, but he has a very distinctive voice which I recognized immediately. I was, understandably, in no position to help him and I forgot the matter. That is, until I acquired information that your FBI had identified the terrorist devices used in those two horrible attacks as essentially M-139 sarin bomblets. I thought it interesting that, while you are being attacked with devices capable of delivering sarin, I was in contact with someone looking for sarin. I believe I am in a favorable position to help you.

This is my proposal. You will send a physician who will make me capable of travel and then take me out of Britain to a very safe place where I will then identify the individual you are looking for and even provide you with an old photograph and some valuable background. You will provide an ongoing safe residence and will not reveal my whereabouts to anyone. Signal your acceptance by placing a wine bottle in the window of your flat (yes, I know where you live).

Faithfully yours,
Maxim Korshkin

"Disingenuous?" exclaimed Karen Hiller. "That's an understatement. That son of a bitch sells nuclear warheads to a Yemeni terrorist, and we lose more than a hundred Marines getting them back. Now he wants to trade for his own hide?"

"Steady, Karen." Wallace was every bit as angry as she was, but there were larger issues at stake. "That operation was hard on everyone. Let's hear everything Alex has first."

The CIA man continued. "Our Chief of Station cabled Langley immediately and we authorized some discrete contact with the British while having one of our senior people here in DC do the same. Not good. The Brits want this guy's hide. We're hearing that any attempt to remove this Korshkin from the UK will be viewed very seriously. If they so much as hear of our people looking for him, or even have any new Agency people enter the country, they promise trouble at the highest levels. And unfortunately, the Brits know virtually everyone in our intelligence agencies, including military."

"I don't get why this is such a problem. Wouldn't something like this be covered by Five Eyes?" asked the president.

"Not exactly," replied Clarkson. "Five Eyes is an intelligence sharing agreement among the five major English speaking countries, but its focus has primarily been signals intel, and each country has at times withheld information it deems of vital interest. And this case involves a British citizen who they regard as a fugitive in their own country. I don't think we can push them too much."

"And there's another problem," said Baker. "We're about to integrate their new carrier, HMS Queen Elizabeth, plus several escorts into our Fifth Fleet to replace the Reagan battle group for operations in the Gulf. You know Reagan's at least six months from completing repairs after that Iranian torpedo attack."

"Yes, and we have just about completed a major post-Brexit trade deal among ourselves, Canada, the UK, and Australia," Wallace said. "A serious British reaction could squash that too. I can see why they're touchy about this guy, but why won't they at least work with us? They usually take a big picture view."

Clarkson paused a second. "Somebody high up in the security services, a fellow called Neville Cathcart. He used to be Korshkin's contact—he worked as a double, you know—and was obviously incensed to learn that he and the entire intelligence community had been snookered by this fellow for decades. Cathcart has apparently made it his mission to take revenge on Korshkin and has used his influence to agitate his superiors, who then got some important MPs involved. Now even the Prime Minister wants his scalp."

"Well, the timing couldn't be worse," said Wallace. "Korshkin probably has nothing and is just trying to save himself, but we can't risk a sarin attack on US soil. We need to make an effort. How will the public react if they knew we could have prevented a nerve gas attack in Iowa, but passed on a chance to identify the terrorist because we didn't want to offend the British?"

"Our scalps would be as much at risk as Korshkin's," replied Sonny Baker. "The British aren't stupid, so we can assume the assets we currently have in country will be under scrutiny and we're limited as to whom we can send. A covert infiltration would be fairly easy—Britain isn't North Korea—but a covert op in a friendly country could really set off the Brits."

"Any kind of op in a friendly country is a delicate matter," Clarkson added, "but when we've already been warned off—that's playing with fire."

Brendan Wallace tented his fingers and thought for a moment. "Sonny, how about this?" All eyes turned from notepads and computer screens and were riveted on the president. As a former intelligence analyst himself, Wallace had more than once surprised the professionals.

"Remember the two officers who were in command of those sailors and Marines that were left behind in Yemen?"

Karen Hiller answered what was obviously a rhetorical question. "You mean that insubordinate Navy doctor who refused an order to surrender and shot his way back to the beach where he wrecked another officer's career by pressuring him to ignore a direct presidential order and pick them up in a landing craft?"

"Yes, Karen, that's the one. Though in fairness, he was not ordered to surrender, he was authorized to surrender. And remember, he was awarded the Navy Cross and that Marine captain with him received the Medal of Honor. Those two are reservists, probably not on the British radar, can obviously handle themselves in a tough spot, and most important they have the skill sets we need. If I recall, their civilian jobs are an ER doctor and a police detective." Wallace gave a small smile of satisfaction, obviously pleased with his own idea.

"There's no exposure for the Agency or for State. Even if the whole thing falls apart, we just tell the Brits a couple of well-meaning reservists overstepped their bounds and apologize profusely. Anybody got a better idea?" This was how Wallace liked to signal he had made his decision. Nobody ever had a better idea.

"Hopefully, we can at least keep those two on a short leash," added Karen Hiller.

"We do have someone experienced in managing missions run by, ah, amateurs," Alexander Clarkson said. "Sometimes people with special access like a businessperson or an athlete and other times individuals from other agencies with specialized skills, but lacking in tradecraft, can still be effective in gathering useful intel. The British GCHQ, similar to our NSA, is very proficient at communication intercepts, but we do have something that should allow reliable contact with them."

"Is this some kind of new encryption the Brits can't break?" asked Baker.

"No," replied Clarkson. "We do have that kind of encryption, but anything like that originating from within their own borders would attract their attention, and teaching complex comm protocols takes time. What I'm thinking of is a frequency-hopping algorithm that uses a part of the spectrum they don't normally monitor. It's very short range, but our embassy comm people can handle it as long as they're in London. Beyond that we'll have to work with the Air Force to have an aircraft nearby on some kind of routine flight that can receive their burst transmission. They could forward it by satellite. Obviously, encrypted traffic from our own military aircraft would attract no attention."

"All right then," said the president. "With our new SECDEF nominee still waiting on a Senate vote, I'll leave it to Sonny to get in touch with the Commandant and get their orders written. You'll need to work up good cover stories for why they're being sent to Britain. Alex, you better let the Chief of Station know, but for God's sake have him steer clear of the whole thing. If our COS gets involved there'll be no denying anything. Karen, I want a daily update from everyone involved. And Frank, don't depend on this little sideshow bailing out the Bureau. We need results on your end—and soon."

To a chorus of, "Yes, Mr. President," Wallace stood and strode from the room, followed closely by Karen Hiller who was still tapping on her tablet while she walked.

CHAPTER 2

MIKE MCGREGOR WAS already tired, and he still had almost three hours to go before finishing his shift at the University of Michigan ER. The day had started with a student texting while riding his bike across campus. He had crashed into a tree and fractured several ribs, punctured his left lung, and ruptured his spleen. McGregor had inserted a chest tube and ordered an emergency CT scan, all the while the young man's blood pressure continued to sag. With transfusions started, he was whisked into surgery.

McGregor hoped there would be a few minutes of peace, but then the heart attack arrived, quickly followed by Hector Ortiz, a well-known professor and author who happened to live next door to McGregor. Ortiz was suffering from advanced pancreatic cancer, the slow-growing kind that had ultimately killed Steve Jobs. He had begun vomiting blood. He told no one, in hopes he would just slip away, but then his daughter stopped by and called 911.

"Michael," he said, "Isabella wants to fight this cancer, but she's not the one doing the fighting. I am, and the fight has finally gone out of me."

"You can refuse treatment," McGregor said. "We may be able to get your bleeding under control, but that won't help the tumor. I'm sure your oncologist has told you that already."

"Of course. But now that Isabella is involved, her sisters will soon follow, and they will all tell me what a fighter I am. How can an old man disappoint his daughters?"

"Isabella's a tiger, that's for sure."

McGregor's own father had died from a rare type of leukemia for which there were few treatments at the time. His mother and sister had encouraged the same kind of prolonged fight and young Mike didn't have the heart to speak up. It was the classic struggle: exhaustion versus the unwillingness to let go. He wished he had a good answer.

"Would you like me to speak with her, before you make any decisions?" he asked.

"Yes, Michael, that would be very kind. And could you feed Maria when you get home? I may be detained here." Maria was Hector's cat, a huge grey tabby he had rescued from the street.

"You know I will."

Just then, one of the front-desk staff poked her head in. "Sorry to interrupt, Dr. McGregor, but one of your Marines is here. Says it's urgent."

Dr. Mike McGregor was also Lieutenant Commander McGregor, battalion surgeon for the first battalion, 28th Marine regiment based at the nearby reserve center just south of Ann Arbor. It was not unusual to receive a call from the staff at the 1/28 while he was at work, but he could not recall one of them actually showing up. This was probably not good news.

He excused himself and walked out to the waiting room where he recognized Lance Corporal Laura Kyle, one of the clerks from the headquarters company. She was wearing freshly pressed alphas, the dark green working uniform, and she immediately snapped to attention.

"At ease," said McGregor. "What's this about?"

She handed him a sealed envelope.

"This just came off the printer from Regiment. Instructions to hand deliver. Corporal Gonzalez is delivering the same message to Captain Moore right now."

He looked at the sealed envelope. Orders. Not again!

Detective Kelli Moore was in the basement of the Ann Arbor Government Center pounding on her computer. She was nearly finished with the arrest report on a guy who had stolen five expensive motorcycles in the last three months. The fact that she had stopped him by opening her car door as he sped past was causing her a fair amount of grief. The door of her squad had been torn off, the stolen Ducati had been seriously damaged, and the thief had dislocated his shoulder and suffered quite a bit of road rash. Careful attention to detail was a must in this report.

"Detective Moore, Marine here to see you," one of the officers at the front desk yelled back.

Moore, after graduating from Annapolis, had served as a Marine MP with tours in Iraq and Afghanistan. Her reserve MP Company, however, had been decimated in an operation the previous year tasked with retrieving stolen Russian nuclear warheads. At the moment, her reserve duty was as assistant operations officer for the 28th Marine Regiment. Not the kind of duty that had Marines visiting her at work.

Moore walked to the front desk where Corporal Tony Gonzalez handed her a sealed envelope.

She gave him a quizzical look to which he replied, "Got no idea Captain. They just told me to deliver this and then make the SCIF ready for a meeting."

The message was brief, in typical military style.

To: LCDR Michael McGregor, MC, USNR,

           Captain Kelli Moore, USMCR

From: Commanding Officer 28th Marine Regiment, FMF

SUBJ: MEETING

1. You will report at 1615 to the Navy and Marine Corps Reserve Center, Ann Arbor.

2. You will meet with such person or persons as the command directs.

3. Civilian attire.

Aaron Mark

Colonel, USMCR

Civilian attire? Mysterious meeting in a secure facility? This couldn't be good.

CHAPTER 3

THE RESERVE CENTER was just south of the city on Stone School Road. The old stone school was still there, but it was currently a daycare center.

Moore had just pulled into the parking lot and was getting out of her BMW Z4 when Mike McGregor pulled in behind the wheel of a ten-year-old Ford Explorer in desperate need of a wash.

Moore gave his ride a long, skeptical look and dryly observed, "Has the University fallen on hard times?"

"I keep thinking about a new car, but this gets me around. And besides my dog likes it. So, any guesses why we're here?"

"Only that it's something we couldn't guess. Though I am guessing it's not good."

The pair presented themselves to the corporal at the front desk who—despite knowing both of them—made a show of inspecting their ID cards. "You're supposed to go right down to the SCIF," he said.

They descended a flight of stairs to a corridor labeled "Secure Classified Information Facility: Authorized Personnel Only." The red "IN USE" light above the SCIF door was out, so they went in. Seated at one end of the small conference table was a scowling man in his late twenties—clearly a Fed with an athletic build, close-cropped hair, and an

15

off-the-rack tan suit. His face was slightly flushed with a hint of jowls. This, combined with his drooping brown eyes, gave the impression of a malevolent bulldog. He activated the "IN USE" light, then held out his hand without saying a word and the two officers correctly assumed he wanted to see their ID's. After a cursory inspection, he said "Sit."

Neither Moore nor McGregor moved towards the chairs. Moore said, "And you are?"

"I'm the man who just told...you...to...sit...down!" His flaring nostrils and clenched fists were flashing the clearest of danger signals.

As an ER physician and a police detective, McGregor and Moore both recognized a bully when they saw one. The urge to push back was irresistible.

"And she's the woman who just told you to identify yourself," replied McGregor. He was senior in rank and felt he should take charge with this disagreeable jerk.

The young Fed stood and regarded the two belligerent reserve officers. After a brief stare down, he produced a cred pack which identified him as Special Agent Craig T. Fuller of Homeland Security. Moore made a show of inspecting his creds a bit too long, and then said to McGregor, "Seems legit." They all sat down.

"You two are being considered for a highly sensitive operation, the details of which are classified way above your level," Fuller said.

"So, we're being considered for a mission you can't tell us about?" replied McGregor. "Being considered by whom? Is this a Marine Corps op, or something out of a DC spook shop?"

"Look, I'm here to assess your qualifications. Period. I'm not here to answer your questions."

"So, we've been selected for something super-secret and the people doing the selecting don't know enough about us to judge whether we're actually qualified?" McGregor glanced at Moore.

"I'm pretty certain we're not qualified for this train wreck," she said. "Can we leave now?"

Agent Fuller slammed his fist down on the table. "Shut the fuck up—both of you! I can see why they had doubts about you two. You're obviously unstable."

"Hey, we're not the ones pounding the table." McGregor pushed his chair back, stood, and said to Moore, "We're outta here."

Fuller was surprisingly quick. He leaped from his chair, pushed McGregor against the wall and got a forearm against his throat. "You aren't going anywhere until I say so, asshole."

McGregor, was getting a bit nervous. Fuller had a lot of leverage, and with only a bit more pressure McGregor's airway would be completely cut off. McGregor raised his foot and slammed it down on the Fuller's instep. This produced a yelp of pain and the pressure on McGregor's throat decreased, but not by much.

Before McGregor could make another move, however, he heard a 'thunk.' Fuller staggered back. Moore had hit him in the side of the head with her SIG P320 and quickly followed this by grabbing his collar and hurling him back against the opposite wall where he slumped to the floor. He recovered fairly quickly, but by then she had her weapon pointing at him. She took a step back, well out of his reach, and said, "Agent Fuller, you are under arrest for assault on Federal property. I'm going to detain you and notify the Federal Marshalls." Her weapon did not waver, and her tone was deadly serious.

"Are you out of your fucking mind? You are going down, lady. You and your pal here are going down hard."

"Get on your feet. Hands against the wall, feet back, and spread. You know the drill." Fuller, sensing Moore was not screwing around, did as he was told.

"Mike, his weapon is on his right side—hip holster. Agent Fuller, do not even breathe while you're being disarmed. I've already got four pounds on a six-pound trigger." McGregor retrieved his weapon, a Glock 19. "Okay, good. Now grab his cuffs. Fuller, do you have a backup weapon? Don't lie or it's going to get very ugly."

"No backup. Look, there's time to walk this back. Once the Marshalls get involved it's the point of no return."

"No backup? Figures. You probably think that big mouth will keep you out of trouble." McGregor dropped the cuffs on the table beside the Glock and after a quick pat down, confirmed there were no more weapons.

Moore took the pistol then told Agent Fuller to sit down. "Put your cuff key on the table, and then cuff your right wrist to the table leg." Fuller looked down to see the table was firmly attached to the concrete floor. He glared at Moore, who pocketed the key to his cuffs.

"I'm sure you know your phone won't work in the SCIF and that nobody can hear you outside the room."

Fuller shook his head in disbelief as Moore and McGregor walked out and secured the door behind them.

On the way out of the building Moore gave Fuller's Glock to the Corporal who had checked them in. She had removed the magazine and field stripped the weapon into parts.

"Corporal, wait fifteen minutes, then go down to the SCIF. You may uncuff Agent Fuller—here's the key—and let him go. Commander McGregor and I are done here."

The astonished Marine replied, "Um...sure.... Yes, Captain."

In the parking lot, Moore said, "Well, that's going to become a shit-storm pretty fast. Any ideas?"

"Yeah, let's grab a pizza. We either proved that we are perfectly qualified for this mission, or we're about to go to prison. Either way, we might not get another for a long time. How about the Cottage Inn? Should be quiet this time of day."

"Why not," replied Moore. "We better get moving. Fuller will be on the phone in..." — she looked at her watch–"twelve minutes."

Half an hour later they were just getting started on a loaded New York thin crust and a couple of beers when McGregor's phone rang. He pulled it out.

"It's the Colonel. I might as well take it. No point in pissing him off any more than he probably is already."

McGregor hit the answer button on his iPhone and immediately heard the raspy baritone of Colonel Aaron Mark. "McGregor, is that you? Is Moore with you? Put me on speaker."

"Uh, yes, Colonel, we're both here. We're in a public place though, sir. Maybe the speaker isn't a good idea."

"I don't care if you're walking down Main Street. Just do it." McGregor activated the speaker.

Moore swallowed. "Captain Moore here, sir."

"I'm not calling to chat. That happens tomorrow. Reserve Center at 0900. Dress blues and alphas. Be there!" Before either officer could say a word, Mark clicked off.

Their water walked up and asked, "Another round of beers for you two?"

They both nodded.

CHAPTER 4

MIKE MCGREGOR ARRIVED first. He took the jacket for his dress blue uniform off its hanger in the back seat and slipped it on. He looked down to be sure his ribbons were straight and the regulation quarter inch above the left breast pocket. There were fifteen ribbons in five rows, a lot for a medical officer, though some were from McGregor's earlier service as an enlisted corpsman. The two that most people noticed first were the Navy Cross and the Purple Heart, both with tiny bronze oak leaves signifying a second award.

A minute later Kelli Moore sped into the lot and hopped out of her BMW. Moore was wearing the Marine Corps Service A uniform known as alphas. This was the dark-green working uniform the Colonel had specified. To McGregor's surprise she was wearing trousers rather than the green skirt—a little shorter than regulation, along with heels a bit higher—which she usually wore. Mike knew this annoyed the Colonel, so obviously even the belligerent Kelli Moore knew when to dial it down.

Moore wore twelve ribbons, including a Bronze Star and a Purple Heart—as with McGregor's, her second. What stood out, however, was the pale blue ribbon with five tiny white stars, the Medal of Honor.

They stood silent for a moment, then McGregor said. "Can I ask just one question?"

"Just one?"

"Why didn't you turn Fuller over to the Marshalls?"

"He was right. That would have been the point of no return. Getting another agency involved would have sent the whole thing out of control."

Mike shrugged, and they walked briskly into the Reserve Center where the same Corporal—this time without asking for ID—nodded towards the stairs. "I never said this, but nice job on that Fed Captain."

McGregor thought he detected a slight smirk from Moore as they entered the SCIF, tucked their covers under their left arms, and snapped to attention.

Seated at the table was Colonel Aaron Mark, commanding officer of the 28th Marines. Next to him was a small, intense-looking man with a long nose, slightly tinted glasses, and a shaved head. He wore an exquisitely tailored pearl-grey suit with the starched white shirt and plain red tie that had become the hallmark of Washington insiders.

"Lieutenant Commander McGregor and Captain Moore reporting as ordered, sir."

Without a handshake or invitation to sit, the civilian began. "I am FBI Deputy Director Wayne Saunders. I head the task force pursuing the terrorists who bombed those towns in Nebraska and Arkansas. I am not here to discuss those cases, however. I am here to resolve the situation with Agent Fuller. Frankly, I had my doubts about you two. The mission you've been selected for is extremely sensitive and requires people who are smart, controlled, and able to exercise the best possible judgment. I sent Fuller to see if you could take a bit of pressure. Turns out he lacks judgment and self-control as much as you two. If it were up to me, I would shitcan all three of you. But it's not up to me. Homeland wants to give Fuller cover, and he's been reassigned to New Mexico. As for you two, I now know that your selection originated well above my pay grade. I need to know if, despite the fiasco with Fuller, both of you can accept this mission in the dark. It's vitally important, that I can tell you. If you agree, you will receive a complete briefing tomorrow. In or out?"

McGregor looked with indifference at Saunders. He turned his gaze to Aaron Mark. "Colonel, we work for you. What's your position on this?"

Mark looked, more than anything, very sad. "Commander, I'm sorry you were treated this way. I had no idea what was being planned or I would have put a stop to it. If Fuller was one of my officers, he would be history. But I wasn't consulted, and Fuller doesn't work for me. The reality is that you are two extraordinary officers who have repeatedly proven yourselves in tough situations. We're asking you—I'm asking you—to take this mission on faith."

"Colonel, you have always been straight with me," replied McGregor. "I'll do it, but I don't know how many of these spook shows I have left in me."

"Captain Moore?" Mark turned to Kelli Moore and gave a slight smile, like a coach letting a player know he thinks she's up to taking the last-second shot.

"What he said, I guess."

"That's what we came for," said Saunders. "Be here at noon tomorrow for a complete briefing. This will be given by someone from the Agency who will actually run the operation from here out. Try to use a bit more finesse, will you?" With that, he picked up a thin leather portfolio and strode from the SCIF without looking back.

Aaron Mark regarded both his officers. "I really can't tell you much. They have kept me in the dark—need to know. I do want you to know this Fuller thing has created a lot of heat, so don't plan on FBI or Homeland sending you any love. I doubt that the Agency cares one way or the other—they would probably have been fine if you had shot the idiot. As for me, I do know that we left you left behind in Yemen and that I will do everything in my power to keep you from being hung out again." He produced two small cards. "Here's a satphone number. It's mine, not tied to the Corps. I'll have it with me 24/7."

"Thank you, sir." Moore seemed genuinely touched.

"One more thing," said the Colonel. "Those medals you're wearing don't come without a price. I'm just asking you to think about that. Something to look at more closely when you're back."

Both officers nodded slightly but said nothing.

"Good luck. At least this sounds like a short mission."

"Right," said McGregor. "The last mission took twenty-four hours, and look what happened."

CHAPTER 5

C IA OFFICER JENNIFER Kim rode in the back of an old Marine Corps van driven by the same Corporal who had greeted McGregor and Moore the day before. In front of her was her security escort. The original plan had been to brief the two reserve officers at Langley, but at the last minute someone above her pay grade had changed his mind. Kim was carrying both documents and hardware so sensitive that commercial air was out of the question, so the Agency sent her in one of their own jets. The aircraft would wait for her at nearby Willow Run Airport while she briefed her new mission, Operation Pegasus.

Kim came from an Agency family. Her grandfather had run high risk missions into China and North Korea in the early fifties, earning him the chance to emigrate to the US after the war. Her father had been an Asia analyst and translator. Kim had been recruited out of Boston College. Her fluent Russian—plus the Korean she had picked up at home—and a degree in International Studies was exactly what the Agency wanted now that Russia was squarely back on their radar. Jennifer had also inherited her Irish mother's long legs and love of sports. She was an avid participant in triathlons, and having completed the grueling Hawaiian Ironman, she breezed through physical training at The Farm, the CIA training camp in rural Virginia.

Kim was assigned to the Directorate of Operations, where she turned in a solid performance in her first two postings to Belarus and Romania. She had been a meticulous case officer with excellent trade craft—until "the incident." One of her agents, an officer in Romanian SIE—successor to the dreaded Securitate under Ceaușescu—had been followed by a counterintelligence officer to a meet near the Carpathian Mountains. Jennifer was armed and had seconds to decide whether to sacrifice her agent or risk an incident by shooting a foreign national. In the end, she delayed too long and her agent was killed in the shootout. Jennifer succeeded in taking out the shooter, but came very close to being killed herself when a bullet fragment barely missed her femoral artery. The Romanians were certain there had been CIA involvement, and Agency operations in that country had been set back for at least a year. And she'd still lost her agent.

She felt she deserved to be canned. The Agency, though, understood that this was a dangerous game and, not wanting to lose a talented young officer, found her a position that seemed well suited to her skills, but largely kept her out of the field. She was assigned to prepare and to debrief American citizens traveling to nations either hostile to the United States, such as Russia or North Korea, or who might be privy to political or technical information of interest to the Agency. These people, known as "the amateurs" to her peers, had included the coach of a volleyball team traveling to North Korea, a ballerina dining at the Kremlin, and several engineers consulting with Chinese companies. Kim was grateful for this second chance and tried to convince herself she was doing important work. Even her skeptical colleagues had to respect the occasional piece of real intel her little operations generated.

Kim knew that several days earlier a group of Agency grandees had a heated discussion about who should run Pegasus. One wanted to dump the whole thing back on Defense; they were, after all, using DOD personnel. Another wanted someone senior and very experienced. They finally agreed, however, that the odds of success were so small, and the chances of a major flap with the British security services so great, that it was best to push running of the op as far down as possible to limit collateral damage.

Kim knew her situation well enough to know she was competent enough, but also expendable—perfect for the job. She would do. And if the whole thing went sideways, they could simply say goodbye to her and suggest that the National Security Council had blundered by choosing a couple of reserve officers in the first place. This was all little more than office gossip, but it had the disquieting ring of truth.

Kim was nervous about Pegasus. Unlike her other "amateur" ops, this involved actual clandestine activity—exfiltration of a source from an admittedly friendly country, but one that was seriously opposed to the US getting their hands on him. She knew that most of the people aware of Pegasus felt this was either a provocation of some kind, or that the subject, Maxim Korshkin, was simply trying to save his own hide. Nonetheless, it was possible that he actually possessed valuable information about the terrorist bombings that now threatened to include use of a nerve agent.

There was one more thing about this op. It was her chance to get back in the game. Or to end her career trying. She was good with that.

Involving military personnel was in itself problematic. These were people used to a well-defined chain of command versus the often fuzzy lines of authority in Agency ops. They liked clear rules of engagement, while the Agency tended to clarify the rules only after the fact. And these two could very well have residual trust issues after being left behind in hostile territory just last year. Nonetheless, they were her people for the duration of the mission, and it was her job to earn their trust.

As she walked into the reserve center, Kim fussed a bit with her shoulder length hair and stopped to smooth her khaki skirt. Her starched white shirt, ubiquitous in the Agency, had come through the flight without a wrinkle. She resented how much professional women were judged by their attire, but bowing to that reality, she had carefully chosen the blue blazer and small hoops to complete her outfit. She knew these two officers had recently seen serious combat and were certainly not going to be intimidated by a power suit—the incident with Agent Fuller had proved that. As a physician and a police detective, she assumed they would respect competence, and she wanted to project the image that she knew what she was doing.

McGregor and Moore rose when Kim entered the SCIF. She extended her hand to each and gave them a warm smile. Her new agents wore camouflage uniforms and seemed relaxed, though each radiated a reasonable skepticism. Showtime, thought Kim.

She appraised her new team. The female officer, Kelli Moore, was a tall redhead, about her own height of five foot ten, with remarkably green eyes. She was attractive without working at it and looked extremely fit. She had an intensity about her that was slightly intimidating. Michael McGregor was a bit taller, lean, but not really athletic, with a relaxed, somewhat detached, demeanor. His eyes were a pale grey, like looking into fog, and gave the impression that there was always something going on behind them.

She put down her heavy case, introduced herself, and asked to see ID, which both officers produced without objection. She presented Agency credentials in turn and they all sat.

"After we leave this room and for the duration of this operation, codename Pegasus, Commander McGregor will be 'Keystone,' Captain Moore 'Empire,' and I will be 'Dover'." You will use these in all communications related to the mission. Your comm device will contain codenames for other individuals to whom you may need to refer. I will be your controller and primary contact."

Mike McGregor smiled slightly at the mention of the codenames, but he said nothing. Moore just nodded.

"I have reviewed both your records and the background of the mission. There is some overlap between your last deployment and this mission, so in my judgement, this is one of those times when transparency will serve better than secrecy. I'll share with you some background I've learned about Operation Ocean Reach—your op in Yemen—and I'll appreciate your answering a few questions for me."

Again, nods from each, but not a word.

"Last August, six Russian submarine-launched missile warheads went missing from a reconditioning facility in Gadzhiyevo, up in the Kola Peninsula." Mention of the warheads elicited an immediate reaction from both officers. Moore leaned forward on her elbows and focused on Kim with those extraordinary eyes. McGregor sat straighter, raised his eyebrows, and assumed a demeanor best described as dark. Kim had expected something like this.

"The theft was believed to have been carried out by the facility manager, Alexi Kovolenko, his girlfriend Anna Voronina, and her brother Boris. All three have disappeared. A source, Stella, jointly run by the Agency and MI6, tipped us off. I'm telling you this because Stella has escaped to Britain and it's possible one of these names might come up. The warheads, as you know, were traced to a Yemeni warlord, Abdullah Nazer. Operation Ocean Reach was activated and the 28th Marine Regiment, your regiment, was tasked with their retrieval from the small city of Arad in Eastern Yemen. When our engineers back on the supporting ships opened the containers, one warhead was missing. At that point Nazer called the President and told him the missing warhead was somewhere on the East Coast and that if US forces were not withdrawn immediately, he would reveal that a nuclear device was hidden in an American city."

Moore finally spoke up. "Naturally, we heard none of this before we were deployed. Who stole them and from where was a mystery until now. I appreciate your including that."

"As I said," replied Kim, "we all need to be on the same page."

"Does the Agency know you're talking like that?" asked McGregor.

"The Agency's given me a fair amount of latitude here. On my end, the information I received about what happened after the warheads were removed from Arad was pretty sketchy. Can you fill me in?"

McGregor looked at Moore and they seemed to agree that he would start. "Orders came down for a rapid egress from the target. Captain Moore and I were with a group of medical personnel, MPs, and wounded just south of Arad and across a deep wadi. Most of the Marines had departed by road to be picked up by amphibious craft. To spare the wounded a rough road trip and to get us back to the ships faster, we were going to be evacuated by two CH-53 helicopters, both of which were shot down. The White House ordered us left behind, and given Nazer's threat, I can understand why. We were on our own."

"Because of that earlier massacre of medical personnel and wounded by Iranian Revolutionary Guards on Queshm Island," Moore said, "the president had ordered that medical units could be integrated with combat units. Commander McGregor was senior, so they called us the 584 Composite Unit and put him in command. We had two Royal Marines with us and they blew the bridge across the wadi, which kept the Yemenis in Arad off our backs."

Kim knew very little of this, but she was familiar with the so-called Queshm Massacre. She was getting a sense of where this was leading.

McGregor continued, "It seemed like our only chance was to get down to the beach. We had enough vehicles, so we just bugged out. Unfortunately, we were pursued from another direction by a company of Yemeni infantry that had just killed Captain Moore's company CO and a dozen of his Marines. Our best bet was to establish a defensive position south of a ridge. That night what has become known as the Battle of Simpson's Notch took place. We lost 12 KIA, but the Yemenis lost a lot more."

In fact, every soldier in that Yemeni company was killed, but McGregor decided not to reveal that to Kim.

"We got down to the beach and were lucky enough to contact a ship whose skipper blew up his career by coming to get us. End of story."

Jennifer Kim nodded. She knew this was not the entire story—she had read Moore's Medal of Honor citation and knew McGregor had received the Navy Cross. She decided though, after looking at her new agents' empty eyes, that she knew all she was going to know about them and about Ocean Reach. It would have to be enough.

"Thank you. Now for the mission brief. Turns out the middleman between the thieves and Abdullah Nazer was a major arms dealer known as Janos. He was quite the mystery. The story was that he worked out of Prague and dealt only in the high-ticket items—things like brokering the sale of that stolen German submarine to the Iranians. The Agency, MI6, Mossad, and others tried to track him down without success. Only after he disappeared from the scene did the British discover there was no Janos. He was actually a small-time dealer and former Russian Army officer working out of London—Maxim Korshkin. Henceforth 'Granite,' by the way. Even more interesting, he had been a part-time agent of the British and fed them bits of insignificant intel while at the same time making a fortune as Janos. The Brits were monumentally pissed, but you do have to admire the guy's chutzpah."

"Amazing," McGregor said, "I think one of our destroyers got that German boat last year somewhere in the Gulf of Oman. I'd wondered how the Iranians got hold of it."

Kim went on. "Last week, this letter was delivered to our Chief of Station in London." She slid a copy—stamped TOP SECRET—across the table and gave them a minute to absorb it.

"So, this guy, who by the way almost got both of us killed, says he has information on the people throwing those bombs." Moore seemed not so much surprised as irritated. "Why not just have your people in London pick him up and exfil out to a ship or just fly him here. I mean it's not Pyongyang."

"It's the politics. The president and the Director want no Agency fingerprints on this thing if it goes south. The British security services want this guy and are absolutely opposed to letting us get our hands on him. Being close allies, they know just about everyone in our own intelligence agencies and senior military. As reservists, you should be below the MI5 radar. You'll have genuine military orders to the embassy consistent with your skillsets, and neither of you has any connection to intel work."

"And if we get caught with this guy Korshkin?" asked McGregor.

"The story is that he contacted you directly and you then acted on your own initiative. I've got to be honest with you. If this thing goes off perfectly, you'll get no credit and if it goes to hell, you'll take most of the blame. I'll get the rest."

"I'm curious, Agent Kim," McGregor said, "why you thought we would believe otherwise? This is not our first intel-directed rodeo."

"It's Officer Kim. Technically, you two are my agents."

"Along that line, will we be covered by diplomatic immunity if our British friends decide to get rough?" asked Moore.

"The work you're going to be doing isn't normally covered by diplomatic immunity and in this particular case we're sure State wouldn't request it even if we asked."

"So, you didn't ask."

"No, we didn't ask."

"And just how was it that two junior reserve officers got selected for this thing anyway?" McGregor asked.

Kim did not like the direction this was taking, but having committed to transparency, she might as well go all in. "All right, what I heard is that the president made the choice. That bit of information, by the way, is close-hold. You do know he has a background in intelligence? I have no idea why he picked you specifically, but he was probably aware of you because of Yemen. Beyond that, they don't tell me much more than they tell you. Frankly, I'm not here to justify the president, I'm here to brief a mission that might help prevent a sarin attack on US soil."

Neither of her new agents seemed chastened by her rebuke.

"Got it," Moore said. "And just how will we find Mr. Korshkin?"

"I was about to get to that. Three days after our Chief of Station put the wine bottle in his window, a courier handed him an envelope as he left his flat. Here's a copy." She slid another paper, again stamped TOP SECRET, across the table.

Message received. I am certain you have concluded, as have I, that because of the delicate situation with the British security services that neither you nor any of your London associates should be involved in my exfiltration.

May I suggest sending someone who will arouse no suspicions by your hosts? I have a source at the embassy who will advise me of new personnel, and I will arrange for contact.

Please thank your government on my behalf and assure them that I will make every effort to justify your assistance.

McGregor said, "That's it? We show up and he contacts us?"

"Pretty much. We have nothing else to go on. You obviously can't start nosing around his properties. So far as we know, there will be no other new staff arriving from the states this week so if he has a source, they should be able to spot you.

"As for your cover, Commander McGregor is assigned to the Naval Medical Clinic London."

"I thought that was closed," McGregor said.

"It was, but when they built the new embassy, they included space for it. With the increased number of military personnel rotating through the UK, the DOD decided it was cheaper to provide care than contract it out. This is a Navy facility with its own commanding officer who does not work for the ambassador. Captain Moore, you will be assigned to the military attaché doing security background checks on non-US citizens hired by the various US military contractors in country. That function has military, FBI, and other civilian personnel and falls under both the office of the attaché and the Regional Security Officer. The RSO works for both the ambassador as well as the Diplomatic Security Service. It's a job that will take you outside the embassy on a regular basis."

"Okay, so Kelli has an excuse to be out on the town, but how do I skip out to go get Korshkin?"

"That could be a bit touchy. You may need to inform your commanding officer that you have classified orders that supersede those to the clinic. The CO, Captain Barbosa, has been around, so he shouldn't give you any trouble. If he does, contact me and we'll have the Navy give him a nudge. Captain Moore, you may not reveal anything. There are just too many people involved, and our Chief of Station has described the office of the RSO as leaky."

"So, we find this Korshkin," said McGregor. "What kind of medical support will I have? We have no idea what kind of condition he's in other than he's apparently too sick to travel. Will I at least have some basic supplies?"

"Yes," said Kim. "We have some people up in Bethesda putting together a backpack with diagnostic equipment and medications they think might be useful. It should be easily portable, about fifteen pounds. It will be delivered directly to you by a diplomatic courier."

"So there's still the getting-him-out-of-the-country part," Moore said. "Have you got a plan for that?"

"We don't know where he is or what kind of condition he'll be in, so no. Once we know, we have some excellent people to work on it, and your Navy friends are going to have some assets in the area. State has so far declined to make Korshkin a US passport, but that's not really a problem. The Agency can produce a passport for pretty much any country as soon as we get a photo. The British are all over every port of exit from the country, so a passport will only be important if you get out through Europe."

"Believe me," Kim added, "if you can find this guy and get him fit to travel, we will get him out. Ideally, at that point, you should return to the embassy, so there's no obvious link between you and Korshkin's escape."

"Pardon my repartee," McGregor said, "but there is a bit more 'trust us' here than I'm really comfortable with."

"Orders are orders," said Moore. "Looks like these are the cards we play."

Relieved, Kim produced a sheaf of papers from her case. "Speaking of which, here are your orders." She handed each multiple copies. "The regular charter to London leaves from Baltimore on Thursday, but you need to report on Tuesday, so make your own arrangements. We obviously can't put you on a military aircraft, too visible. As for housing, you have hotel reservations for three nights, but after that you need to make your own arrangements. You can submit travel claims after you're back."

"Not a problem," said Moore with a finality that surprised both Kim and McGregor. "We'll make our own travel and housing arrangements, and they won't cost the government a dime."

"Really?" asked McGregor.

"Now you need to trust me, Officer Kim. I'm on this."

Kim weighed her options. This was an accomplished professional woman from a wealthy family, not some twenty-year-old corporal. If she said they would get to London, she believed they would. Not a battle she wanted to fight.

"All right, but you need to be there no later than 0900 Tuesday."

"Done. Is there anything else?"

"Yes. Communications." Kim pulled what looked like a tablet computer from her bag.

"This is a highly classified piece of hardware. Though it looks exactly like a tablet computer, it is, in fact, a sophisticated short-range comm device that functions on one of the few frequencies the British GCHQ—their NSA—doesn't monitor. It's short range, but as long as you're in London everything will be forwarded to us through our station comm people at the embassy. If you travel outside the city, we'll make other arrangements, probably a military aircraft. You log in with facial recognition." She used the tablet's camera to snap photos of each. "You need to send me an update every day, even if nothing's happening. And do not take this device into the embassy. The RSO is not cleared for it, but he can legally search anything you bring into the embassy. Clear?"

"Clear as it's going to get." McGregor turned the unit on and reviewed the home page. "Looks like the menus are idiot proof. And this thing gets to us how?"

"By courier," replied Kim. "You'll also get an encrypted satphone with emergency contacts already loaded. That is for serious emergencies only. As soon as GCHQ picks up an unknown encrypted satphone they're going to get curious, and curious is bad. Finally, we will provide you with regular cellphones, identical to the ones you have except they have been modified so they can't be tracked. Leave yours at home."

"How do you even know what phones we have?" asked McGregor.

"For God's sake, Mike, they're the fucking CIA," Moore said.

"So now, is there anything else?"

"Two things. First, this mission should be short and simple. You aren't in Yemen, so keep the paranoia tamped down. And do not get caught with a weapon. The UK is not the US: the British take this incredibly seriously. Finally, I am available twenty-four seven. I will monitor your comms and keep my satphone with me at all times—it's the first number on the list. This isn't my first rodeo either, Commander. Are we clear?"

McGregor seemed to suppress a smile. "Crystal." He turned to leave, but Moore didn't move.

"Officer Kim," she said, "I do have two questions for you."

Kim nodded.

"You know where we've been and what we've done. How about you. Have you ever lost an agent?"

Kim's face became tense. "Yes, I have."

"And have you been required to kill anyone in the line of duty?"

"Yes again. Same mission. Now, if you don't have any more questions, I think it's time to get on with business."

"One more thing, Officer Kim," said Moore. "We're going to need your complete file on Mr. Korshkin."

"File?"

"Look, I'm a police detective. This is essentially a missing-persons case. The way to find people is to learn everything about them—their habits, finances, travel history, family, friends, work. Everything. Don't even try to tell me the CIA didn't think of that."

Kim paused. The Agency was worried that the more these two knew, the more likely they were to freelance and somehow blow the mission. Best to wait for contact and leave it at that. On the other hand, what she asked for made perfect sense. She hated being put in this position. "I'll get what I can and send it with the courier."

"It could be a deal breaker, Officer Kim."

"I'll remember that."

The two officers left the SCIF without looking back.

Jennifer Kim began to pack her gear. She carefully inventoried every piece of paper to be sure nothing was missing. The briefing, particularly Moore's questions, had left her shaken. She stopped and pulled McGregor's Navy Cross citation from his personnel folder. The description of his leadership convinced her that his detached attitude was a carefully constructed act. Mr. Korshkin, she decided, was in good, if unorthodox, hands. Moore worried her. She had no doubt of her courage and skill, nor her commitment to the mission. But something was there that only another woman who had faced death could understand. She retrieved the Medal of Honor citation. It read:

> FOR CONSPICUOUS GALLANTRY AND INTREPIDITY AT THE RISK OF HER LIFE AND BEYOND THE CALL OF DUTY WHILE SERVING WITH THE 584 COMPOSITE UNIT, OPERATION OCEAN REACH. ON THE NIGHT OF SEPTEMBER 13-14, 2017 CAPTAIN MOORE WAS TASKED WITH DEFENDING A GEOGRAPHICAL LOCATION KNOWN AS SIMPSON'S NOTCH. DURING AN ATTACK BY A GREATLY SUPERIOR ENEMY FORCE CAPTAIN MOORE REPEATEDLY RALLIED HER MARINES TO DEFEND AGAINST AND TO COUNTERATTACK THE ENEMY. IN DOING SO SHE CONTINUALLY EXPOSED HERSELF TO ENEMY FIRE AND PERSONALLY ENGAGED THE ENEMY, KILLING AT LEAST SIX WITH SMALL ARMS FIRE. SHE SKILLFULLY MOVED HER MARINES TO ALTERNATE POSITIONS MAKING MAXIMUM USE OF TERRAIN AND THE FIRE OF AUTOMATIC WEAPONS TO INFLICT HEAVY LOSSES ON THEIR ATTACKERS, ULTIMATELY DEFEATING THEM IN DETAIL. WHEN HER CORPSMAN WAS SERIOUSLY WOUNDED BY GRENADE FRAGMENTS, CAPTAIN MOORE, WITHOUT HESITATION, PROVIDED FIRST AID WHILE UNDER CONTINUOUS ENEMY FIRE AND THEN GAVE THE WOUNDED SAILOR HER OWN BODY ARMOR. IN A FINAL ACT OF BRAVERY, SHE ENGAGED THE ENEMY COMMANDER, KILLING HIM IN HAND-TO-HAND COMBAT AND WHILE DOING SO SUSTAINED A CRITICAL CHEST WOUND. CAPTAIN MOORE'S LEADERSHIP, COURAGE, AND EXTRAORDINARY DEVOTION TO DUTY PREVENTED AN ENEMY BREAKTHROUGH INTO THE REAR OF HER COMMAND, THUS TURNING THE TIDE OF BATTLE. HER ACTIONS REFLECT GREAT CREDIT UPON HERSELF AND UPHELD THE HIGHEST TRADITIONS OF THE UNITED STATES MARINE CORPS AND THE NAVAL SERVICE.

For a moment Jennifer Kim was back in the Carpathian Mountains. But this time, like Kelli Moore, she did not hesitate. She took the shot and saved her agent.

CHAPTER 6

ABOUT THE SAME time Jennifer Kim finished her briefing, the Uzbek was peering into the video screen of the Tarot T-18 drone. He had been working on the machine for months—he had acquired the major components separately, so it had taken some time to get it flying. He was sitting in the back of his old Winnebago not far from Georgia's Lake Lanier, a large artificial lake north of Atlanta with numerous parks and recreational areas and, of course, million-dollar waterfront homes.

His target was Laurel Park, about a half mile away. The drone had launched from the roof of a boathouse just across a narrow channel from the park. The Uzbek had placed it there the previous night from a small kayak. As soon as it took off it would be visible, but that was no matter; its mission would last but a few minutes.

Using a remote antenna on the roof of his RV, he did not have to actually observe the small aircraft—the on-board video camera would show him where it was going. The green plastic sphere suspended from the machine was the payload. In its center was a charge of one hundred grams of RDX covered by half-inch ball bearings. These were surrounded by a thick layer of finely powdered CS, a tear gas popular with many police departments.

The event was a picnic for one Roy Bedford, a prominent citizen celebrating his ninetieth birthday. The Uzbek had chosen it purely by chance when he saw a poster at a local convenience store. Though the overall plan was for him to avoid participation in actual missions, this one he simply could not resist. His instincts told him that this attack would create a greater reaction than the last two. The introduction of an actual chemical weapon, albeit a fairly benign one, would set social media ablaze.

The drone circled the park for a few minutes until people began to crowd together near the parking lot. The guest of honor, it seemed, was arriving. As the drone glided over the crowd, a few looked up and assumed someone was recording the event. One idiot even waved! When the old man was wheeled from his van to the center of the crowd, the Uzbek dropped the drone to about ten feet and pressed a small button.

He could not hear the explosion from inside his vehicle, but there was a visible puff of smoke above the trees. Without hesitating, the Uzbek started the engine and drove away. In a few minutes he was on I-985, heading south.

CHAPTER 7

BRENDAN WALLACE WAS livid. Four hours ago, another terrorist attack on US soil, this time a park in Georgia. And again, his advisors had nothing to offer.

Wallace turned his ire on FBI Director Frank Branigan. "All right, Frank, when we talked an hour ago you said you would have something for us. Well?"

The FBI man straightened in his chair and looked at the president, failing to make eye contact. "Here's what we have so far, Mr. President. The bomb was definitely delivered by a drone, but nobody saw whoever was controlling it. As of a few minutes ago, twelve dead and eighteen injured—the fact that the device was detonated overhead caused a lot of penetrating head injuries which contributed to the fatality rate. The projectiles were half-inch ball bearings, and the thing was also packed with CS tear gas. Like in Arkansas, the chemical component slowed EMT response and complicated hospital care."

"You said this was in a park. What was going on before the attack?"

"Birthday party for a local guy. He had just turned ninety, a Korean War vet. Ironically, he was in a wheelchair so the people around him took all the hits. He did suffer some respiratory trouble from the CS,

41

but they think he'll be okay. Apparently, he was a local politician years ago, so naturally the internet is full of conspiracy theories."

"Could there be something to that?" demanded Wallace.

Branigan hesitated, giving Karen Hiller an opening to speak up. "Not likely. He was active in the seventies and eighties. Ran a lumber yard after that. Million to one that the terrorists knew anything about him."

"Well, we need to squash this conspiracy talk. Get with communications on that. And Frank, the FBI knows nothing about a political conspiracy. Right?"

"Absolutely right, sir. Nothing."

The president moved quickly to the CIA director. "Alex, anything to report on that British lead?"

Alexander Clarkson displayed little emotion in his response. "Mr. President, one of our people just finished briefing those reserve officers. They should be in London tomorrow."

"I'm concerned about this, Alex. Very concerned. My gut says this whole approach by Korshkin is bogus, and that we'll blow things up with the British. If there is so much as a whiff of trouble, I want to know about it."

Turning to his National Security Advisor, Wallace asked, "Sonny, have you heard anything from London?"

"Quiet on my end, sir. I think we need to let this play out for a while. It's the only lead we have right now." Baker was less concerned about the CIA operation than he was about the president's increasing anxiety. If he pulled the plug too soon, it could torpedo their best hope for a breakthrough.

"If this thing is the best we've got, then we all need to be working harder. A lot harder." He peered around the table and all present nodded in agreement.

Wallace looked back at Clarkson. "So what if we do locate this Korshkin? Do we have a way to get him out clean?"

"I have no doubt we can get him out. How we do it will depend on where he is and what kind of shape he's in. We have a group of first-rate exfil specialists on call to put together a plan on short notice. And the Navy is starting to position some ships to be available if needed."

"What about that Sonny?" asked Wallace.

"Last I heard, sir, the *Makin Island* Group is leaving soon for an exercise with the Norwegians. I'm looking into putting them in position to assist within the week."

"About that, Mr. President..."

All heads turned to Oliver Sharpe, the newly confirmed SECDEF. Sharpe was a retired four-star admiral from the submarine community who had also headed Strategic Command, America's nuclear forces, as well as being the Vice CNO.

Wallace cut him off. "Good to hear from you Oliver, do you have some kind of problem with what Sonny just presented?"

"Yes sir. We are about to embark on a multi-year integration of US and UK naval operations that will greatly relieve our overstretched forces. If we step on British toes right now, the whole thing could blow up in our faces. I've been hearing concerns from the CNO as well as NavEur."

"I understand your concerns and I share them," Wallace said. "We are simply putting forces into position to cover contingencies. We must remember that American citizens have been the victims of three terrorist bombs, each more deadly than the last. Oliver, have you seen the news coverage of these attacks? People are starting to avoid public places. There are conspiracy theories being floated on every media outlet. I get that we have to balance our priorities, but until we find a better way proceed, this is our best option."

Chastened, the SECDEF replied, "Understood, Mr. President."

"Okay then," said Wallace, "I guess we'll have to wait for developments. Karen, with that many deaths and a possible political angle, we better look into attending some kind of memorial service—we obviously can't go to a dozen funerals. Also, set up a press conference. Frank, you need to be there for questions. Alex, call me for so much as a peep out of London."

To a chorus of, "Yes, Mr. President," Wallace stood and left the room.

CHAPTER 8

KELLI MOORE WALKED down the stairs from the Gulf-stream G650 that just landed at the Cambridge City Airport northwest of London. She had flown on this aircraft before and was confident she could arrange for the flight. McGregor, who descended right behind her, was still trying to figure out what was happening. Though the Gulfstream had all the luxurious trappings of a high-end business jet, the flight crews—there were two sets, one for each direction—had been introduced simply as Tony, John, Ashley, and Tim. They looked and acted, however, like they should have been called "Flight Lieutenant" or "Group Commander." And the cabin attendant's safety talk prior to takeoff was more like a mission brief than the mono-tone speech everyone had heard a hundred times before.

They pulled up the hoods of their windbreakers to ward off the wind and heavy mist. The flight crew followed, and they all walked to an open hanger.

They were greeted by Ian, a very fit-looking man in his mid-thirties with close-cropped blond hair and eyes that seemed to miss nothing. He informed them that Sir Charles had been unavoidably detained. Both Moore and McGregor were impressed when an official from Immigration Enforcement met them in the hanger, took a quick look at their passports, and welcomed them to the UK.

Their bags were swiftly loaded, and they settled into the buttery-soft seats of an Audi A8 for the ride into London. Ian advised them that their late afternoon arrival would put them into the worst of London traffic. He pointed to a wicker basket on the floor and invited them to help themselves. Inside they found several cheeses—hard and soft; a fresh baguette; fruit; a thermos of coffee; and a bottle of Macallan 18.

"Sir Charles?" asked McGregor while munching on a piece of baguette.

"It's been years, and I don't think I've ever heard him called anything else. Being a banker, he tends to be a bit formal."

"Right. And you call him Sir Charles as well?"

"No, I call him 'Grandfather,' of course."

The trip into London passed agreeably with the aid of the smooth, aromatic whisky. The Audi drove around Sloane Square, an area once frequented by Lady Diana Spencer before she became Princess Diana. They turned onto Sloane Gardens, a street of nineteenth-century red stone townhouses with luxury cars on the street and well-dressed residents walking well-behaved dogs. Surprisingly there was an open place in front of the house Kelli recognized as belonging to her grandfather. On reflection, perhaps not so surprising.

Ian paused for a moment to look up and down the street, then led them to the door where he entered a long code into a security panel. "Been a lot of changes since you were last here, Miss." The massive front door swung silently on hydraulic hinges and Kelli saw that the door was really a sandwich of wood with about a half inch of steel in between. That was new.

McGregor noticed it too, as well as the inch-thick windows. McGregor whispered, "Your Grandfather isn't an ordinary banker, is he?"

Despite the Edwardian exterior, the interior was Scandinavian modern—lots of glass and steel with high-design LED lighting. Before either could comment on the décor, however, they were approached by a tall, lean man with a grey pencil moustache. He shared Kelli's athletic grace, and his ramrod-straight posture emphasized the tailoring of his three-piece dark blue suit. Most dramatic, though, were the glittering emerald eyes both Moores shared.

Stepping forward to hug his granddaughter, Sir Charles broke away and approached Mike McGregor. "Charles Moore. A great pleasure to meet you, Commander."

"The pleasure is mine, Sir Charles. Thank you for extending the invitation."

"First of all, we shall dispense with this Sir Charles nonsense. It's Charles. And may I call you Michael? I feel I already know you."

Kelli was surprised. She could not remember her grandfather ever inviting anyone to call him by his given name.

"Of course, Charles," Mike replied.

"Ian will see to your luggage. I hope you will find the accommodations satisfactory."

Kelli laughed. "Much better than the Marine Corps would have provided."

"Don't worry, I won't be disturbing you. I have a nice flat down in the City now and will be staying there most of the time. I hope you won't mind if I drop in though, just now and then, to see how you're getting on."

"Are we not in the city now?" asked McGregor.

"The actual City of London is just a small area around St. Paul's. It's been there since Roman times, but it's mostly the financial district

47

these days—ruling the world through different means. I have quite a bit going on there right now so it will actually be quite convenient.

"Before I go, though, could I persuade you to join me for dinner? I actually am a passable cook."

He led them into a large, modern kitchen which was—in defiance of energy standards—equipped with top-of-the-line American appliances. He took off the jacket of his elegant suit and donned an apron. He then put together a dish of pasta and fresh mussels with a homemade marinara sauce, while they sat at the butcher-block island and watched.

Sir Charles displayed the pleasure of a true chef in watching his guests devour his work. He cleared the dishes, refusing help—which he declared "so American"—and then poured snifters of an aromatic Armagnac.

"So Kelli," he asked, "what brings you and Michael to London?"

"That's a long story," she said. "And one I'm not actually authorized to tell you."

"That's quite all right, my dear," he said. "I have my own sources and can make my own guesses."

CHAPTER 9

Port of Baltimore, Maryland

THE MV PISCES *Union*, a midsized container ship, was half-way through unloading at the Seagirt Marine Terminal when a truck bearing the name Connover Welding Supply parked by the brow. On seeing the truck, two crewmen wheeled a dolly containing an empty oxygen and an empty acetylene cylinder down to the dock. They were exchanged for full tanks, and with payment authorization signed, the truck departed, and the crew brought the new cylinders aboard.

In fact, there were already two cylinders on board, virtually unused. The empties had been brought aboard a week before during a stop at Port of Caniçal in Madeira. The oxygen cylinder actually was empty, but the one labeled "Acetylene" contained fifty kilograms of sarin.

Thirty minutes after picking up the cylinders, the driver and his assistant transferred them to an unmarked van, and in minutes were on I-70 heading west. An hour after that, one of the unconscious Connover employees woke up and began kicking the side of their truck. They were finally noticed and released by police, but by time their report was filed and the movements of the van reconstructed, the Pisces Union had sailed and was in international waters. It made no difference: the ship had not been a scheduled stop for Connover, and nobody at the port thought delivery of welding supplies was at all out of the ordinary. There were no witnesses, and police found no forensic evidence.

The Uzbek smiled when he received the confirming text. Two minutes after that, the phone on which he received it was in a dumpster.

CHAPTER 10

L CDR MIKE MCGREGOR had settled into his small office in the Naval Medical Clinic, London. He was filling in for Lieutenant Alexandra West, who had been sent away on temporary orders to a destination unknown to her colleagues or any of the corpsmen. With his background in emergency medicine, though, everyone seemed happy to have McGregor on board. There was one other physician working that day, a young family doc whose last duty had been at a clinic in San Diego. There was also a nurse practitioner just in from Bagram Air Base in Afghanistan. She was also a lieutenant commander, and judging by her ribbons had also done some sea duty as well as time in Iraq. She had eyed McGregor's Navy Cross and Purple Heart, but had refrained from asking.

McGregor had been there barely an hour and was just figuring out the clinic's organization and patient flow when he received a message that the CO wanted to see him. This was routine, but meeting a new commanding officer always had to be approached carefully — particularly when engaged in a clandestine mission. Mike had worked with commanders who were among the most dedicated and honorable people he had ever known—Colonel Mark, for example. He had also worked for the incompetent and the self-promoters. He knew he had to

51

size up what was expected of him and try to deliver, all the while actually working on an entirely different mission. No problem!

The commanding officer's suite was small, with a first-class petty officer at the front desk. She told him to knock, which he did.

"Enter."

McGregor was surprised to see a compact man of about fifty in tailored dress blues wearing a SEAL Trident, a Navy Cross, and the insignia of a Medical Corps Captain. The two men regarded each other for a moment, then the Captain walked around his desk and extended his hand.

"Jose Barbosa." He directed McGregor to a cluster of chairs. "Please join me."

"I've never seen a medical corps officer with a Trident before," said McGregor. "There must be a story there."

"Simple enough. My people were Portuguese fishermen who moved to Nova Scotia for the cod and then to Maine for the lobsters. It seemed to me that if I was going to make my living being cold and wet, I might as well be serving the country. Got an appointment to the Academy and wound up in Team Three. Helicopter crash during an op in Africa resulted in a detached retina. They did a laser procedure at Landstuhl, but there was still some loss of the visual field. I had more than ten years in at that point, so I convinced the Navy to send me to USUHS, the military medical school up in Bethesda, for medical training. That's about it. And what got you into the Navy? Your record shows you began as a corpsman."

"Yessir. I was in college at Michigan and working part-time as an EMT to pay the bills, but just couldn't stay ahead. I thought a few years in the Navy would let me save enough to finish my degree and then use the GI Bill for medical school."

"And that's where you got that Navy Cross—the first one? Details were mostly redacted in your personnel file."

"About what you'd expect. Spook show into Syria with the Marines."

Barbosa nodded. Nobody serves with the SEAL teams without understanding how those kinds of missions go wrong. "And the second was Ocean Reach? That I'm familiar with."

McGregor was surprised, and he showed it. "Ocean Reach is still very close hold. May I ask how you know those details?"

"I was the senior medical officer on the *Essex* for that op. I was there when we sailed off and left you behind. Your colonel went absolutely ballistic, by the way, but I suppose you know that."

"I do. It's still a very sore point with him. And to be honest, with me."

"Understood. Well, nothing like that is happening here." Barbosa outlined McGregor's duties and a few policies unique to his command. He surprised Mike again when he asked, "Do you know where they sent Lt West, the officer you're replacing?"

"No sir. The staff seems to be in the dark."

"Diego Garcia. It's a little island in the Indian Ocean. Air Force operates B-52s out of there, but at the moment there are none on site. There's intel and communications and a small port operation in the lagoon. Now West is a competent young physician, but she has no particular qualifications that would make BUMED pluck her out of this clinic and send her to the Indian Ocean. Her orders were for only ninety days, so I wasn't expecting anyone to replace her. In fact, we had already adjusted our schedule to cover her when I heard you were coming. A guy deployed just last year and wounded? A Lieutenant Commander with a high-profile ER job sent to cover a primary care position? Does that seem odd to you?"

McGregor knew his mission had been put together on the fly and that his cover was weak, but they had been hoping nobody would be alert enough to notice. So much for that. He debated telling his CO, someone obviously familiar with sensitive ops, more about his mission, but he didn't get a chance.

"You don't need to answer," Barbosa said. "In fact, I prefer that you don't. I just want you to know that I believe they sent West to the Indian Ocean just to create an opening for you to fill. If you do have orders that supersede your duties here, this command will do whatever it can to support and assist you. Do what you need to do, Commander. I will personally cover any days you are the medical officer of the day, but need to be elsewhere." He handed McGregor a card. "These are my cell and satphone numbers. Call anytime. The third number is a throwaway cell I picked up in Belgium. Single use. I think you understand what that means."

McGregor just took the card. "Thank you Captain, but I'm just here to work in your clinic."

"In that case, Commander, welcome aboard. Enjoy your time in London. Perhaps we can get together for a beer sometime."

"I would like that very much, Captain. Is there anything else?"

"No, you are dismissed."

McGregor rose, did an about face, and left his new commanding officer's office. On the way out, the petty officer noted McGregor's slight smile of satisfaction. She stepped into Barbosa's office and was not surprised to see he had the same smile.

Later that evening, McGregor was pouring one of Sir Charles's single malts while he described to Kelli Moore his interaction with his new CO. "He even invited me for a beer. I think Captain Barbosa and I will get along fine."

"Two blokes sharing stories of classified missions over a pint. Charming."

"Well, how did things go in your office?" he asked.

"The guy who directs the office is an Army lieutenant colonel. Bernard Schmidt. Wasn't in uniform, in fact nobody was. Apparently he prefers it that way, so I guess I have some shopping to do."

"Did he seem like an agreeable guy?"

"Yeah, remember Fuller?"

"I see."

"Schmidt's another one. First thing, he made it clear he had not requested me and that he had not previously had anyone assigned to him that he hadn't personally selected. All the while he was looking me over like a leg of lamb."

"So, did you cuff him to a table?" asked McGregor with a chuckle.

"No, I was afraid he might have enjoyed that sort of thing."

"Anything else?" asked McGregor.

"Yes, in fact. We only talked for about five minutes, but the guy reeked of DIA."

"Defense Intelligence Agency? Why would they have a senior DIA officer running a small shop doing routine background checks? And he personally picks all of his subordinates? Do you think there were other intel types?"

"You're becoming quite the investigator, Michael. As to your first question, I have no idea. Maybe he just wanted a cushy assignment. Or maybe they're running some kind of op out of that office and I just blundered in because the Agency put this whole thing together on the fly and failed to coordinate with other agencies."

"Wouldn't they have other intel assets then?"

"Maybe they do, but they're not as obvious as Schmidt. There's a woman from the FBI who looks like she's been around since Hoover and a young guy from Army CID. They're the other investigators. There are a couple of civilians and a few enlisted people–or at least they say they're enlisted–doing the grunt work. Just try to remember our mission and don't worry about what other people are doing."

"Unless what they're doing interferes with what we're doing." McGregor's latent paranoia about intel missions was beginning to surface.

"I considered that, but our friend Dover seems too low on the food chain to be mixed up in anything with too many moving parts."

"Unless, as you say, we got dropped into another agency's party. A left hand/right hand thing."

"Well that would be just fucking great wouldn't it? But I think we should probably assume that isn't the case and simply stick to our mission. And let's not get young Dover too spun up until we know something more."

"Agreed," Mike said. "But the fact is that our cover stories were pretty thin from the outset, and it looks like they're getting really threadbare on our first day. She does need to know that."

Before heading out to dinner McGregor sent his first report:

From: Keystone
To: Dover

Keystone and Empire in place. Keystone's CO very suspicious that there is another mission in play. Indicates willingness to cooperate as necessary. Empire's supervisor seemed suspicious as well. Could be a problem.

Nothing from Granite.

CHAPTER 11

IT WAS ONE of the smaller malls in upscale Scottsdale. The customers were gathering for a huge sale, however, so there would be a dense crowd in a contained space. Perfect for what the Uzbek had sent him here to do.

Raoul had been a low-level mule for one of the cartels in El Salvador when the Uzbek approached him. A week before he was recruited, a chest X-ray—the only medical test he could afford—showed a large cancer in his right lung. The doctor told him this explained his cough and weight loss and regrettably meant he would not likely survive more than a few months. What the doctor didn't tell him was that the X-ray actually showed evidence of tuberculosis, treatable with drugs even Raoul could afford. The Uzbek, however, had paid the doctor to tell a different story.

Confronted with leaving his mother and young sister with virtually no source of income, Raoul had been persuaded to travel to the United States for what was certainly a suicide mission. But what did that matter to a man dying of cancer? He was offered five thousand dollars and promised another five thousand would be delivered to his family when his mission was complete. Raoul had already sold his soul working for the cartel, so he took the offer, gave his mother the money, and drove away with the man who called himself "the Uzbek."

Raoul had a simple mission. Walk into the mall, turn the dial on top of a green plastic ball to the number "2," press on the dial until he heard a click, then toss the ball into the air. If he could escape, so much the better, but two seconds was very little time. He knew the ball contained an explosive, and the way it had been transported gave him the strong sense there was something poisonous inside as well.

At this last moment, doubts began to eat away at his insides. His mother would not want this, even to survive. And besides, she already had more money than she could imagine.

But he had agreed. And if he backed out, the Uzbek seemed perfectly capable of killing his mother. He had no choice.

Raoul turned the dial, pressed until he felt the click, then held the ball at arm's length and waited.

CHAPTER 12

BRENDAN WALLACE GLARED at the FBI Director. "Six dead?"

"Yes Mr. President. Definitely six. Several first responders were stricken before they realized it was sarin. Then there were three people in the parking lot who were close enough to get a high dose, and of course the bomber himself, who was killed by the blast. At least a dozen have been hospitalized so far."

"Hats off to the EMS personnel who realized what it was and called for doses of the antidote. The contamination will spread beyond the parking lot, though, and there are bound to be additional casualties. What we don't know is why he didn't deploy it inside the mall. Could have been ten times as many killed—easily."

"Probably just screwed up," Karen Hiller said. "A suicide bomber would certainly have tried to maximize casualties."

"That's our thinking as well," replied Branigan. "Now that the WMD threshold has been crossed, everyone's going crazy. Demands to close the borders, schools being closed, and sporting events cancelled. Conspiracy theories of every kind are sprouting up online. The bombers are getting exactly what they wanted. Chaos."

Wallace turned his attention to the CIA Director. "Alex, how about that operation you're running in London?"

"Those two officers are in place, and we have reliable communication. Nothing to report so far."

"The operative word being 'nothing'." Wallace was interrupted by a staff member who handed a message to FBI Director Branigan.

The FBI man read the single page. "The van that transported the bomber to Scottsdale was picked up on a security camera just outside the parking lot. It was pulled over by State Police north of Phoenix. When the officers got close, the van exploded. Estimates are a hundred pounds of C-4, or something similar. Hardly anything left of the driver, one officer killed, one injured. Van was stolen more than a year ago—we got lucky on the VIN. Plate was fake, matched a similar vehicle owned by a business in Tucson."

"So this thing has been in the works for more than a year," Alex Clarkson said. "They're obviously well organized and supplied. We need some kind of break if we're going to get ahead of this."

CHAPTER 13

IAN HAD DROPPED them back at Sloane Gardens after they finished at the embassy. On the drive home McGregor had bored Kelli with a minute description of a complicated skin condition acquired by a senior officer in Afghanistan.

Mike was currently trying to figure out the espresso machine in Sir Charles's kitchen.

Now that they were alone, Kelli decided to bring up something of more immediate interest. "You might be surprised to know who stopped by my desk today," she said while rummaging in a drawer for a suitable container in which to froth a little milk.

"Who was that?" asked Mike while trying not to burn his fingers.

"Sergeant Leach."

"What? Your platoon sergeant from Ocean Reach?"

"The same. She stayed on active duty after that op and wound up in the Marine Corps Security Guard School at Quantico. Assigned here just a couple of months ago. We didn't really have an opportunity to talk, but she did slip me this."

It was a small card, the size of a regular business card, but with nothing printed on it. On one side was written in a neat script, "The Antelope, tonight, 1900." It was signed "Singh."

Moore added, "The Antelope is a pub on Eaton Terrace, just a few blocks from here."

"I assume this is Captain Singh, but why the cloak and dagger?"

"I don't know, but he must have a good reason. Obviously, we have to go. Do you think this could be related to the mission?"

"Now there's a question. Given that our bosses saw through our cover on day one, we have to assume they aren't the only ones. My instinct is that we should trust him."

"Mine too," said Moore. They each sipped on a double espresso, unconcerned about the effect of that much caffeine. "Let's plan to leave around 1845."

Just before 1900 McGregor and Moore stepped into the Antelope, a cozy pub just over a block from nearby Sloane Square. There was a buzz of conversation from a largely after-work crowd of young professionals in Saville Row suits clustered at tables and standing around the bar. Moore was wearing black jeans and a blazer while McGregor was in tan slacks with a leather jacket. They both felt underdressed. In less than a minute, they spotted a big man wearing a turban and a grey pinstripe suit. His dark beard was beginning to show a few streaks of grey, but his smile at seeing his two comrades was warm and genuine. As they approached his table, he rose and gripped both of their hands with great energy.

"Please sit, my friends. I have taken the liberty of ordering for you. American bourbon for the doctor and the Macallan 18, which I believe is your grandfather's favorite."

"You know my grandfather?"

"We have...crossed paths."

"Captain, I thought you would be back with your regiment by now," said McGregor.

"It's 'Major' now," said Singh. "Official just a few weeks ago. The reason I'm posted here in London is that this hand"—he held up his left palm which showed several surgical scars—"has taken a bit longer than expected to heal."

Moore and McGregor both toasted to the promotion. McGregor added, "I'm not surprised. That shrapnel hit you took in Arad must have caused a fair amount of damage. Palm of the hand is a sensitive area."

"So I discovered. Chap at the King Edward Hospital has done several operations, though, and I'm about finished with my therapy. Should be getting orders back to the field any time now."

"What are you doing in the meantime?" asked Moore.

"Liaison between the Royal Marines and the security services, mainly MI6. They have their own operations people, of course, but sometimes on foreign ops they need a bit more muscle, as it were."

"And you arrange for the muscle?"

"Precisely. My work does bring me into contact with a number of people well up in the services. Which brings me to why I'm here."

"And how do we figure into the security services?" asked McGregor, afraid of the answer.

"I think you have both heard the name Maxim Korshkin in the context of Ocean Reach. It turns out he engineered the whole thing, and now he's on the run. MI5, and particularly a chap called Neville Cathcart, is furious at being played by this fellow. Cathcart had been his handler for years and now has a number of people in the services as well as the government out for his blood. Your people want to question him in regard to those bomb attacks in the states, but my government is determined to keep you from getting your hands on him."

The two Americans tried to look surprised.

They apparently failed. "So...are you looking for Korshkin?"

McGregor made a snap decision. Singh was a Marine, he was no spook. They had fought together, literally side by side. The mission was on the cusp of being blown anyway, so he had to trust someone.

"Yes, Major, we are."

Kelli Moore took a sharp breath. She was shocked McGregor had revealed their mission, but after a moment she considered two things. First, McGregor was senior. Also, Singh had trusted them by revealing what was happening in the security services regarding Korshkin, something their own handlers from CIA had not really explained. She gave a slight shrug of her shoulders.

"I suspected as much," Singh replied. "You must be very cautious. This whole thing seems highly irregular, too much pressure, too many people involved. This is not how we operate. This man Korshkin may be able to help a close ally, and we are making a maximum effort to prevent that. I don't know why, but something strikes me as quite wrong."

He took a sip of tea. "The second reason I wanted to see you is this." He took a small USB drive from his pocket. "This morning a messenger handed it to me as I left my building. It was wrapped in a paper that said only, 'McGregor.' Obviously I could not just meet you at the embassy. I knew Sergeant Leach had been posted here, so I took a cab up to your new embassy on the chance she had guard duty at the gate. She did and she recognized me. I stopped long enough to say hello and slipped her that card you received during a handshake."

Moore examined the USB drive. "What is it?"

"I have no idea. Seemed best to leave it to you to find out. My guess is that it somehow relates to Korshkin, but that is only a guess"

"So you didn't turn it over to the security services. Interesting. Major Singh, have you gone rogue?"

"Probably have, Commander. But I thought about the captain of the *Bataan* who sent those landing craft to pull us out of Yemen. I heard he was retired as soon as he got home—and that impressed me. He had to choose between duty and loyalty and he chose loyalty. For better or worse, I'm doing the same."

McGregor regarded the big man for a moment. "We're honored you feel we're worthy of that kind of loyalty. Thank you."

"We won't forget this," said Moore. "I also think you're right about the USB drive. Our handler told us we would be contacted with further information."

"Then that's probably it. Interesting that someone affiliated with Korshkin knows about our connection." Singh looked at his watch. "We should probably be leaving now. It would be unwise were I seen by someone from the services out with the two of you."

"Quite right," said McGregor. "Thank you, Major. I guess we're on our own now."

"You're never on your own," Singh said as they all walked towards the door.

As the three officers walked towards the main street, they were suddenly confronted by two shabbily dressed young men who had obviously been waiting for them. The two were out of place in this upscale part of Chelsea. That point became crystal clear when both snapped open flick knives.

The taller of the two, clearly the more experienced street fighter, moved towards Singh. He held his knife in his right hand out to the side, preparing to slash. He expected the well-dressed man to draw back, so he moved aggressively.

He was surprised when Singh moved in on him, and in a lightning move, grasped the assailant's wrist with his left hand and delivered a hammer blow to the forearm with his right fist.

There was a sharp crack.

The young punk let go of the knife and Singh moved his right hand up to the elbow, pushed the arm down, and followed almost immediately with a brutal upward thrust with his knee.

There was a nauseating crunch.

The young man dropped to the pavement, his forearm was bent at a forty-five-degree angle. As he fell, Singh applied a quick elbow to the jaw which caused McGregor to wonder professionally if the blow was hard enough to fracture the mandible.

The shorter of the two was distracted by Singh's three-second destruction of his partner. By the time he turned back towards the two Americans, McGregor's foot was already in motion. He connected behind the thug's left knee.

As he went down, Moore sprang forward and planted her heel on his genitals. McGregor wondered if he would ever forget the man's animal cry of pain.

The trio walked around the two writhing men, crossed the street, and did not look back.

CHAPTER 14

BRENDAN WALLACE SAT in the Situation Room and glared at the figures seated around the table. "All right, let's have it."

"Nothing but bad news, I'm afraid," Frank Branigan said. "The guy with the bomb has been tentatively identified as belonging to a Salvadoran gang, but to be honest, that ID is soft. He was torn up pretty well by the explosion, and the body is so contaminated that everyone who gets near it has to be in Level A hazmat protection. Also... the tentative ID slipped out."

"Slipped out?" Karen Hiller said. "What do you mean slipped out?"

"One of the techs told a family member. She's now on administrative leave."

"So that's how the disaster at the border got started," Wallace said.

"I'm afraid so, sir. Once word got out that a potential illegal was involved in a nerve-gas attack, a group of locals attacked some people crossing the border. Two killed, one wounded, as well as an injured Sherriff's deputy. The remainder of the group—perhaps a dozen—dispersed and have disappeared."

"Well Frank, that's just great. And what about Detroit?"

"We know more about that. A couple of our agents were tracking down that information about an Arab kid being involved in the produc-

67

tion of parts for these bombs. They went to interview the owner of a machine shop in Dearborn, a suburb with a large Arab population. He's Jordanian and has been in the country for decades. Naturalized citizen and completely clean, but our people just wanted to ask if he knew who this kid might be. He got spooked when he heard there were FBI agents in the building, took off, and was hit by a pickup truck while running across a busy street. He's in critical condition, and there was a demonstration by members of the Arab community at the hospital."

"So, we have an Arab kid, a Salvadoran gang member, and vague descriptions of others who could be just about anyone. Frank, you need to get a handle on your people. Another fiasco like this, and things are going to get out of control. Fast."

"Things already are," Hiller said. "The number of airline passengers has dropped, traffic at fast food outlets is down, and fewer people are going to movies. The actual numbers are small, but there is a definite trend. A couple more of these events and there could be a significant economic impact."

Alex Clarkson from CIA added, "One of my analysts has suggested the geography of the attacks and their escalating nature is most consistent with an intent to cause social and economic disruption rather than just maximizing casualties. If so, it sounds like they are getting exactly what they want. We need to be thinking outside the usual terrorist suspect list. This is more than just a cell of fanatics in a basement somewhere."

"Alex," Wallace said, "it's easy for you scholarly analyst types to think outside the box, but when the American public sees a nerve gas attack they think terrorists. If we start talking about other possibilities, it's just going to make it seem like we don't know what the hell we're doing."

"We don't have to announce this line of investigation, but we can't ignore it either. And to answer your next question, nothing yet from London."

"Don't try to do my thinking for me, Alex. Why don't you head on back to your smart people and start demanding some results? That goes for all of you. Now get back to work. Karen, you stay here. You and I need to do some thinking of our own. Apparently nobody else is."

CHAPTER 15

AS MOORE AND McGregor walked with Major Singh down Eaton Terrace and away from their would-be assailants, a small crowd gathered around the two men still writhing on the ground. Mobile phones were produced, and calls made to the Metropolitan Police. Singh produced his own mobile, and opened an app which he showed the others—a street map of the area with red arcs indicating the field of view of the area's CCTV monitors.

"Developed by a chap at MI5. I convinced him to load it for me." Using the device to avoid the ubiquitous cameras, the trio worked their way back towards Sloane Gardens.

"I think we should avoid going in the front door in case there are people waiting for us," Moore said. "It's not exactly a secret where we're staying."

"What?" asked McGregor. "We just climb the garden wall and go in the back?"

"We could do that. Or...there may be another option." She took a quick look at Singh's phone and led them a few blocks to a tiny corner pub. When they entered, McGregor saw the pub was dimly lit with few patrons. The barman looked up, smiled, and said, "Good evening Miss. It's been too long."

Moore walked up to the bar and took a seat. "Yes, Henry, it has. Unfortunately, we're just passing through. I promise, though, I'll be back."

She turned to Major Singh. "Major, do you have a knife?"

"Always."

"If you don't mind, just step into the Gentlemen's and retrieve a key that's behind the upper right part of the doorframe."

He was back in less than a minute and handed Kelli an ordinary looking brass key. Kelli turned to Henry and nodded slightly, to which he responded with a nod and a small smile. She led them down a short hallway, used the key to open a door, flicked on a light, and motioned for them to join her. They did, and she relocked the door behind them.

They found themselves on a platform above a rickety looking set of stairs. They descended—one at a time—and at the bottom they stood in a dimly lit tunnel, about a quarter the size of a typical London Tube tunnel.

As they began making their way down the tunnel, Kelli added, "During the war, this connected the Sloane Square Station and the Duke of York's Headquarters, and later to a nearby American Headquarters as well. That American headquarters, by the way, was heavily damaged by a V-1 rocket in 1944." They walked down the damp, dimly lit tunnel for a few minutes until they were blocked by a brick wall. On the left was a metal ladder. Moore climbed quickly to the top, released a catch, and opened a small trap door. She climbed through. "Come on up," she shouted from above.

The two men ascended to find themselves in the garden shed behind Sir Charles's townhouse. Moore used the security system to open the back door, and they quickly entered. Singh walked immediately to the front and discreetly checked the street. "Looks clear from what I can see."

Kelli opened a large burl elm cabinet in the sitting room and removed a SIG P320, which she handed to McGregor. She offered a second to Singh, who simply opened his suit jacket to reveal the venerable Browning he had carried in Yemen.

"Compliments to your tailor. I completely missed it," said Moore. "But why didn't you use it at the Antelope?"

"On those fools? No need. Besides, this is London; gunshots still attract far too much attention."

"Good point. Are you going to report this little dustup to your superiors?"

"I think not. It would give rise to awkward questions."

"We should probably follow your lead," Moore said. "Who knows what kind of drama that would provoke from our Officer Dover."

"We do have to tell her about that zip drive, though," McGregor said.

"Naturally, but it might be nice to know what's on it first. Grandfather has quite a computer room. I'm sure he has something we can safely use in case it contains some kind of malware. In fact, I'll give him a quick call."

Moore used a landline to call her grandfather. After a minute of conversation, she thanked him and hung up.

"He has a computer not connected to the Internet—or to anything else here—that has some specialized security software. Let's have a look."

They ascended a stairway to the second floor where Kelli led them into a room with an entire wall devoted to computer monitors and other electronic devices. She found the computer she was looking for, booted it up, opened a program, and inserted the drive.

"Quick scan shows there's just a JPEG image file. A very large one. No sign of viruses or other malware, though. I'm going to open it." She did.

"It's one of those gigapixel photographs of a stadium crowd," said Singh. "In fact, it looks like the O2 Arena. I was there just two days ago with my nieces. They were very excited about seeing that Swedish singer, Ingrid, but my sister fell ill, so I took them."

"Is the O2 the same as the Millennium Dome?" McGregor asked.

"The arena is part of the dome. Fantastic place. Here let me show you were we were sitting." Singh moved the mouse and then began to zoom in to an area quite close to the stage.

To everyone's surprise, there was a smiling Singh with two teenage girls.

"So that was taken just two days ago," exclaimed Moore. "We had just arrived. Somebody is well connected at our embassy. Do you think there's something in this photograph intended for us?"

"We should assume so," replied McGregor. "Let's start a search. Begin at the front row, go all the way around, then up a row. This could take a while."

It took about ten minutes. They found a young man with bushy blond hair and a short beard sitting in the third row. He was wearing a t-shirt printed with three rows of text.

"McGregor"

"5th"

"Kneecap."

"It's obviously intended for me, and I assume the 5th refers to tomorrow. But Kneecap?"

They used another computer and after a few minutes of searching found nothing useful.

"It has to be a place rather than an action — you know like knee-capping someone. Or the body part."

McGregor looked up from the screen. "Wait a minute. I took a run yesterday. What's the road that goes by the old building that says 'Michelin' on the front? It has that famous restaurant."

"Brompton Road," answered Moore. "Why?"

Because just down Brompton Road there's a club called Patella. It caught my attention, so I took a look. It's a twenties theme and the sign has a flapper doing the Charleston and she has orange neon patellas—kneecaps!"

"Could be," said Singh.

"Sounds like all we have." Moore looked up the website on her phone. Photographs showed the typical London club crowd with bartenders and staff wearing twenties outfits. In one there were two women on the stage dressed as flappers. "Looks like we have a plan. I'll be taking tomorrow afternoon off. I need a haircut and something to wear; dress for this place is way beyond anything I packed." She looked over McGregor's leather jacket, plain white shirt and khakis and added, "Mike, you could use a little wardrobe upgrade yourself."

McGregor just shrugged.

"With that, I think I'll say good night," Singh said. "I texted one of my people for a ride and he will be here shortly. Still looks quiet outside. Good luck, my friends. You know how to reach me." With that, Singh headed towards the door.

Once he left, Moore said, "Better get a report off to our minder."

CHAPTER 16

APRIL 4

Washington, DC

J ENNIFER KIM READ, then re-read, the brief report from London.

From: Keystone
To: Dover

First contact. Received a USB drive via a cutout. Photograph shows a man—not Granite—in an arena wearing a shirt saying "McGregor, 5th, Kneecap".

We believe this means a meet tomorrow at a local club called Patella. Will attend the meet and report.

This was good news in the sense of contact. The means of contact was weird, though when dealing with amateurs they sometimes did what they imagined intelligence agents did rather than what they actually did. Kim was concerned about the brevity of Dover's reports. Usually, her agents were compulsively detailed. She had a nagging sense that there was something he wasn't sharing.

On the other hand, she had already decided not to include the details in her own report. She did not want some Agency sleeper showing up at this meet. She was going to report contact and that a meet was scheduled. She was curating the information she passed on and McGregor was probably doing the same. What could possibly go wrong?

CHAPTER 17

KAREN HILLER STEPPED into the Oval, waited for Brendan Wallace to gesture for her to approach, and then stepped over to the big Resolute Desk.

"Mr. President, I just received a call from Alex Clarkson at CIA. There has been contact in London. A meet has been arranged between those two officers and someone, probably not Korshkin though. A cutout, I assume."

"That's progress," said the President. "Any details?"

"No, sir. CIA is keeping this op close to home. Either he chose not to tell me where the meeting will be held, or he doesn't know. I suggested using one of our London sleepers to tail those two officers. They both have a history of being loose cannons, you know."

"And how did Alex respond?"

"Rejected the idea out of hand."

"I would agree. Either this meet bears fruit or it doesn't. Surveillance will just increase the chance of blowing it while adding nothing. No, we need to trust our people. Why do I have to keep reminding you that those two officers brought their people—our people—home after we left them behind? We had a good reason—or thought we did—but it was not our finest hour."

Hiller's face flushed. "Of course, Mr. President. I just have an issue with people who routinely disobey orders."

"Remember this. Out of our entire federal response to this crisis, they are the only ones with any hope, so far at least, of making real progress. Now that there's been contact, we need an exfil plan. The Navy is dragging its feet on this. They don't want to piss off the Brits. I get that, but we need to impress upon the CNO that they are getting on board, like it or not. Give him a call and have him begin to put some assets in place. If he asks to talk to me personally, tell him he wouldn't like it."

Hiller, who liked kicking the butts of military brass more than just about anything, said, "Actually, sir, Sonny has a meeting set up with an Admiral Piotrowski early tomorrow to discuss that. He thought we probably had more leverage with him than with CNO or NavEur, both of whom are about to retire and are pretty much beyond political pressure."

"Right, Piotrowski. Yes, we did give him top cover on that Castelli thing last year, and he owes us. Let me know how that plays out."

Karen Hiller replied with a snappy, "Yes, Mr. President," turned, and left the Oval Office.

CHAPTER 18

IAN DROPPED THEM off at Patella at about 2000, which was early for the London club scene. Kelli Moore was in a short black sequined dress, black tights, a chunky gold choker, and strappy heels. Her normally straight red hair was now layered and had a bit of a curl. McGregor, who had never been to a nightclub in his life, wore black jeans and T-shirt with the same leather jacket he had worn to the Antelope. He was aiming for modern nonchalant casual, but Moore thought he looked like a drug dealer. Oh well, it was too late to find anything different. The club was in an aging building that had been hastily remodeled to take advantage of the current fad for 1920s culture. It would probably be gone in a year. The crowd was sparse, but the music loud and the few couples who were dancing did so with great energy.

They found a table near the back and away from the stage. Moore ordered gin and tonic for both.

"I hate gin and tonic," said McGregor.

"I know that, but we need to blend in, and this way you won't drink too much. We need to stay sharp."

After a half hour of sipping their warm drinks and watching the dancers, a young man with bushy blond hair approached their table. He was the man in the photograph that had led them there.

78

"May I sit down?" he asked with a heavy Russian accent.

"Please do," replied McGregor. "Would you mind telling us just who you are?"

"Call me what you wish, but I was once known as Boris Voronin. And yes, I do know Korshkin. You can probably guess how."

"You were involved in the theft of those nukes, weren't you?" Moore asked.

"What can I say? I am a thief by nature and if you were trapped in the dismal Arctic outpost we were in, you might have considered doing the same. I hope your military told you that those warheads had been disabled. They were not going to go off no matter what."

"I heard a rumor," McGregor said. "Well, thanks. But that didn't help all the people who were killed trying to get them back."

"No way we could have known you smart Americans would find them. But that is old news. You want to find Korshkin, or don't you?"

"That's what we're here for," said McGregor.

"All right then. At some point Korshkin knew the British security services were on to his real role in handling the sale of those warheads, and now they are going all out to lay their hands on him. Korshkin has a flat in Glasgow, so he went up there, but he soon got word that MI5 was sniffing around for real estate holdings in Scotland. At the same time, he began having some kind of spells."

"Spells?" asked McGregor, suddenly very interested. "What kind of spells?"

"He would feel very weak and short of breath for a few minutes, then back to normal. These spells started happening more often and lasting longer. We kept in touch with single-use mobiles and he told me he was going to Edinburgh to stay with a woman friend."

"Were they..."

"I don't think so. She is some kind of artist. He supported her work until she could make a living at it. I visited him there just once."

"Do you have her name or an address?" asked Moore.

"I can give you directions. Korshkin thought staying too long in Edinburgh might put her at risk so I'm sure he's moved on. But she can probably tell you where he is."

Boris paused for a moment, apparently trying to recall the details. "Start at Deacon Brodie's Tavern, it's an Edinburgh landmark. Go east down the high street past Parliament Square. Not far after that, on your right, there will be several small passages that lead to spaces that were once stables and lodging for the grooms and coachmen, and are now blocks of flats. The doors are mostly just plain wood or black, but one is bright blue. Beside it is a decorated tile with the letter 'M.' That's the best I can do."

"That's it?" asked Moore.

"I found it easily. No reason you can't." Boris stopped suddenly and looked towards the door. "There's trouble. Could you have been followed?"

"Possible," said Moore. "We weren't really looking out for surveillance."

"Well I was, and he didn't follow me. I cannot believe they sent amateurs for Korshkin. Christ—Americans!"

Moore glanced around as surreptitiously as she could. No one stood out.

"Look, I have a motorcycle out back," added Boris. "I'm getting on it and not stopping until I am out of London. I think a vacation is in order. A very long vacation. Good luck."

"Tell us what's going on," Moore demanded.

"See that big guy who just came in? Shaved head, blue suit."

McGregor glanced towards the entrance. "Yeah, who is he?"

"Looks a lot like a guy called Viktor Belov. Does freelance work for all the Russian crime bosses in the UK. There's a rumor he works with a little guy who actually does the wet work. Viktor gets your attention, chases you around, and sets up the little one for the shot. That's the story, anyway. No one has seen this small man. At least no one still alive."

Without another word, Boris stood and hurried out a side door, looking quickly left and right for the little guy, who was apparently not there as a few seconds later they heard the roar of his motorcycle.

"You think there's anything to that?" asked McGregor. "Is this guy the escalation after those punks with knives?"

"We're about to find out. If he follows us out, then we have to deal with this very differently."

"Wouldn't it be easier to give Ian a call and just have him come get us?"

"Easier, yes," she replied, "but then we wouldn't know if this guy is a real threat or if young Boris just has an overdeveloped sense of paranoia."

"Just remember, we're not armed and if this guy really is Belov, you can bet he is."

"Speak for yourself."

Moore opened her shoulder bag, rummaged for a moment, then pulled out what looked like an oversized fountain pen. She held it below the table, pressed the clip, and a five inch, very thin triangular blade dropped out. "Watch out," she said. "It's incredibly sharp." She turned it so the blade was up, pressed the clip again, and it retracted. She handed it to McGregor who put it into his jacket pocket.

She then pulled up a small flashlight and dropped it back into her bag. "It's brass. Surprisingly heavy."

"Do you have a SIG in there too?"

"Probably should, but no."

"Officer Kim will be pleased to hear we followed her instructions."

The two officers exited the club by the same side door Boris had used. They crossed Brompton Road and walked down a side street— slowing occasionally to look at shop windows or restaurant menus. At one small bistro, a couple sat outdoors. He was eating a pizza and she was working through a big pot of mussels. They were unaware of the drama next to them on the street.

McGregor looked down several alleys and saw they were not as dark as he'd hoped. He looked up at the moon, just a day or two short of full, perched in a cloudless sky.

"Grandfather says they used to call that a bomber's moon," said Moore.

"And I guess we're the target."

After two blocks, they stopped and looked back in the direction they came. In the middle of the previous block stood Belov, looking directly at them with dark, deep-set eyes. His hands were on his hips in an attitude of complete confidence.

"One question answered," said Moore. "Let's see if we can lose him."

They picked up the pace and walked two more blocks, turned left, and after a minute entered a small pub. They walked through the bar out to a small courtyard with tables. From there they walked out a back gate and onto a street a block from where they had entered. They crossed the street, took a right, and turned the next corner.

At the end of that block they looked back. There was Belov, his shaved head gleaming under a streetlight. He waved at them. Dammit!

"Cocky, bastard," McGregor said. "Any more ideas?"

"Sure. We take him out."

"So...you're talking about killing a professional assassin on a London street using what are essentially hand tools."

"Exactly," she said. "And I know right where to do it." She sat on a step, took off her heels, and jammed them into her bag. She pulled out a pair of folded ballet flats and put them on. "We might need to move fast."

After several turns and three quick blocks, Moore directed McGregor into a narrow passage between two buildings—narrow enough they had to pass through sideways. After about ten feet, it widened out, and beyond that was a courtyard surrounded by dimly lit buildings.

"There are several ways out of that courtyard, all facing on different streets, so he will probably choose to follow us in rather than trying to guess where we'll come out. We're going to take him right here. He's going to come through sideways like we did, so we'll be waiting for him on either side of this opening. Whoever he faces has to do something to hurt him enough to buy a second or two for the other to take him down."

"I'm guessing he'll lead with his gun hand. We have to be pretty quick or he is going to start shooting."

"He's too damn sure of himself, doesn't think we can hurt him. That's our advantage," replied Moore.

Less than a minute later they heard heavy footsteps that paused at the other end of the passage. Moore and McGregor both had the same thought. He's wondering if we're waiting for him.

He apparently made a decision as they heard him shuffling quietly along the Victorian-era paving stones.

His right hand emerged first, holding a Glock. In two seconds, he was out of the passage and spotted McGregor in the dim light. Less than a second after that, the narrow triangular blade McGregor held was plunged into Belov's sternum.

Lots of nerves there, so the blow was intensely painful. Stunned, the Russian froze for a second, but then he bellowed something in Russian, and the Glock began to swing up towards McGregor.

McGregor was still gripping the blade. He gave it a quick twist and the Russian made a guttural noise, but it did not stop the progress of the muzzle. Before he could get off a shot, however, Moore struck him on the side of the head with her weapon and the hitman slumped to the ground. A flawless execution of their plan.

As he went down the blade pulled from his chest. McGregor looked down and was surprised that the man, though stunned, was still conscious. McGregor jumped on him, pinned his shoulders down with his knees, and thrust the blade into his throat. This produced choking and gasping. Moore knelt beside the hitman and delivered several more blows to the same spot on his head. With the third impact there was an audible 'crack.' After that, he was still.

McGregor unbuttoned the man's shirt. "Russian prison tattoos."

Moore pick up the Glock, and a quick search produced a Beretta Nano from an ankle holster. She handed it to Mike.

"We need to get rid of the weapons we used. His DNA is all over both of them." She dropped the flashlight down a heavy steel grate.

"Won't that be the first place they look for evidence?"

"That shaft goes down to one of London's underground rivers. There's a lot of flow to clean away any forensic evidence. Besides, I doubt this grate has been removed since the war."

"Keeping the guns is risky, but if the small guy is for real, we may need them. We can ditch them later."

Moore replaced her heels and, arm in arm, they passed back onto the street from which they came. Just two people heading home from an evening out.

Indeed, in the following days, the London Police questioned a number of people who had been out that evening in the area of Brompton Road. They were asked if they had seen anyone suspicious. None of them had.

CHAPTER 19

APRIL 5

Norfolk, Virginia

REAR ADMIRAL VINCE Piotrowski picked up his office phone and asked his Chief of Staff to step in. As Commander, Naval Surface Forces Atlantic—COMNAVSURFLANT—Piotrowski had administrative, but not tactical, control of all surface ships stationed on the East Coast. When deployed, his ships were attached to operational commands such as NavEur, Naval Forces European Command. It was a complex overlap of authority, but it generally worked.

Captain Ron Weiss stepped in. Piotrowski didn't bother with formality and discouraged the snapping to attention ritual. "Ron, we have a touchy situation and I'm going to need your help."

"Of course, Admiral. What's up?"

"This is something that normally would end up on NavEur's plate, but for a couple of reasons, it hasn't. The National Security advisor met with me this morning and laid out something the President wants handled—quietly. He subtly brought up the fact that his boss backed me last year when I let the skipper of *Bataan* retire after he disobeyed a White House order and pulled those Marines out of Yemen. CNO wanted to come down hard on that guy, and by inference, on me. The White House let it be known they were satisfied with the outcome, so that was that."

"Captain Castelli. I remember. I was a bit surprised myself." Weiss had been more than surprised. He had been strongly opposed to allowing Captain Castelli to walk away with his pension. He knew, though, that during the first Gulf War Piotrowski, as skipper of the missile frigate USS *Bowman*, had skirted orders to extract the crew of a downed B-52 from the same area of Yemen where Castelli had recovered the sailors and Marines. This led Piotrowski to be somewhat lax with skippers who took the similar view of mission first, orders second.

"It was the right thing to do, but now we're in a 'no good deed goes unpunished' situation. The White House wants me to do something CNO and NavEur don't want to get involved in."

Weiss was inwardly pleased that his boss was now getting squeezed for his prior misdeeds, but then realized that the pressure was about to be passed on to him. "What situation is this? I haven't heard of anything in our wheelhouse that could get CNO excited."

"You are now. I'm reading you in on an op that originated out of the White House. By the President personally, in fact."

"Is this about the nerve-gas bomb?"

"That's it. Well, there seems to be someone involved with those Russian nukes that wound up in Yemen who may know the individual behind these attacks. The informant is in Britain and wants out, but the Brits don't want us getting our hands on him. Two reservists—that Marine and the Navy doc involved in the Yemen extraction—have been placed in our embassy and charged with finding this guy and organizing an exfil plan. They have apparently made enough progress that the White House wants the Navy to be in a position to support them. The problem is that the big dogs up the chain don't want to touch it. They are committed to closer integration with the Royal Navy and think this is a fool's errand that's just going to screw up that relationship without solving the terrorist problem."

"But the White House thinks otherwise?"

"Obviously. It's essentially the President's plan."

"So where do we come in?" Ron Weiss had a bad feeling about the answer.

"I've worked up the best option I can on short notice. Since we normally lack operational control once our ships get underway, we need to get involved while they're still in port. The *Makin Island* and a couple of destroyers are about to depart Norfolk to participate in Nordic Watch, that big NATO exercise off Norway. GE wants to install an upgrade to the operating software for their gas turbines, but the squadron commander recommended delaying until after the exercise. In order to put them where we need them, though, I've decided to go ahead with those upgrades which will hold them back a day, maybe two. The delay will put them off the coast of Scotland about the time they'll be needed. If they are needed."

"And I...?"

"Will visit the skippers of *Makin Island* and the two destroyers escorting her. You will pass along these orders"—Piotrowski handed him several large envelopes—"which instruct them to proceed with the upgrade and to use the time after departure to do the required engineering tests. Because they will be performing those tests, they will remain under SURFLANT control until they enter the exercise area and chop to control of Task Force 64, which is the naval element of the exercise."

"Admiral, a day or two of engineering trials isn't unusual, but I've never heard of an Atlantic crossing under control of SURFLANT. And what about PHIBRON 6? Aren't we just cutting him out of the chain of command?" *Makin Island* was part of Amphibious Squadron Six commanded by Captain Alonzo Kane. Kane was between Piotrowski and *Makin Island* in the chain of command, and something like what this would normally go through him. Weiss was concerned that he and his boss might be stepping on too many toes.

"Don't worry, Ron. I've informed Captain Kane that there are unusual circumstances here. PHIBRON 6 won't be a problem."

Weiss knew that Alonzo Kane was a protégé of Piotrowski and that they had managed back-channel deals in the past. He suspected the skipper of *Makin Island* was probably tight with Piotrowski as well.

"Of course, Admiral. But I'm still not clear how the change to Makin Island's schedule helps this mission."

Piotrowski ignored his question. "In addition to delivering written orders, you will inform *Makin Island* that a representative of the Central Intelligence Agency will be coming aboard." Piotrowski consulted a notepad. "An Officer Kim."

"She will be listed as a technical representative. She should be provided with private quarters and given full access to comm facilities. She also has—and this is the touchy part—been authorized by the National Security Advisor to request assistance from *Makin Island* and her support vessels in the performance of her mission."

Things were now becoming very clear to Weiss. The Admiral had found a way to circumvent NavEur and the exercise commander, both of whom were very tight with the CNO, in order to put one of his ships in position to assist a CIA mission dreamed up by the White House. And he was the point man to make it happen. Weiss felt the sudden need for an antacid tablet.

"And NAVSEA? How do we inform them of the turbine upgrade without CNO finding out?"

"Yeah, that is a problem. Sea Systems Command is in the CNO's shop, but the upgrade is a routine maintenance issue. We'll send instructions for the upgrade to PHIBRON 6 who will endorse and forward to *Makin Island*, copy to NAVSEA. Could take a week before it gets there. By then it may turn out that *Makin Island* isn't even needed."

"And if they are needed?"

"The CIA agent will make a formal request, but they should not expect the White House to issue them direct orders. Frankly, if the skipper complies and the whole thing goes sideways, he could end up like Castelli. On the other hand, if the Navy fails to prevent another nerve gas attack on US soil—well, you can imagine how that would work out."

"Geez, Admiral. I'm starting to understand just how Captain Castelli felt."

CHAPTER 20

JONAS LANKA, THE embassy Regional Security Officer, picked up the single-use phone, one in a series bought by cutouts from street vendors, and destined for the bottom of the Thames.

"Yeah."

"They're dead."

"Both of them? How?"

"Yes, both of them," said the man with the harsh Russian accent. "Belov had his head bashed in and was stabbed with an icepick. The small man's neck was broken."

"They were supposed to be the best."

"They are, or were. I have never heard of anyone laying a hand on either of them. You told me these people were amateurs. Are you sure? Could they be specialists operating with some kind of deep cover?"

"It would have to be the deepest cover I've ever heard of," Lanka said. "They both have ordinary jobs back in the states and there is no doubt they are who they're supposed to be. I just don't see any connection between them and Korshkin. On the other hand, if they're starting to cause trouble, we may need to get them out of here."

Lanka paused for a moment, then added, "Didn't they have help outside the Antelope? Maybe they had help again."

"Probably," said the Russian. "The small one was two blocks from Belov when he got it. Belov was herding them in his direction. All the CCTV footage showed was that an arm reached out and dragged the small man into an alley. Belov was killed with two different weapons, so he was likely taken down by your people."

"It may be time for a change in tactics," Lanka said. "We tried to scare them off at the Antelope and that went sideways; and now this. By the way, have those two morons from the Antelope told the police anything?"

"What could they say? This was just a robbery that went badly. No concern there. If they become a problem, we can deal with them very easily."

"As I was saying, we couldn't scare them, and we couldn't kill them. Perhaps it's better now to see if they will lead us to Korshkin and then take them all out at the same time."

"That is going to take a lot of people for surveillance. We have to assume they will have help from Sir Charles. Watching them will cost a fortune."

"I am told," Lanka said, "that there are unlimited funds available. If I need to, I can ask for some specialists to be brought in."

"Hopefully better than our recently departed specialists."

"Remember this, there is one thing that is certain: Korshkin cannot be taken to the United States. That would end badly for both of us. One other thought. If your people have any doubt they can maintain surveillance on these two, and the opportunity arises, tell them to make another—better—attempt at removing them."

"Yes, yes. They cannot be lucky every time. And what will you be doing while we are doing all the legwork?"

"I'm going to get the ambassador to call them into the embassy for a confrontation. That might push them into making a mistake. Send me whatever you have from CCTV or private security cameras."

"I will also send photographs from the crime scenes and from the autopsies."

"I did not realize you were that well connected," remarked Lanka.

"As you Americans like to say, the Metropolitan Police and MI5 leak like a sieve."

CHAPTER 21

From: Keystone
To: Dover

1. Successful contact with Russian national believed to be Boris Voronin, one of the individuals responsible for the warhead theft at the center of Op Ocean Reach.

2. Voronin states Granite is in Scotland, recently in Edinburgh, but likely moved on from there. He provided a source in Edinburgh who presumably knows Granite's current location.

3. Our intent is to travel to Edinburgh to investigate. Expect a day of preparation tomorrow, with departure the morning after.

4. Keystone's CO will cover absence. OPSEC requires you to arrange for Empire's section head to do the same. Suspect he is DIA so this may have to come from very high in Army chain of command.

5. While returning from meet, we were followed by a presumed Russian assassin. No choice but to eliminate him. Very unlikely either Keystone or Empire can be tied to this action. Monitor and advise if this changes.

McGregor finished his report to Jennifer Kim, sent it off, and slumped back in his chair. He finished his whisky and poured another.

"We're going to need help from Grandfather to get to Edinburgh." Kelli leaned against the doorframe, also sipping whiskey. "And we should probably be better armed."

"I'll say." McGregor turned to look at her. "I'm sick of being outgunned. And I'm sick of pretending we're undercover when everybody seems to know what we're really up to."

"I texted Grandfather to meet us here tomorrow morning. He may have some ideas.

"And can you help me with this dress?" She turned around and McGregor unzipped her. He expected her to head for her room.

Instead the dress dropped to the floor.

The closer people have come to death, the greater the desire to feel alive, and that was true on this night in London. For a few moments, Mike and Kelli were free from thoughts about driving a high-tech icepick into the Russian's heart or cracking his skull. They did not have to wonder if this was duty, or self-defense, or if they had just lost it.

McGregor had been surprised, but in truth, this was not the first time they'd been at this point. On Christmas Eve, only a few months after both were wounded in Yemen, McGregor had asked her over for chili and Christmas movies. It was near the end of "Love Actually" that McGregor pulled her close and kissed her. What followed then was more healing then passion. The next morning Kelli Moore had dressed, about to head to her brother's for Christmas, when she said, "That was pretty amazing."

"Yes, very therapeutic." McGregor had rarely been smooth when it came to women. He instantly realized what a stupid thing he had done and waited for the inevitable rebuke.

"It was. Very." On the way out the door she added, "Merry Christmas, Michael."

Early next morning, Kelli sat on the side of McGregor's bed. "Mike, I think there are some things I need to tell you."

"Go ahead, I'm happy to hear whatever you want to say."

"I think it would be easier if I wasn't sitting here naked. I'll be back in a minute." As she walked away it was not her lithe figure that attracted McGregor's attention, but the scar just behind her left breast where a Yemeni officer had inflicted a near fatal knife wound. She had survived only because her knife work was more effective than his. McGregor had been there and had watched one of the other battalion surgeons place the chest tube that had saved her life.

Five minutes later she returned wearing Naval Academy sweats and carrying two cups of coffee. McGregor had changed into jeans and a Michigan hockey T-shirt. They sat down in the matching wing-back leather chairs and she began.

"I think it all started when my grandmother divorced Grandfather. She wanted to live back in the States, and he didn't. It was tough, but grandfather always put work before everything else in his life and Grandmother was tired of not being his priority. When they were old enough, he put my dad and his brother, my uncle Tim, in charge of one of his US businesses. This caused more issues with my grandmother. Tensions grew between the two because she felt that having their sons take over the business was a way to control them and take them away from her. These were stresses I was unaware of at the time."

Kelli took a deep breath to calm the tension building in her chest. "It happened when I was thirteen. My family and my uncle's were at a park along the river outside Detroit. My little brother and cousin Sarah were with the adults, while my sixteen-year-old cousin Alex and I were some distance away. We were lying under a picnic table talking when he started kissing me. I was surprised, but I must admit I was liking it, which added to my sense of confusion. Then he put his hand in my shorts and started pulling them down."

"Kelli, you don't have to..."

"Yes, I do. I was a pretty strong kid and I pushed him away and punched him a couple of times. He got furious, jumped on top of me and started choking me. I picked up a rock and hit him in the face. Apparently, it damaged his eye. I can still remember his scream."

"I imagine he lost that eye."

"Not lost, but there was a lot of damage to the retina. Even after several operations he can only see light or dark. I felt really bad, at least I did until about a week later. What happened that day changed me and my family forever."

McGregor raised his eyebrows, surprised at her intensity, and by his own anxiety at what more she might be about to reveal.

"Dad told me he and Uncle Tim had reached an agreement. There would be no charges against me for assault, but I would go to a special school for girls with emotional and violence problems. I asked about what would happen to Alex for attacking me, and he just slapped me. Called me a 'stupid girl'. Told me if I said anything more it would ruin everything, and that what happened was my fault and I needed to forget about it."

"I can't believe ... Jesus." McGregor was truly shocked, but he was also beginning to understand the trauma that had shaped her life and had been part of what prevented the relationship that McGregor had wanted for some time.

"I couldn't either. I ran out of the room crying and my Mom explained to me it was to keep peace in the family, and it was best for me to stay quiet for the time being. She was acting strange, and I was worried she agreed with what my dad was doing. I assumed it was mainly to keep the business together. But then Grandfather showed up.

"It was only a few hours later. He flew over on his jet as soon as he heard—I think Mom must have called him, which probably explained her behavior. He was angry, and it was that kind of cold, no-forgiving-ever kind of angry. He told my father that if he went through with this plan that he would take away the business and leave him and Uncle Tim with nothing. The alternative was that I would live with him in London until he felt it was safe for me to come home. He would split the business with Tim getting the commercial real estate and Dad the investment banking. He handed Dad papers that gave Grandfather custody of me and allowed him to take me out of the country. He stood there glaring at my father while he signed. We left an hour later.

"I lived for three years in this house—it wasn't quite as nice as it is now though. I attended a lovely girl's school a few blocks from here. Grandfather taught me to shoot, to fish, and to sail. He really is an extraordinary man and I'm so grateful he took me away. He's the only person I had growing up who really cared about me and had the power to stand up for me no matter what came along. I think he's the reason I can be strong in the face of danger now."

"After a moment, McGregor said, "That's...incredible. I'm so sorry that happened, but I'm glad Sir Charles was able to step in."

"For better or worse, it made me who I am. I went back to Michigan for my junior and senior years in high school. I'll admit, I did a lot of acting out with my father. Pretty much everything he wanted, I did the opposite."

"I suppose that accounts for the Academy and the Marine Corps."

"You would have loved the reaction at dinner when I told him I had turned down Yale and Michigan and was going to the Academy. Incredibly satisfying."

"So, this is the endgame? We're here living with Sir Charles, winging it on some kind of spook mission, and being chased by Russian killers."

"I suppose that's true. I never dreamed I'd be working to exfil a nuclear weapons dealer out of Britain when I entered the Academy, but I'm starting to think we're exactly who they need on this mission. We aren't reacting like they expect us to because we're not professionals. We can pull this off—find Korshkin, get him fit to travel, and do the exfiltration. Do you remember what you said when we were outnumbered in Yemen and they called for us to surrender?"

McGregor paused for a moment. "Didn't I say, 'We're going to kill every fucking one of them?'"

"Well Michael, it's time to start thinking like that."

McGregor waited for her to address the previous evening, but she did not.

A moment later, they heard the front door open. McGregor and Moore got dressed for the day, Kelli stopping for just a second on the way out of Michael's room to glance back at the bed they had shared. They walked downstairs and found Ian and Sir Charles in the kitchen chatting and cooking omelets.

CHAPTER 22

THE UZBEK PULLED his RV onto a side road in a remote area of the national forest, adjusted his satellite dish, and logged into a website for nature photographers. He recognized one of the photographs as a subject used by his handler to transmit messages to him—a bluebird at a feeder. He downloaded it and began running the software that would extract the encrypted characters from the background of millions of pixels.

The Uzbek was not actually an Uzbek at all. He was born in Uzbekistan in 1980 while his father, Alexander Ulanov, was stationed there with the KGB. They had lived there long enough for him to learn some of the language and customs before moving back to Moscow after the fall of the USSR. The KGB was disbanded, but the need for its services remained. His father was by then well placed in the SVR, the new foreign-intelligence service. He had groomed his son, Alexi, to take on foreign assignments for the service. He was kept away from most of the SVR hierarchy, so few in the service even knew who he was. Since he began foreign missions, he was referred to only as the Uzbek, and that is how he was known now—when he was known at all. This, along with his entirely nondescript appearance—medium height, dark hair, soft brown eyes—made him a perfect candidate for foreign operations.

Realizing Uzbekistan would offer few opportunities for important assignments, the Uzbek studied English, ultimately speaking both the British and American versions with native fluency and accent. His motivation was more than professional, though. After the attacks of 9/11, when the Americans and the British became involved in Afghanistan, the elder Ulanov was dispatched to that forlorn "graveyard of empires" to gather intelligence and to disrupt Anglo-American covert operations. He was discovered by western operatives, probably CIA, and he and his team were assassinated by a missile strike. After that, Alexi dedicated himself to operations against the British and Americans. It became an obsession.

Recently, he had been an active participant in the Brexit campaign, where he ran a disinformation website and had actually become the speechwriter for an influential MP. His current assignment had the potential to weaken another enemy of his homeland even more. But there was no margin for error. What he was doing absolutely could not be traced back to Russia or to its President. The Uzbek must not be captured—under any circumstances.

His laptop had extracted and decrypted the message. Once he read it, all evidence that it ever existed would be erased and there would be no record on any server.

The news he received was not good. One of the few—the very few—people who could help the Americans identify him had contacted them and was trying to arrange exfiltration from Britain in return for this information. The Uzbek knew that the service had important contacts in the US embassy and that they were apparently trying to obstruct the mission to retrieve this man. He also knew there was a highly placed contact in the British government—Codename Asher—who was feeding information back to the SVR via Russian organized crime figures in London. The Uzbek had made use of Asher several times during his recent mission in Britain. The man was ruthlessly ambitious. He asked for no money, but rather he demanded the service find ways to derail the careers of people who might block or otherwise frustrate his advancement.

This was a refreshingly Russian way of thinking: British traitors were usually political zealots and the Americans simply greedy.

The Uzbek's mission had been planned as a prolonged campaign of terrorist nerve-gas bombings that would serve two purposes. First, to disrupt the social and economic life of the country as more and more people became fearful of public places. And second, by utilizing people of various ethnicities to deliver the weapons, to aggravate the already-boiling tensions over immigrants and minorities, with the goal of slowly imploding American society.

This part of the mission was proceeding very well, indeed. After the second attack, specialists in the suburbs of St. Petersburg had released a veritable army of Internet bots onto social media platforms and their effect was magnified by so-called media influencers and commentators, some in the employ of Moscow and others simply useful dupes. The Uzbek had been disturbed by Internet stories blaming Russia for the attacks, but naturally without evidence. Though counter to his natural instincts, he understood that erasing negative stories about his homeland would be a beacon of Russian involvement to the American security services.

Despite his successes, this threat from Maxim Korshkin made his handlers wary of exposure. They were demanding an acceleration of the attacks and preparation to shut down the operation on a moment's notice. They were skittish fools. The Uzbek wanted to see the job to its end, and to do it his own way.

The Uzbek, though, was a thorough professional. He knew his operation was but one in a series of acts designed to slowly, relentlessly destabilize the enemy. And the escalating tensions over immigration and race were testaments to their success. Once his op was shut down, there would be another. The SVR played the long game. There was always another.

The message was deleted, and the Uzbek reached into his small refrigerator, removed a bottle of chilled vodka, poured a glass, and sat back to think.

CHAPTER 23

THE FOUR PEOPLE seated around Sir Charles's dining room table had discussed in some detail the meeting with Boris Voronin and the subsequent confrontation with Viktor Belov. Kelli and Mike had already agreed they were going to need help for the next steps and would have to trust her grandfather, who seemed to have the kind of connections they needed. There would be no more cover story—Sir Charles would know everything.

Sir Charles pulled an encrypted mobile from his pocket and sent a text. "I have arranged for you to meet with someone this afternoon who can provide several items you may find useful in future confrontations."

"Grandfather," said Kelli, "I've told Michael what happened back in Michigan. I thought he needed to know."

When Sir Charles smiled at her, his green eyes shone with real affection. "I am very glad you have someone you can trust. Michael, if Kelli trusts you completely, then so do I. And in that case, there are a few things you probably should know about me as well." He refilled his tea.

"Back in the sixties, I joined the Royal Navy—family tradition. After a few years on the decks, I became an intelligence officer. They sent me back to Cambridge to study Russian, which was where I met Sarah, Kelli's grandmother. She was from a wealthy Michigan family and living in Britain studying economics. I think she wanted to escape the political discord back in the states. To be honest, she found me disagreeable at first. Remember, Viet Nam was nearing its peak and American college students had a natural aversion to all things military. Nonetheless, I finally wormed my way into her heart and after she graduated, we were married at a village church near my parent's country home down in Sussex.

After a few years, I moved over to MI6 where they arranged for me to do business in Eastern Europe. It was a perfect cover, as the Cold War made anyone who did business with Communists a pariah in the UK, or at least in the business community. The Reds assumed I must be real to expose myself to so much grief."

"He received death threats from a number of conservative activists," Kelli said. "And even a couple of MPs."

"By the time my cover was well established, though, we had two sons—John, Kelli's father, and Tim. Their mother wanted me to leave the security service and move with her back to the States. But I was just too deeply into the intelligence game to leave, and after butting heads once too often, I impulsively told her to just leave if she wanted. She did and moved back to Detroit. I visited when I could and spent time with my sons. To be better connected to them, I started a business there—commercial real estate and investment banking. These were boom times in the States, and even though the city of Detroit was fading along with the auto industry, there were still plenty of opportunities, and in time I set the boys up to run the business. It felt right at the time for us to separate, but now I wish things had been different—obviously, growing up without their father was difficult for my sons, and they have made choices that, well, disappointed me. I knew that I bore some responsibility for what happened to Kelli. That was part of the reason I took her in. I saw that they were putting their business before their family just as I had done—but with dramatically more severe consequences. I was determined that she would have a caring father, the father I wished I'd been for my sons."

Kelli looked down to her lap for a moment, the past was difficult for her to think about, and it had been coming up a lot these past twenty-four hours

"If you don't mind my asking," Mike said, "how did an MI6 officer manage to afford an investment in Eastern Europe?"

"An excellent question, Michael. To get me started, Six arranged for a business loan through Barclay's Bank, no direct connection to the service. I repaid the loan, and despite the fact that the business was primarily a cover, I did very well—and I owned the whole thing. Because very few people were willing to do business in the East, I had a clear field. Following the 1989 demise of the Soviet Union and the breakup of their empire in Europe, I quit the service and continued to run the business. In short, I was well funded to invest elsewhere, including the US, though at the time Six was not entirely happy."

"Can you tell me anything about your intelligence work?" Mike asked.

"Some intelligence gathering, but mainly reporting on economic activity, and developing dossiers on the people I did business with. A secondary function was to aid the infiltration and exfiltration of our people, and occasionally of agents they were running."

"I think you need to mention the American connection," said Kelli.

"Considering why you're here, I probably should, though it's nothing exotic. Because I had family in the US as well as business interests, I was approached by the CIA about doing little off-the-books jobs for the Agency. Mainly helping with exfil and with filling in details about people they wanted to recruit. I knew Six wouldn't like it, but I did have a strong connection to the US, so I just took it on as a sideline. It really was very small stuff."

"I'm getting the feeling that your relationship with both MI6 and the CIA has not been entirely severed," Mike said.

"Ah...mostly."

"Aha!"

"Just the occasional small job for both. Last time I did anything for the Agency was a few years ago. They had lost a local agent, and one of their people was wounded in Eastern Europe. They had shockingly limited local contacts—all their assets seemed to be in the Middle East—so I arranged the exfil. Had to buy a helicopter to do it; a beat-up old Ka-27 Helix. Thank God that at the time Ian still had a valid license. A small gratuity convinced the seller to waive the need for a type certificate. It was a miracle we all got out."

"Excuse me Sir Charles," said Ian, who had until now been quietly observing the conversation. "That was bloody fine flying considering I can't read Russian and had never seen one of the damn things before."

"Yes, Ian, you really were brilliant. I was thinking more about the condition of the aircraft."

With that remark, Ian seemed mollified. He toasted Sir Charles with a glass of juice and went back to observing.

Mike's mobile rang. He listened for a moment and hung up. Everyone looked at him, and there was a sudden chill in the room. They were somehow expecting the worst.

"Jonas Lanka, the Regional Security Officer at the embassy," he said. "Says the Ambassador wants to see us. Right now. I have a bad feeling about this."

"Considering what happened last night, I would tend to agree," added Sir Charles. "Do you have any kind of backup here?"

"Maybe. Do you have an untraceable mobile?"

Sir Charles stifled a laugh and looked to Ian who said, "About a dozen." He stepped out, and in a minute, he returned with two.

McGregor dialed and put the phone on speaker. After one ring it was answered. "Barbosa."

"Captain, it's McGregor. Well, you were right about our mission. Now we could use your help."

Mike explained the situation with the Russian in the most oblique terms, trusting that an experienced operator like Barbosa would understand exactly what he meant. "Now the RSO has called telling us to report to the Ambassador immediately."

"I don't like it," the Captain said. "Lanka is at best a snake, and at worst something much more dangerous." He did not elaborate, and McGregor did not ask for details.

"I will meet you in the lobby of the embassy when you arrive. I'm going to assume your mission is important enough to permit a certain amount of latitude on my part." Barbosa ended the call.

"I wonder what he meant by 'latitude'?" Kelli asked.

"Well, he struck me as the kind of guy you don't screw around with," Mike said. "I'm inclined to trust his judgement."

"And I am also not—as you so elegantly put it—the kind of guy you screw around with," Sir Charles said. "Ian, I'll be joining you on the drive up to the embassy. First, however, I believe you and I should take precautions."

Ian stepped into the sitting room and returned with two SIG P320s. He handed one to Sir Charles while placing the other into a nicely concealed shoulder holster.

Five minutes later they were on their way.

CHAPTER 24

THE AUDI PULLED up in front of the embassy, located west of Sloane Square, across the Thames in the area of London known as Nine Elms. As the two officers, now in dress uniforms, exited the vehicle, Sir Charles said, "We'll wait down the street. When you leave, we'll be right up to collect you." Ian drove off as Sir Charles rolled up his window, leaving Moore and McGregor on their own.

They presented identification to the guard and were admitted to the embassy. In the lobby they found, as promised, Captain Jose Barbosa, also in dress blues. He gestured towards the elevator. "Don't want to keep the Ambassador waiting."

McGregor shook his hand. "Captain, I appreciate your coming to meet us, but I don't think the Ambassador or the RSO really want anyone to join us."

"And if they had a choice, that might matter. But you are not under their authority, you're under mine. Naval Medical Clinic London is not a subordinate command here, we are simply a tenant. I'll be there—or you will not. Captain Moore, it's a pleasure to meet you. I don't have any command authority over you, so you'll have to use your own judgement, but I would strongly advise you against attending this meeting alone."

110

Moore studied the Captain for a moment and apparently liked what she saw. "I agree, sir. Let's go."

They proceeded to the elevator that took them up to the Ambassador's suite. His assistant, a middle-aged woman with salt and pepper hair, looked them over for a moment, gave the barest hint of a smile, and then said, "The Ambassador is expecting you. Go right in."

Ambassador Oliver Crane looked exactly like an ambassador should look: tall and lean with thick black hair just greying at the temples. Scion of an old Massachusetts political family, he had attended Harvard, as had five generations of his forebears, and then had gone on to graduate study at Georgetown. After a stint at the Center for Strategic and International Studies, he had become the foreign policy advisor to the new congressman from South Carolina, Brendan Wallace. This gave him the political chops to move into the Foreign Service where his work was competent, if not spectacular. When Wallace ascended to the White House, Crane's path to the top of the Foreign Service was cleared. He was appointed Ambassador to Afghanistan, but after an unspecified family problem, he was transferred to London.

The Ambassador came around his desk and greeted McGregor and Moore with the insincere handshake of a true political animal. "Captain Barbosa, I don't recall inviting you to this meeting. I'm afraid I'll have to ask you to leave."

"And I'll to have to refuse, Ambassador. You have no authority over Commander McGregor, and I have decided that any meeting that includes one of my subordinate officers must include me as well."

"Jonas, what's your position on this?"

The Regional Security Officer spoke from a dark corner of the large office. His obscure location was clearly intended to surprise their guests, but all three officers possessed a high level of situational awareness and had noticed him as soon as they entered.

Lanka looked at the trio of officers, who looked intently back at him. He did, in fact, have broad authority to deal with security issues within the embassy. The subject they were about to deal with, however, was one that absolutely must not leave the room. He considered the issue for a moment. "I'm sure we can include Captain Barbosa, Ambassador. He may be interested in what his subordinate has been up to."

As if nothing unusual had happened, Oliver Crane showed his guests to a comfortable sitting area at the far end of his office. Lanka picked up a remote and pressed a button. The window glass turned dark, and a projector switched on. The white wall served as a screen and showed a grainy image of Sloane Square.

"You recognize this?" asked Lanka.

"Sloane Square," Moore said. "We're staying near there. But then I'm sure you know that."

Lanka pressed the same button again. The image closed in on an intersection almost two blocks away. On the corner stood the two punks who had assaulted, or tried to assault, McGregor, Moore, and Singh only a few nights ago. "You recognize these two?"

"Should we?" replied McGregor.

"Let's see what happens." The video advanced to where three people appeared and were confronted by the two men, who had just produced knives. "The video quality is poor, but those two look a lot like you."

"They do, kind of," Moore said.

"Is that you?" demanded the RSO.

"Don't remember it. You, Mike?"

"Not me."

"How about the guy with the turban?"

"Can't help you." Moore was getting eager to know the point of this exercise and where they were going with it.

Lanka advanced the video to show the first man having his arm brutally broken. "This man is in Guys Hospital. They had to amputate his forearm. Too much damage to blood vessels and nerves."

"I can see why," McGregor said. "That much angulation would cause a huge amount of damage. I'm curious, was his jaw fractured too?"

"Michael, for God's sake," Moore said.

"Professional curiosity."

Captain Barbosa leaned forward, apparently curious as well.

"To answer your question," said Lanka, "yes, his jaw is wired."

The video was advanced to the moment that Moore's heel landed on the second man's genitals.

"Impressive move," the Captain said.

Lanka glared at him. "Testicles destroyed, surgically removed. They may be able to save his penis."

"I'll assume you two know absolutely nothing about this incident."

McGregor and Moore stared at him without comment.

"Maybe we should move on."

The video switched to Brompton Road and was much better quality. It showed Sir Charles's Audi pull up in front of Patella, where McGregor and Moore stepped out and entered the club.

It was the Ambassador who spoke. "Now that is the two of you. And Captain Moore, I must say you look exceptionally good."

"Ambassador, do I really have to tell you just how obnoxious that remark was?"

"Watch yourself, Captain. It was just a harmless observation"

Lanka ignored the exchange and fast forwarded to a brief segment where a large bald man entered the club. "Viktor Belov. A significant figure in Russian organized crime here in London."

He moved on to a segment showing McGregor and Moore leaving via the side door and less than two minutes later Belov leaving by the front. "Why did an organized crime figure follow you out? Did you meet with him?"

"How do you know he followed us," McGregor replied. "Maybe he just left at the same time. Probably didn't like that twenties music. And no, we didn't meet with him."

Lanka went on. "Here's a picture of the two of you crossing a side street about three blocks from the club. And here's another, two blocks from that."

"Captain, I see you changed your shoes, the Ambassador said. "Why was that?"

Moore glared at him. "I think Mrs. Crane could probably explain it to you."

"If you look at the locations on the videos"—Lanka showed a street map with three locations marked—"you can see this photograph is from a location between the two images showing you."

Moore recognized it as a crime scene photo, with evidence markers scattered around. It showed Viktor Belov on his back, shirt open, and quite dead.

"Doctor, perhaps you can enlighten us. What are we seeing here?"

It was an autopsy photo with Belov's chest—open. His heart was a purple mass. McGregor said, "Looks like a pericardial tamponade. A wound to the heart can allow blood to collect between the heart and the membrane covering it—the pericardium. That would compromise the heart function. Often fatal if not rapidly relieved."

"And how about this?" The next picture showed Belov's larynx opened to reveal a puncture wound, swelling, and a large blood clot.

"Doesn't take much trauma to close off the trachea," he said.

"And this?" It was from a CT scan of a head.

"Depressed skull fracture, and an epidural hematoma. Those are very serious, and rapidly fatal."

"So, Mr. Belov sustained three fatal injuries?" asked Lanka.

"Seems so."

"And how about this?" There was again a clip from CCTV that showed a short man in a raincoat walking near the corner of a building. An arm reached out and dragged him off the sidewalk.

"This X-ray is from his autopsy."

So that's what happened to the small man. "Not a great film," McGregor said, "but his neck is obviously broken. Did you just bring us here to get my medical opinion?"

Ignoring McGregor's question, Lanka continued. "The Metropolitan Police don't have his name, but he is believed to be an associate of Belov. He was found about two blocks from where Belov was found. You two would have walked right past him, but he was probably dead by then."

"Guess we didn't notice," Moore said.

Lanka slammed his palm down on the desk. "I'm getting sick of you two and your lack of cooperation. Two men are dead. Murdered. It's obvious to me that you're somehow involved in these two homicides. I'm detaining you until the Metropolitan Police can take you in for questioning."

Captain Barbosa stood. "Mr. Lanka, you're not detaining anyone. Something smells here and I'm not about to let you to interfere with these officers. McGregor, I suggest you and Captain Moore leave right now. I will sit with the RSO and the Ambassador until I see you've left the embassy. We have such a nice view of the street from up here."

"I can call the Marines and have them stopped," Crane said.

"And yet, I don't think you will. That would result in questions you don't want asked. Besides, you may find it difficult to make that call." He pulled up his right trouser leg just far enough to reveal a small automatic in an ankle holster. "Some habits are hard to break."

"We don't want to jam you up, Captain," said McGregor.

"Don't worry. After I leave the Ambassador's office, I'm going to stop by the clinic, where three SEALs on assignment to the SAS are being seen for training injuries. They have similar habits."

McGregor and Moore left the office, smiled at the Ambassador's assistant who smiled back—this time more obviously, and then left the building. As promised, the Audi appears in less than a minute and they were whisked away.

They were back at Sloane Gardens in a few minutes. There, the two officers changed out of their uniforms. After a brief discussion they agreed that Kim needed to know about the Ambassador's involvement. McGregor sent her a message and they all left together.

CHAPTER 25

"**W**HAT THE HELL were you thinking?" demanded Oliver Crane. "Detain them?"

"Okay, I overplayed our hand. I was going to squeeze them a bit, then act like I changed my mind and let them go. You could have pretended to talk me out of it. They might have let their guard down. Made a mistake."

"Instead, you made a mistake. I had no idea what you were thinking. And now that cowboy Barbosa is involved. He still has a lot of connections with that special warfare crowd, you know."

"Bastard. How could I know he was going to show up?" Lanka hit the table with a clenched fist. "If he hadn't had that pistol, I would have kicked his ass."

"No, you wouldn't. You're lucky he brought that gun, or he might have just killed you with his bare hands."

Lanka knew that was true. He liked to use his size to bully people, but he never took any chances. When he'd started his career as a Boston cop, he had always made sure to be partnered with an actual tough guy. And later in Homeland Security, he had always been able to avoid going one-on-one with a suspect. As RSO, he had no cause to ever be involved in physical confrontations, but that didn't stop him from acting like he could.

"Okay," Lanka said, "we're behind the curve. How do we catch up? I'll have to report to the Russian. What the hell do I tell him?"

"God damn it, Jonas, you're their agent; I just got sucked into this because of my son. Why must I do all the thinking? I'm just about at the point cutting the little bastard loose and letting them release that tape."

Lanka sensed the Ambassador was reaching the end of his rope, but he couldn't afford to let him break. He needed Crane in control of the embassy if they were to have any hope of getting hold of Korshkin—or of eliminating him.

A year ago, Lanka had arranged for his Russian handlers to film Crane's son giving a teenage girl in Copenhagen a fatal injection of heroin. There were supporting fingerprints and DNA, so Crane was given the stark choice of cooperating with Lanka or seeing his son doing a long prison term. The stress was obviously getting to him.

"Okay, Ambassador, you're right. I need to handle this. But you have to know that if Korshkin gets interrogated by American intelligence, the Russians might burn us both as payback. And it won't just be your son; they have evidence of your involvement, too."

"I hope whatever they're paying you is worth it."

"No, it's not, but I'm in deeper than you are and now there is no getting out of it. I've come to grips with that reality, so now we have to get this Korshkin thing under control. I'm starting to think that the best out for both of us is just to get fired. We would be of no value to the Russians; maybe we could walk away."

"No Crane has ever been fired!"

"How many have been convicted of treason?"

The Ambassador groaned. "All right, do what you have to do. I'll see if I can somehow smooth Captain Barbosa's feathers."

"I have some calls to make." Lanka left the room, leaving Ambassador Oliver Crane staring out the window as a light rain began to fall.

CHAPTER 26

THEIR NEXT STOP was more than a half-hour drive from Sloane Square into West London. They were in a commercial area with mostly new, but some pre-war, buildings. One Victorian brick building—by far the oldest on the street and identified only by a street number—seemed out of place. The Audi pulled up to a gate, where several discrete security cameras inspected the vehicle and its occupants. The gate retracted and they drove into a small courtyard. After Ian had parked, Sir Charles got out, and the rest followed his lead.

An elderly man in a white lab coat came through a large oak door, waved to Sir Charles, and walked towards their vehicle.

He was a short man of about seventy, with a bushy grey moustache and thinning grey hair. Despite his age, his step was light and sure. McGregor was surprised to see him throw his arms around Sir Charles and give him an enthusiastic hug.

"My old friend," the man said, "it's been too long. Much too long."

The man shook hands with Ian then turned to Kelli Moore. "It is a pleasure and an honor to meet you, Captain Moore. I am Dieter Wolff. Welcome to Wolff Waffenfabrik. I have owed your grandfather so much for so long. I am very pleased to be in a position to offer a tiny payment on that debt." He turned.

To McGregor, he said, "A pleasure to meet you as well, Commander. I have heard much about your exploits."

Turning abruptly, Wolff strode towards a nearby door, assuming everyone would follow. They did. They passed into a room that looked like the floor of a very small factory, with classic tools like drill presses and metal lathes, as well as computer-driven multi-axis milling machines. Two men, both in their fifties or sixties, were assembling pistols. Reaching the far end of the room, Wolff pulled open a heavy door and they entered what was clearly a modern pistol range.

He gestured to the two Americans. "Sir Charles described to me your encounter with Viktor Belov and suggested you could use something more effective than that fountain pen." He winked. "What did you think of it, by the way?"

"Nicely made and obviously got the job done," McGregor said. "Sorry we had to dump it."

"It was the right thing to do," said Wolff. "My gunsmiths made up a few last year as gifts for our best clients."

Moore looked at her Grandfather with a raised eyebrow. "Best clients?" He waved off her remark with an enigmatic smirk.

"I also heard from other sources about the demise of Ernst Grosse. Were you involved in that as well?"

"No," said McGregor, "we weren't." He paused, then added, "Was that Belov's partner?"

"The so-called small man?" Sir Charles said. "I thought he was Russian."

"East German, worked for the Stasi, but very tight with the Russians."

"You're the only person who seems to know his name," Sir Charles said. "How is that?"

"He murdered my wife. She was suspected of passing information to the West, and even then, as a very young man, Grosse was a killer. Shot her from an alley in Berlin as she walked by." Though his voice was calm and measured, the old German's face was taught with anger and grief.

"I did not know that, Dieter. I am very sorry. If I learn who took him down, I will certainly pass it along to you." Wolff nodded.

McGregor was about to respond but caught himself and remained silent.

Wolff continued. "I have selected these." He pointed to two identical pistols at the first firing point.

"Walther PPK's?" asked Moore.

"They have a similar appearance. I find our clients prefer weapons of a design they are familiar with. In this case, these are modeled on the older PP model, chambered in 7.65 mm. They are much lighter than the original PPs, however, being made entirely of titanium, carbon fiber, and composite. They also have a locking breech, which reduces recoil and lightens the tension on the operating spring. As you can, see they have a reflex sight. You may know it as a red dot sight."

Kelli walked over and picked one up. Indeed, where the rear sight would normally be, there was a piece of clear plastic extending up a bit less than half an inch and no front sight.

"Any pressure on the trigger activates the sight. It's powered by a little battery down in the grip. A gentleman in Switzerland makes them for us, and you won't find better. Place the dot on your target and fire. Unlike lasers, only you see the dot, the target cannot."

He turned smoothly toward the targets and fired the pistol once. It made a sound like a loud cough.

"Each comes with an integrated suppressor made mostly from carbon fiber. Not only reduces the report, but alters it so it isn't recognizable as a gunshot. These weapons are designed for close-in work—less than ten meters—in an urban setting. They are not very durable, though. The light construction makes the pistol good for about a hundred rounds and the suppressor for less than fifty before there's some loss of accuracy. These are not built for days at the range or for shootouts, but rather for situations like you and Belov. One shot. Two at most. If I have misread your needs, I have several other options."

"No," said Kelli. "I think this is what we need. Mike?"

"I think so. I assume we would be well-advised to dispose of them after use."

"Precisely. Never possess a weapon that has been used in a shooting. Dispose of it if you must, but we can also retrieve it anywhere in the UK and provide a replacement. Just call us." He handed both a card.

"I think you should each fire one magazine to familiarize yourselves with the weapons."

Mike and Kelli each fired one eight-round magazine and were amazed at the performance of their new weapons. They were remarkably light, recoil was virtually absent, and the suppressor masked the sound far better than expected. They were also impressed by accuracy of the sight.

"I'll have one of the gunsmiths clean those and get you two loaded mags and an additional box. We have our ammunition custom made. Subsonic, of course, with a fragmenting bullet. Will not penetrate body armor, so be alert. Also, we have a variety of custom leather and nylon holsters. Take whatever you need."

"And here is something else you might like." He handed McGregor a worn messenger bag. "Slip you hand in here."

McGregor was surprised to find that the bag was split on one end and contained a space just large enough for a pistol to be secured by a clip. "Remarkable. You can't tell there's an opening until you reach into it."

Wolff turned to Kelli. "We have some really beautiful Italian hand-bags similarly modified. And here's a leather messenger-type bag that's very popular with our female clients."

Moore picked up one of the pistols and slipped it into the concealed cavity in the bag. "Love it." She returned the weapon to the table and slipped the bag over her shoulder.

Dieter Wolff turned abruptly and led them out of the range. They passed through the shop and entered another room where he intro-duced a plump, ruddy-faced woman. "This is Angela, my daughter. She manages our protective gear."

"Protective?" asked Mike.

"That's right." Angela had an incongruous British public-school accent. "We have the most advanced body armor available anywhere." She handed him a piece of a heavy silvery-white fabric. "This is made from a very fine titanium thread, a fiber similar to Kevlar, and a thread made from the silk of the Darwin's bark spider."

"Are you serious?" exclaimed Moore. "How do you get the spiders to make all those webs?"

"Actually, a biotech company in Finland inserted the gene into a bacteria, and they can make pounds of it which they somehow make into a thread. These threads are much stronger and more elastic than fibers like Kevlar and are actually stronger than stainless steel. We have to use lasers to cut the fabric."

"So, you have body-armor tailors?" Moore asked.

"We will measure you by laser and then have the fabric cut. We will put it together and deliver it to you tomorrow morning. Let me show you an example." She pulled a vest from a drawer. The surface was dark, rather than shiny like the fabric sample. It was lined with something very soft and had a Velcro closure in front. "The women's model closes in the back."

"Naturally," Moore said.

"One aspect our ladies do seem to like is that you won't need to wear a brassiere. The fabric has a lot of support."

"Sort of a bullet-proof corset."

"Just so," answered Angela, without a hint of humor. "If you would accompany me into the next room, I will make the measurements."

It took about fifteen minutes, during which Wolff showed Mike around his small factory.

"Would it be impolite to ask what kind of customers you serve?" asked Mike.

"About what you might expect. A number of government agencies here and abroad. Some people with private security needs. A few military specialists. Nobody like Belov or Grosse, though." The last he said with some emotion.

After Kelli reappeared, Mike went into the adjoining room for his own fitting.

"Grandfather," she said, "Angela told me the most interesting story. About how you smuggled her and Mr. Wolff out of East Germany through Czechoslovakia."

"Yes, Miss, it is true," Wolff said. "After my wife was killed, I knew I would be next. We had both passed military information to West

Germany and to Britain through Sir Charles. I worked as a gunsmith for the East German army and he had a license to export small amounts of specialty alloys. That's how we met."

"He drove us to Prague in a hidden compartment in a truck, then after a few weeks, we entered Austria with fake West German passports. Sir Charles financed my purchase of this building and many of the tools. Perhaps you now understand the nature of my debt."

Sir Charles smiled, remembering his own early life of missions into the East and the thrill of bringing something—or someone—back out. "Dieter, you make it sound much more exciting than it was. I just drove a truck across a border."

Both men managed to deflect most of Kelli's additional questions until Mike reappeared.

Details for delivery of the weapons and body armor to Sloane Square were arranged for very early the following morning. Wolff answered a few technical questions as they walked back to the Audi.

"Well, thank you Dieter," Sir Charles said. Both men seemed a bit awkward about expressing the strong emotions they were feeling, so he simply added, "We should be going. Several more stops before dinner."

As they left, Dieter Wolff added, "Be safe, my friends. And good hunting."

CHAPTER 27

WENDY HILLER OPENED the Oval Office door. "The president will see you now, Alex."

CIA Director Alexander Clarkson found the president sitting in a wing-back chair sipping coffee. Wallace was skilled at making the most choreographed situation look casual. Clarkson was equally skilled at discerning such nuance, so the performance was wasted on him. Nonetheless, Wallace was the boss, so he played along.

"Alex," Wallace began. "Have a seat. Can I get you some coffee?"

"I could use some, Mr. President, thank you." Wallace walked to a sideboard, poured coffee from a carafe, added a dash of cream—Clarkson's preference—and sat it down in front of the CIA man. Wallace served coffee much as FDR had mixed martinis. It was a way to put people at ease and to play the genial host.

Clarkson made a mental note that if ever he became president, he would mix martinis.

"All right, Alex, what was worth a trip all the way in from Langley?"

"We heard from our people in London."

Wallace leaned forward. "Good news?"

"There's progress, but the situation is complex." Wallace frowned. "They made contact with someone who knows Korshkin and received information that he is hiding out somewhere in Scotland. They were given a further contact that should be able to point them in the right direction."

"Sounds a bit cloak-and-dagger, doesn't it?"

"Well, Mr. President, Korshkin is obviously being cautious, probably too cautious. On the other hand—and this is the bad news—our people were followed from the meeting by a known Russian hit man. They felt at risk, so they had to take him out."

"You mean they killed a Russian mobster on the streets of London?"

"Apparently so. There was also a second man believed to be working with the Russian who was also found dead in the same area. Our people deny involvement in that."

"Did you have someone providing backup? Is that how this other guy was taken out?"

"Absolutely not, sir. We have no hint as to who might have done it. Perhaps our people have local resources we know nothing about."

Wallace stared at him for a moment. "Alex, you have that look you get when you haven't told me all the bad news."

"Yessir, there is one other thing. This morning our people were called to a meeting with the Ambassador and the Regional Security Officer, who as much as accused them of being involved in these killings. Threatened to hold them for questioning by the Metropolitan Police."

"Christ, that's all we need. Are you're telling me they're being questioned by British authorities?"

"Fortunately, not. The doctor's CO, a Captain Barbosa, is a former SEAL, and he somehow intervened. Our people left the embassy and are preparing to leave for Scotland early tomorrow. They did not mention Captain Barbosa in their report. That came from our Chief of Station, who apparently has one of his people working as the Ambassador's personal assistant."

"Wait, wait. You're spying on our own Ambassador? To Britain?"

"I should probably look into that," replied Clarkson, who obviously was going to do nothing about it.

"All right, fine. So what do we know about this Captain?"

"Rock solid. As I said, former SEAL, Navy Cross, injured in action, and went to the military medical school up at Bethesda. He will certainly know to lay low and stay quiet. I'm more concerned about the Ambassador and the RSO. They are obviously working against the mission, and we don't know if it's intentional or not."

"This could be politically touchy. I have a personal connection to Oliver Crane: he used to work for me. Don't know anything about the RSO, do you?"

"Pretty basic," Clarkson said. "Former Boston cop, then worked for Homeland before becoming an RSO. We did turn up one thing, and you're not going to like it: he has a girlfriend back in Boston who has an account in Bolivia with $650,000 in it."

"Meaning you think he might be dirty and channeling money to his girlfriend?"

"Could be. She works at a financial services firm and knows the systems."

"All right, we need to get on top of this. We don't know exactly who we can trust at the embassy right now." He turned to his Chief of Staff, "Karen, get Branigan on the phone. We need to get some of his people to London ASAP and fly both the ambassador and the RSO back here for a chat. Remember, we have nothing on Crane so tread very lightly. Tell him I need to talk with him."

"And you might want to have the FBI bring in that girlfriend up in Boston," Clarkson added. "If she gets a hint of anything gone awry in London she could be in the wind. God forbid, but she might be more than his girlfriend. Worst case, she's SVR."

The president's shoulders slumped. "And what isn't worst case these days? You better have Branigan see to that as well."

"Yes, Mr. President, right away." Hiller walked out of the office.

"Alex, is there ever going to be a day, just one day, without a disaster, a crisis, or some other mess?"

"You knew that about the job when you took it, Mr. President."

Wallace added, "Alex, on your way out, ask the steward to come in and remove this damn coffee."

CHAPTER 28

O N THE WAY back from Wolff Waffenfabrik, the Audi made several stops for an assortment of gear and clothing. Their final stop before Sloane Square was at Sir Charles's favorite fishmonger for a fresh Faroe Island salmon.

Back at the house on Sloane Gardens, McGregor was about to send a brief update to Kim when he saw an alert that they had received an urgent message from her. He opened it and read aloud:

URGENT

From: Dover
To: Keystone/Empire

1. Reliable source indicates RSO has contacted security services about your possible involvement in deaths of two Russian organized crime figures.

2. Same source indicates discussion now taking place to consider detaining and questioning you both. Best information is they will either detain or place you under close surveillance after you leave current location tomorrow. Believe attempt to enter your current location is unlikely due to owner's political connections.

3. Evade if possible and proceed with mission. However, DO NOT resist if approached by security service personnel.

4. If approached by security personnel activate self-destruct on this device. This is VITAL.

5. Dover will arrange to have aircraft in place to monitor comm traffic throughout UK north of London starting NLT 0600.

6. Advise status NLT 0900 tomorrow.

7. Just received information that ambassador and/or RLO are likely compromised. DO NOT return to embassy under any circumstances. Do not contact any embassy personnel. Consider yourselves detached from USEMBASSY LONDON as of now. Orders to that effect are pending.

8. Acknowledge receipt immediately.

9. Dover affirms complete confidence in you and your mission. Standing by to assist.

"Well, that changes things," Kelli said. "Suddenly we're fugitives. Grandfather, I suppose it's good to know you're so well connected they won't try to break down the door."

"Not that they could," said Ian with a bit of a grin. "Sir, I imagine you'll want to make some calls. How many phones will you need?"

"Let's start with six, Ian. All right, let's get to work. We have a big night ahead of us."

CHAPTER 29

TITO PANAY PARKED his newly leased Tesla S in the parking lot of the Mariner's Club in Miami Beach. He was dressed as a waiter in a black suit and bow tie, but nobody gave him a second glance. This was Miami Beach, after all; even the waiters drove Teslas.

He reported to his supervisor who briefed him on his duties for the big Mariner's Club Man of the Year banquet that was about to start. Tito had been working there about a month, mainly as a bartender, and was enjoying himself. In another life he might have considered staying, but not in this life. The Uzbek was not paying him to pour drinks.

Tito Panay was from a large family on the southern Philippine island of Mindanao. He used family connections to become a police officer in Davo City, which at first was a satisfying career. As more of the police and military on Mindanao were drawn into the ongoing war with the Dawlah Islamiya fundamentalists, Tito grew tired of the relentless violence, assassinations, and breakdown in the usually gentle Filipino community. Ten years ago, he walked away from his job and signed on as a deckhand on a freighter, one of thousands from his nation so employed.

One night in a Singapore bar, he got into a fight and killed a Malaysian cook. Several men took his side and quickly smuggled him across the straits into nearby Jahor. They were pirates, he discovered, and unable to return to his ship, he fell in with them.

Their business model was simple. At night they ventured into the heavily traveled Strait of Malacca where they boarded pleasure craft and small commercial ships. They stole anything of value and often ended up killing their quarry. Tito, now known as Bolo, after the large machete-like knife popular in the Philippines, proved a ruthless and proficient pirate. He rose in their ranks and seemed destined for a leadership role, but that all ended when most of his crew was killed and he barely survived a running gunfight with the Singapore Defense Force. Singapore regarded pirates like the Romans had—enemies of all people—not deserving of a trial, only a bullet. He fled back to sea on a small godforsaken regional tramp freighter, constantly fearing his fake identity would unravel.

Things began to look up when he encountered a man in Bahrain. Known only as the Uzbek, Bolo surmised he was probably Russian, but never knew for sure. The Uzbek made him a simple proposition. He would receive new identity papers and would continue to work as a seaman, unless the Uzbek had a job for him. After which he would return to the sea, albeit a little richer.

The jobs ranged from smuggling papers or packages ashore in a variety of ports to the occasional assassination. The man paid well, planned his missions with care, and usually minimized the risk. His Cayman Island bankers invested wisely, and his accounts grew in size and diversity. Something was destined to go wrong, though, and it finally did. It was the shooting of a British politician—a prominent opponent of Brexit—on the M1 motorway. The killing was captured on the dashcam of a passing truck, and Bolo barely escaped by boat to France, where the Uzbek drove him to Genoa and a new life as a fugitive.

After that, he became increasingly skilled at moving across borders undetected, doing the Uzbek's bidding, and slipping away.

Bolo's current job was the best paying so far—and with good reason. Just getting into the US had required multiple stops and a lot of cash. Tonight, in the middle of the event, he was to leave his station, climb a stairway to the balcony above the banquet room, retrieve a device concealed in a fire extinguisher cabinet, activate it, and toss it over the gathered plutocrats and their bejeweled wives and girlfriends. He knew something small enough to toss and worth what he was being paid had to be some kind of WMD. But what? Biological? Chemical?

On reflection, probably best not to know too much.

He was reassured that the Uzbek had agreed to his detailed escape plan, which suggested this was not a suicide mission. To be sure though, he had made all the arrangements himself, at the Uzbek's expense. Nonetheless the man was cunning and well financed, so his escape could still be cut short after the mission. But somehow, he didn't think so. He was too useful to kill.

At about 9:00 pm, business at the bar was slow. Dinner was winding down, and the tedious speeches had begun. Bolo walked to the door leading up to the balcony and climbed the stairs. At the top of the stairs, he located the fire extinguisher case, opened it, and removed an object about the size and weight of a grapefruit that was covered in bubble wrap. He unwrapped it to reveal a dark green plastic sphere.

It was suddenly clear to him what he was about to do. This device looked exactly like the one described from the nerve gas attack in Arizona two days before. Nerve gas! He was about to commit an act of terrorism.

But he had killed before and there was nothing to do but go ahead.

He turned the small black knob on top to "3", pressed it down, and lobbed it high over the room below. He immediately turned and fled down the stairs. He was only on the fifth step when a heard what sounded like a loud "pop". Then screams.

Bolo emerged outside the banquet room to find one of the security guards running towards him. Without hesitation he produced a Glock 43 from his jacket pocket and shot the man in the throat.

A few seconds after that, the door opened and a woman in a short red dress stumbled out, coughed, clutched her chest, stumbled, and fell at his feet. He ignored her and walked briskly towards the main entrance. He saw more security and shouted, "There's been an explosion in the banquet room. Hurry." He pointed to the door where additional diners could be seen trying to leave, but unsteady on their feet, mucous streaming from their noses, and falling onto each other.

Bolo continued out the door, took off his coat and tie, and walked to his Tesla. He drove away and headed towards the Venetian Way causeway that would take him to his house on San Marco Island. The house, rented from a recently bankrupt hedge fund manager, was comfortable enough, but its main attraction was the dock where he kept his Hatteras 58 sport fisherman, "*Shark Fin*." Unlike the house and car, he owned the boat.

Using a remote, he opened the gate and drove into his garage just as emergency vehicles—lights flashing and sirens blaring—rushed by, headed towards Miami Beach. He ignored them.

It was time to go. In a few minutes it would become obvious that this had been another sarin attack and the area would be locked down and flooded with police and federal agents. He stopped in the house only long enough to change clothes. Everything else he needed was already on board the boat. He performed a quick inspection, and finding all in order, he turned over one of the two big Detroit Diesel 8V92 engines, cast off, and headed southeast towards the channel known as Government Cut that would take him between Miami Beach and Fisher Island, and then into the Atlantic. He had both radar and night vision, but neither were necessary. The moon was nearly full and the shoreline a veritable Christmas tree of multicolored lights.

Once away from land he cranked up the second engine and pushed the throttles to allow a cruising speed of twenty-five knots. A good speed, but not one that would attract attention. He slowed as he neared Andros Island where he used his radar and GPS to navigate through the cluster of small islands and reefs that made Bahamas shipwrecks so numerous. He docked in Nassau about 7:00 am and walked a few blocks to another pier, where he boarded the MV Pisces Union, recently arrived from Cuba.

An hour later two men dressed for fishing boarded the *Shark Fin*. They stopped at a nearby marina and topped off the 775-gallon fuel tanks, picked up some provisions, and a few cases of beer. They headed south into the Caribbean where they would work their way down to the island of Barbados. There, *Shark Fin* would have her engines traded for ones with new serial numbers, have some cosmetic changes made, and be issued a new name and registration number. Thereafter, *Shark Fin* would cease to exist.

CHAPTER 30

THE NIGHT HAD been a whirlwind of activity. Sir Charles had sent texts and made encrypted calls, while at the same time people had come and gone via the tunnel ending in the garden shed.

A middle-aged woman arrived and informed Kelli and Mike she was going to make a few changes to their appearance. Specialists in disguise know that small changes are often the most effective, particularly if they alter a subject's most prominent features. For Kelli, this meant changing her red hair to a straw blond with a few tasteful streaks of magenta. Tortoiseshell glasses with slightly tinted lenses obscured her brilliant green eyes, making them appear an ordinary hazel. For Mike, the scar below his left eye, courtesy of a bullet fragment encountered years before in Iraq, was expertly covered. He was fitted with steel-rimmed glasses, also with tinted lenses that made his watery grey eyes appear bluer. A quick buzz cut made him look younger. Both selected expensive sportswear, and the result was the appearance of a trendy London couple on holiday.

After that, Angela Wolff arrived with two satchels. The smaller contained their weapons, ammunition, spare magazines, holsters, and messenger bags. There was also a large, familiar-looking fountain pen.

The larger of the two held their body armor. In turn, each stepped into another room while Angela judged the fit. Finding it perfect, they then dressed, this time wrapped in the stiff fabric they both hoped would live up to its reputation.

At about six that morning, a young couple left the Sloane Gardens house and got into Sir Charles's Audi. The woman had short red hair and brilliant green eyes. The man wore a Trilby hat and sunglasses.

Kelli was watching discretely from the front window "Won't those people impersonating us run into trouble with the police or security services?"

"Not much, I suspect. The young woman is Lady Vanessa Finch. She handles my real estate holdings—a really exceptional mind. Her father is a senior MP and a close advisor to the current Prime Minister. The gentleman is Andrew Sinclair, recently retired from the SAS and the Parachute Regiment. Awarded the VC for action in Afghanistan. He is engaged to Lady Vanessa and thought this might be just the thing to get him out of the office. MI5 will, no doubt, be miffed, but cooler heads will prevail and that will be that."

What Sir Charles did not mention was that, prior to attending the London School of Economics and entering his employment, Lady Vanessa had been Captain Finch, an intelligence officer in the British Army. She had been awarded the Military Cross for the same action that resulted in Sinclair receiving the VC. Neither had any intention of falling into the hands of the security services.

With Sinclair at the wheel, the Audi's engine raced and it sped down Sloan Gardens and around the corner onto Holbein Place. The waiting MI-5 officers, surprised by this reckless maneuver, took a few seconds to react. As the Audi rounded the corner, an elderly couple walking two terriers entered the intersection and created an additional delay. By time they were able to proceed, a lorry had backed onto Holbein Place from the drive beside a commercial building. They demanded the driver allow them to pass, but by then the Audi was long gone. The helicopter they had relied on for air surveillance had been delayed when the pilot developed food poisoning, apparently related to a delivery of Thai curry the night before.

Sir Charles had had a busy night.

An hour later, the Audi returned to the space in front of Sir Charles's building. The driver, an ill-tempered elderly woman accompanied by a menacing German shepherd, said she had borrowed the vehicle from her friend Sir Charles Moore. Finding no sign of Kelli Moore or Mike McGregor, the surveillance team allowed her to leave. Had they investigated further, they would have discovered she was recently retired from the London stage, a World War Two veteran, and the ninety-four-year-old great grandmother of Vanessa Finch. But they did not investigate.

Ian spoke up. "I don't imagine the security services will be quite so forgiving of your involvement, if you don't mind my saying so."

Sir Charles chuckled. "Quite right, Ian." To Kelli he said, "Don't worry my dear. We have made our own arrangements."

A few minutes later, Kelli, Mike, and Sir Charles slipped out of the pub at the other end of the tunnel, and then squeezed into an aging Mini after stuffing several bags into the boot. With Ian at the wheel, they crossed Chelsea Bridge, passed Battersea Park, and headed west out of London, ending in the town of Maidenhead.

There the Mini pulled up in front of a small office building. Ian got out, unlocked a gate, which he slid up, and they entered a parking area under the building. He parked next to a Land Rover and a battered stake-bed truck bearing the name "Keane and Sons Brewery."

"You own a brewery too?" Mike asked.

"Wish I did, but no. Arthur Keane is a friend from the old days and owns what you in the States would call a microbrewery up in Cambridge. Allows me the use of one of his lorries now and again." He opened one of the doors, pulling out two cloth caps and worn leather jackets. He donned cap and jacket and tossed the others to Ian.

Mike and Kelli moved their bags to the Land Rover. Sir Charles showed them several hidden compartments where they could conceal their weapons. The glove box contained two mobile phones, a few maps, and two Canadian passports in the names Gerald and Jessica Ryan. There were driver's licenses bearing the same address in an upscale building in Vancouver and ID cards for The Royal Bank of Canada, London.

"Here is the address of your lovely flat at Plane Tree House in Kensington." He handed them each a card. "The entry code is on the back."

"Is anyone living there?" asked Kelli.

"You are. It's being leased by Gerald and Jessica Ryan. Stop in, if you have the chance. It isn't Sloane Gardens, but it is very nice."

"Oh, I almost forgot these." He pulled several credit cards from his breast pocket.

"One more thing. Your identities have been scrupulously maintained so they should stand up to close scrutiny, particularly outside of London."

"I'm sorry we got you into this, Grandfather. Not only will MI5 be looking for you, but now we're all being hunted by the Russians."

"Nonsense, my dear," replied Sir Charles with a smile. "They have no idea who they're dealing with." This he said with a kind of grim finality.

With a quick handshake for Mike and a hug for Kelli, Sir Charles Moore and the enigmatic Ian hopped into the truck. Watching them, Kelli could see it was like they had always been together. Was Ian the son her grandfather had always wanted, capable and loyal instead of the feckless bastards so consumed by their business interests they were willing to cast off his beloved granddaughter?

As they began to back out, Sir Charles rolled down his window. "Take care of yourselves. And each other." With that the old truck rumbled out the rear gate and onto the busy street.

Mike and Kelli reviewed their planned route, concealed their weapons, and then with Kelli at the wheel—Mike had to admit that having him drive on the left would have been a disaster—they left the garage and headed north.

CHAPTER 31

BRENDAN WALLACE RUSHED into the situation room, Wendy Hiller and Sonny Baker right behind. Everyone rose and Wallace gestured for them to be seated.

"I'm just back from the Pentagon," Wallace said. "Sonny, why don't you give everyone here a quick update on what's happening in Iran before we move ahead with other issues."

"Last night, Iran attempted a repeat of the Qeshm Massacre. I'm sure you all remember two years ago when they infiltrated Quds forces onto Qeshm Island in the Strait of Hormuz and attacked an Army Hospital. One-hundred-eighty-one of our people were killed, mostly wounded and medical personnel. This is what led to our integrating medical facilities with operational units. Last night, under cover of a mortar barrage, about sixty Quds fighters attacked the Navy Expeditionary Medical Facility located adjacent to the 7th Marines, who just arrived from Twentynine Palms to begin relieving the Army 1st Infantry Division. This time the hospital had beefed up security and an infantry company there with them. All but two of the attackers were killed, but we still lost about a dozen of our own and at least twenty more wounded. The president and the Joint Chiefs are discussing our response. I think I'll leave it at that."

"Thanks Sonny," said the president. "Yes, I think we should keep our response plans very close hold for the moment. Right now, we need we need to discuss Florida. Frank?"

Frank Branigan, holding a sheet of notes, stood to address Wallace. "Mr. President, the terrorist attack at the Mariner's Club last night was definitely sarin. The chemical composition matches that used in Arizona. This time, because of the enclosed space and high density seating, the casualties were much worse. Eighty confirmed dead including Congresswoman Valeria Bautista and her husband, as well as Eric Young—we just got confirmation on Mr. Young."

"My God, Eric was the Chairman of my Florida Committee," said a shaken Wallace. "And I campaigned for Val."

"Yes sir, and there were a number of other prominent individuals from the Florida business and political communities. My staff is handing out that list right now."

"So you think this event was targeted specifically?" asked Karen Hiller.

"Hard to imagine that it wasn't. I think they're escalating by making it personal," replied the FBI Director. "The guy responsible was picked up on several security cameras. He's a smuggler and occasional contract killer known as Bolo. Filipino, but hasn't been there in years. He's been in place working as a bartender for at least a month, so this was planned well in advance."

CIA Director Alex Clarkson, who had just walked in, asked, "Wasn't he responsible for the assassination of that anti-Brexit MP on the M1 outside London?"

"The British think so. He's been off the radar since. Looks like he rented a house nearby. Miami Beach is heavy with security cameras, so we were able to see him escape by boat immediately after. It was reported docked briefly in Nassau and a few hours later it was spotted heading south. We have no idea if he's still aboard. Coast Guard and some Navy assets are looking for it now."

"So another dead end. Goddamnit, Frank. All we have are dead ends."

The FBI Director looked chagrined, but pushed ahead. "There's more. The Mariner's Club apparently released his name and photograph to the press."

"What the fuck," shouted Karen Hiller. "Didn't local police take control of that information?"

"Apparently not soon enough," Branigan said. "Once it showed up online, there were several incidents involving Filipino and Indonesian businesses. Small-time vandalism, but worrisome. And there are already conspiracy theories popping up on social media."

"Why Indonesians?" asked Wallace.

"My guess is the morons who did it couldn't tell the difference."

"You have more, don't you Frank?" Wallace was tired and wanted to get through all the bad news at once.

"I'm afraid I do, sir. Ambassador Crane and Jonas Lanka, the RSO, are both in custody now in a secure facility at Quantico. Both lawyered up as soon as they landed. Won't say a word."

"You haven't given them access to attorneys yet, I hope," said Alexander Clarkson.

"Being a serious national security case, no, not yet. But we can't delay for long. I suppose you could Alex, but we don't work that way."

"Look, Frank," Wallace said, "I know Oliver Crane. I need to speak with him."

"Mr. President, I can't even count the number of ways that's a bad idea."

Alex Clarkson added, "I've got to agree with Frank on this, Mr. President. I just can't see how that helps us."

"You're both right, of course, but I'm doing it anyway. Set it up."

"And for God's sake keep it absolutely secret." Karen Hiller pointed at Branigan, her finger thrusting in the air like a dagger. "Are you listening, Frank?"

Branigan ignored her. "All right, Mr. President, I'll make the arrangements. We'll need some time to coordinate with the Secret Service. You can't just take a motorcade or Marine One out to Quantico. We can come with something secure that will get you there without raising any questions."

"Thank you, Frank. This may be more productive than you think. Anything else?"

"Just one, but it's small. Agent DeSantos up in Detroit—he's the one who got hold of that metal disc—finally ran down the Arab kid who picked up the discs from the plant that produced them. As we suspected, he was just an Uber driver hired for an errand. He did provide one lead though. He also picked up several boxes from a small factory that does injection molding in Plymouth, a small city just west of Detroit. One of the boxes had a loose top, and when he took a look, he saw green plastic balls. The plant says it was the same as the metal stamping—order came in by computer and payment was in cash."

"Another goddamn dead end. Does anyone have something useful to add?"

Alex Clarkson responded with an almost imperceptible nod. "Last night, we received information from a source in the British Security services that before Frank's people pulled him out, the RSO informed them that our two officers in London, Lieutenant Commander McGregor and Captain Moore, were probably involved in the death of two Russian mobsters. They had planned to detain and question them, but they apparently eluded their security people and are now on the move. Captain Moore's grandfather, who I must admit has had some past Agency involvement, used the daughter of a senior minister and her fiancé to facilitate their escape. Looks like those two got away clean, but if their involvement becomes known, it's going to ruffle some feathers in the government."

Karen Hiller glared at his CIA Director. "Well?"

"What?"

"Did they kill those Russians?"

"Looks like only one of them. The other one, probably not. In fact, we have no idea who did that."

"Well, now I feel so much better," said the president, who already knew about Belov, but apparently wanted to act like it was news to him too. "Two American military officers are fugitives in an allied country, but are responsible for only one of the two homicides they're suspected of. Then, of course, her grandfather has CIA connections and facilitated their escape using well-connected British nationals. For God's sake Alex, can this get any worse?"

"Mr. President, the man they took out, Viktor Belov, was a notorious killer and I have no doubt this was self-defense. We have also learned that the RSO, and quite possibly the ambassador, are actively working against our mission. That's important when we consider why they were talking to the British in the first place."

"You're right Alex," the president said, a bit calmer now. "That bit of information may prove to be useful leverage. And it also makes treating this as a national security case imperative."

Everyone was distracted when an aide handed Sonny Baker a note and he excused himself to take a call on one of the secure phones that lined the wall. Returning after only a minute, the national Security Advisor looked grim.

"Mr. President, that was Bill Granger from my office. A contact in the CNO's office pulled him aside after the meeting and told him the Chief has been in contact with Admiral Billings, commander of Task Force 64. That's the Navy element for the big amphibious exercise off Norway. He's also been in contact with the skippers of the two destroyers with *Makin Island*."

"Would you just get to the point?" said Wallace.

"He's telling them that whatever mission Admiral Piotrowski had been briefed on did not go through his office or NavEur. He emphasized no entry into UK territorial waters or airspace without authorization. My guess is that he didn't contact *Makin Island* because he knows their skipper is close to Admiral Piotrowski."

"Goddamn Navy politics. When is the CNO retiring?"

"His term ends this summer, but he's been angling to be reappointed."

"Not a chance. Not after this. Do you think we should lean on him?"

"I would advise against that Mr. President," said Karen Hiller. "The CNO, or more likely NavEur, would probably leak to the British, and we would be in a position of explaining why we're trying to extract two military fugitives from their soil."

"You're right, Karen. What a shit-show that would be."

"So we're cutting them loose?" Sonny Baker said. "Yemen all over again?"

"No, we are not cutting them loose," replied Wallace. "Let's see how this develops. Alex, exfiltration is your wheelhouse. Don't you have clandestine assets that can help?"

"We've been counting on the Navy, but once we know where they are and their situation, we can get working on it."

"Make it happen." The president had heard all he wanted to hear. He stood, and without looking back, strode from the room, with Karen Hiller, as always, at his heels.

CHAPTER 32

MIKE AND KELLI had decided to stay overnight outside Edinburgh. They chose a country bed and breakfast about an hour south of the city. Their ID and credit cards had attracted not a second look, and both had slipped easily into their personas as Canadian bankers. They slept very little, though. The tension of the previous day and the excitement of finally being on the hunt for Maxim Korshkin kept them up.

Kelli sat on the bed wearing Manchester United sweats, arms and legs crossed. McGregor, in jeans and a fleece pullover, was lying on a large sofa.

Kelli was channel surfing—looking mainly for news about her grandfather or mention of her and Mike's escape from Sloan Gardens and current fugitive status. What she found was a headline on Sky News titled "80 confirmed dead in Florida nerve-gas attack."

As she read, Kelli exclaimed, "I can't believe they killed eighty people in one room."

"Sarin in a confined space is the perfect WMD. That number will probably go up," Mike said. "The question is how do the Russians figure into this?"

"So, what do we know?" asked Kelli.

"Well," Mike answered, "we know that for some reason the Russians really, really want to derail the mission. Those idiots at the Antelope were obviously there for us. They just hadn't counted on Major Singh."

"And Belov was a big-time Russian mobster, no doubt that's how he got on to us. You have to admit we were lucky to take him down."

"Maybe," said Kelli. "Even those big-time killers can get careless. I doubt he ever had to deal with an ambush like ours. But we were lucky to have someone deal with that other one. Grosse, wasn't it? What do you make of that, anyway?"

"I have some thoughts, but can't really put it all together. The other thing I can't put together is exactly what interest the Russians have in Korshkin. I can't believe they're just pissed off that he scammed them as Janos. He says he knows who is running the terrorist operation back home. Could the Russians be behind the whole thing?"

"Nerve gas on US soil—that would be so high risk. But yeah, I'm starting to think the same thing. It would sure explain why they want to keep us away from Korshkin."

"We're really in their crosshairs now," Mike said. "We need to be sharp tomorrow. Let's try to get some rest."

For the rest of the night, each got a few hours of fitful sleep while the other watched the window and kept a pistol nearby.

In the morning both lingered over a large breakfast of eggs and smoked salmon with crusty fresh bread. Kelli put down her fork, took a sip of coffee, and said, "Time we get going. One more bite and I'll have to take off this damn titanium corset."

"Yeah," Mike said, "I've been eating a bit too well on this trip." Still, he did finish off his salmon before standing up.

As planned, they drove to the Edinburgh airport, a trip of just over an hour, where they used a long-term car park on site. They walked about a quarter-mile to the tram stop and took the short trip into the city. They exited the tram once, walked a few blocks while watching to see if they had been followed. Seeing nothing suspicious, they again boarded the tram and reached their destination, Princes Street. From there, they walked uphill to the High Street, the famed "Royal Mile," which ended at Edinburgh Castle. By midmorning, the street was already buzzing with tourists from dozens of countries, which made spotting surveillance more difficult. They found Deacon Brodie's and spent a few minutes at the classic old tavern, where they limited themselves to a cup of espresso.

On leaving the pub, they headed downhill, each on different sides of the street, with Mike slightly behind and watching for anyone following. So far, no signs of a tail. In a few blocks, they passed the St. Giles Cathedral and Parliament Square. Beyond that, the street narrowed, and it wasn't long before they saw the first passage described by Boris Voronin. It was brick-walled, just wide enough for two people to walk side by side, and seemed to pass through the building that faced the street.

Mike crossed the street, and while he did, an elderly man with a walking stick came out of the passage and another, younger, man entered. After that, it was quiet.

Kelli said, "Watch the street. I'll check it out and be back in a minute. If there's no blue door we can go on. If it's there, I'll come out and we'll go back in together."

Mike nodded and she disappeared down the passage. A few minutes later she had not reappeared. He looked carefully up and down the street, and then entered the passage—all senses on high alert.

The passage opened onto a small square covered by paving stones, with an area of grass and planters in the center, a few benches, and a bike rack. On the left were a series of doors to the flats that stretched in a curve to the back of the square. There they ended, and after about thirty feet there was a series of what had once been stables, but were now obviously used for storage and parking for scooters or motorcycles.

Moore was nowhere to be seen.

Mike walked along the row of flats. As he neared the end, he heard a voice with a Russian accent. He tensed and moved slowly forward. At the end of the last flat was a set of ancient stone steps leading downward. He peeked around the corner and was shocked to see Kelli Moore at the bottom of the steps, facing a brick wall with her hands against the wall and her feet spread. Behind her stood the man who had entered the passage a minute before she had. He held the collar of her jacket in one hand and a long knife in the other. The blade was just below her ribs on her right side.

He said in that harsh accent, "Where is he? Where is Korshkin? Talk now or you will lose your kidney. Do you want that?"

Mike slipped his pistol out of the shoulder bag, silently thanking Dieter Wolff for the quality of his work. The moment he touched the trigger, the sight lit up. His first thought was for a quick head shot to eliminate the threat. But they needed answers. How were they found? Who was he working for? He moved the red dot down to the man's right calf.

Suddenly the man tensed. Something had alerted him and as he began to turn, he shoved the knife hard into Kelli's back. The blade cut through her jacket, but was stopped cold by her body armor. A second later there was a barely audible sound of a cough and the bullet struck his calf. He yelped and fell as Mike bounded down the steps, kicked the knife away, and pointed his pistol at the man's face.

Kelli turned, but seemed unsteady. A large bruise on her forehead explained why.

"What happened?" he asked.

"I'd walked past the flats and was about to head back when this asshole stuck his arm out from around the corner and threw me down the stairs. Next thing I knew, he had me on my feet, facing the wall, and that knife at my back. My head was just starting to clear, and I was thinking about the best way to disarm him when you took the shot."

"I'm sure you were," Mike said. "Looks like that corset really works."

"For knives, anyway." She paused and looked around. "We can't just stand here. Check that door." She produced her own weapon. "I'll keep an eye on our new friend."

The door to the lower level of the building was unlocked. Mike stepped inside and found a light switch. It was a storage area with a few old trunks, a rusty bike, an umbrella stand, and a stack of flower-pots. They dragged the Russian inside and closed the door.

Kelli conducted a quick search which produced a small Ruger LCP .380 pistol concealed in the small of his back. He was also carrying a wallet. "Igor Krensky," she said. "Lives here in Edinburgh. And, oh look, a phone!"

While she looked through his wallet, McGregor opened the first aid kit in his bag and applied a pressure dressing to the man's leg wound. He turned his attention to Kelli. A quick look at her pupils and eye movements, and he was satisfied that whatever head injury she had was not an emergency.

Both Kelli and the Russian were surprised when McGregor pushed the man flat on the floor, got his knees on his shoulders, and produced the fountain pen. He snapped open the blade.

"Igor," he said, "here's the thing. We don't have much time and there are things we need to know."

"Typical American," said the Russian. "Big talk." He tried to spit, but his mouth was too dry. "Am I supposed to be afraid of that thing? If you wanted to kill me you would have done it already."

"You heard about Viktor Belov? You must have heard about Belov."

The man's expression showed that he had.

"That was us, Igor. Used this." McGregor drew the razor-sharp blade along the Russian's cheek, leaving a trail of blood. "Jammed it into his trachea. About here." He tapped the blade on the man's throat.

"For you Igor, I'm thinking right through the eyeball."

In a single, swift motion, Mike brought the blade to within a millimeter of the man's left eyeball. It was hard to tell who was more surprised by the doctor's sudden change in demeanor, Kelli or the Russian.

The Russian, who had no loyalty to Russia or to his mission and very little to his bosses, had suddenly become concerned this American might do exactly what he was threatening to do.

"Very well. What do you want to know? I do not know much."

"For starters, how did you find us?"

"I was lucky," he said. "They sent us pictures. They are in my phone."

He gave Moore the code for his phone and in less than a minute she found the photos. "They're from our Michigan driver's licenses." She glared at Igor. "And you just happened to be on the High Street?"

"Believe it or not, yes. They have more than a dozen people in Edinburgh looking for you. Two here on the High Street. There are people in every large city in Scotland, most train stations and airports, and some even driving the major highways."

"Who is 'they'?" Mike asked.

"I work for Andrei. He runs Edinburgh for the Russians. I run a few dealers, a little gambling, and a house. I'm nobody."

"A house?"

"Girls, Mike. Prostitution." Kelli was often amused by her partner's innocence.

"Right. And who hired this Andrei?"

"A guy called Sergei Volodin. Very big down in London. Everyone knows he is connected with the SVR. Sounds like he is running the Korshkin search for them."

This was no surprise, the connection between the Russian intelligence services and organized crime went back to the czars. And a connection to Russian intelligence would explain their clandestine access to the Michigan DMV.

"What were your orders?"

Igor seemed less certain about answering. McGregor gave him a nick to his lower eyelid and he blinked as blood oozed into his eye. He reconsidered.

"They told me to call in if I spotted you."

Kelli checked his outgoing calls. "And yet, you didn't."

"No. I knew Volodin was offering big money to whoever got hold of you and even more for finding Korshkin. I wanted in on that, seemed easy enough. When you stopped in front of the entry to this place, I could not just stand in the street, so I decided to walk in and then follow when you started off. When the girl came in"—he looked at Kelli—"I found the stairway and it seemed like fate had offered me a chance to ask a few questions of my own. I didn't realize you two were psychopaths with guns—and that thing." He nodded towards the blade McGregor continued to hold near his left eye. It was hard to tell what made Igor more indignant, being overpowered by these two Americans, or the fact that his own people had not warned him that they had taken down Belov—a legend in Russian criminal circles.

"This might be your lucky day, Igor." Kelli was pulling a set of zip ties from her bag. "This has a device that I can set to release your wrists in"—she adjusted the small cylinder in the middle of the nylon restraint—"three hours. You think he'll survive that long?"

"Oh, sure. Bleeding has slowed down a lot. And Igor, I suggest you find a good story about how you got shot. If anything happens to us, people will be back for you. The kind of people you really won't want to meet."

The Russian said nothing as Kelli tied his legs and pocketed his phone. The pair of Americans left the Russian laying on the cold stone floor of the storage room, blood still oozing from his leg as well as the cut on his face.

Coming to the next passage, they decided to enter together. In two minutes, they found there was no blue door and they left, finding nobody suspicious lingering on the street.

The third passage was identical to the first two. The row of flats was also the same, with one exception: the last door was painted a dark blue and to the right of the door was a large tile decorated with the letter "M."

They stepped up to the door and looked at each other. Kelli nodded, Mike knocked, and they waited. This was it.

In less than a minute, a tall woman in her forties with short blond hair opened the door. She smiled. "You're the Americans, aren't you?" This she said with an accent that was primarily Scandinavian, but with a bit Edinburgh around the edges.

"We are," said Kelli. "May we come in?"

They were shown into a two-story room lit mainly by a large skylight. The furniture was modern, and there were paintings of Scottish landscapes on the walls and sitting on several easels.

157

Kelli inspected several paintings, each of which was signed simply with an "M." She looked at the woman. "You're Marta."

"I am," the woman replied.

Mike was confused.

"Marta is a very famous painter of Scottish landscapes. Think John Constable, but highlands rather than Sussex. Grandfather owns one of her paintings.

The woman brightened. "Which one?"

"The Isle of Skye. He bought it at your first show in London."

"Oh yes, that was one of my first sales. I remember him. Charming older gentleman. I think he referred several other buyers who really made that show a success."

"I saw you at that show. I'm sorry we didn't have a chance to meet. I didn't realize you were Swedish."

"Norwegian, actually. Marta Andreessen, from Stavanger. I came here for college and fell in love with Scotland. Been here since."

"I'm sorry Marta," Mike said, "but we don't have much time. Can you help us find Maxim Korshkin?"

"I think so. We became friends some years ago when I first started painting. He had a flat in Glasgow and some business interests here in Edinburgh. He supported my work and introduced me to the gallery in London where I had the show. I liked him. He reminded me a bit of my father. But something happened recently, I'm not sure what. People were looking for him. I let him stay here for a few weeks, but he wanted to get out of the city. I immediately thought about my Uncle. Korshkin apparently knew my Uncle Vegard from the old days, back when he was still in Norway. I'd heard some stories from my father that Vegard had a shady side. I'm not sure of the details, but I do know he worked in supply with the Norwegian Air Force. Might have been why he left Norway. He lives up in Orkney now."

In response to Mike's questioning look, Kelli said, "The Orkney Islands. They're just north of Scotland."

"Right," said Marta. "Vegard immigrated before I did and worked in the crab and lobster business before he got involved in salmon farming. He retired two years ago and bought a deserted building on the west side of Hoy. It's the big island on the south side of Scapa Flow—the large, sheltered anchorage used by the Royal Navy in both wars. The navy built a lifeboat station in a small bay on the west side of Hoy due to the heavy ship traffic during the war. After the war, they manned it off and on during exercises, but when part of the headwall collapsed and damaged the breakwater, they abandoned it. Vegard has been living there a bit like a hermit, but it seems to suit him. He agreed to bring Maxim up by boat until he could find a way out of Scotland. That young Russian, Boris, drove him up to Gills Bay where Vegard picked him up. Sounds like a rough crossing in his little boat, barely more than a skiff. But they made it."

"How was Korshkin's health when you saw him?" asked Mike.

"He had started having spells just before he moved from Glasgow. He would get weak and short of breath, but they lasted just a few minutes and then he would seem fine. They started happening more often after he got up to Hoy and now Vegard says poor Maxim is weak and breathless most of the time. He is afraid to move him."

"How do you communicate with Vegard?" asked Kelli.

"He has a satellite phone. Calls now and then."

"We're going to try to get Korshkin some help and then move him off the island," Kelli said. "Michael is a doctor."

"Do you think you can help?" asked Marta.

"Maybe. What you're describing sounds like a heart problem. There might be something I can do to get him well enough to travel. We'll get him to good specialists."

"Can you show us on a map where your uncle is located?" Kelli asked.

Marta went to a bookshelf and pulled down an atlas, flipped through the pages and settled on a large map of the Orkney Islands. "Here's Hoy. See this little bay on the west side? That's it. I've never been there, but Vegard says a boat up to forty or fifty feet can get in near high tide. It's possible to climb down the rock wall too, but you would need rope."

Both Kelli and Mike studied the map. "You weren't exaggerating about the seclusion," said Kelli. "Your uncle is a hard man to reach. I can see why Korshkin would want to stay there."

"Like I said, he prefers his solitude. Just him and the fish; perfect for a true introvert." Marta had become quite chatty with the two Americans and Kelli thought her fondness for her uncle very sweet. It was a nice contrast to her own life experience.

Mike, who had been studying the atlas said, "Maybe we can get something more detailed from the Defense Mapping Agency. Looks like we're going to need more equipment too."

"Marta," Kelli said, "you need to be away for at least a week. Don't go anywhere you've ever been before. Buy a few throwaway phones and use each one only once. Best to pay with cash. Do you have enough?"

Marta seemed to pick up on what was really going on. "I have some. Probably best not to use the bank. Right?"

"Exactly." Kelli rummaged in her shoulder bag. "Here's five hundred pounds. Do you have a car?"

"My neighbor had hip surgery. I've been using his."

"Perfect," said Kelli. "Pack a small bag and we can walk you to your car."

In a few minutes, the trio walked three blocks to a garage where Marta drove off in a well-used Volkswagen. Mike and Kelli returned to the airport, retrieved their Land Rover, and headed north.

After crossing the Queensferry Bridge over the Firth of Forth, they stopped for coffee in Rosyth. There McGregor was able to acquire a communications link.

From: Keystone
To: Dover

1. Successful contact in Edinburgh. Granite located in Orkney Islands. Old lifeboat station in a small bay on the west side of Hoy. Keystone and Empire are en route now.

2. Empire was intercepted by a Russian organized crime figure hired specifically to find us. She suffered a minor injury. Russian suffered GSW to leg.

3. Interrogation revealed Russian intelligence service has contracted organized crime to follow or terminate Empire and Keystone.

4. Anticipate final report with condition of Granite and exact location for exfil within 24 hours.

CHAPTER 34

PRESIDENT BRENDAN WALLACE entered the secure holding facility by a side door. He had traveled from the White House in a regular Marine Corps helicopter, not the ultra-secure and meticulously maintained Marine One. It had taken some time to overcome the objections of both the Secret Service and the crew of Marine One. Wallace finally prevailed, as they all knew he would, and his arrival was as secret as anything could be in the nation's capital.

Wallace and his small party of agents, his Chief-of Staff, and FBI Director Branigan were shown to a room furnished with grim steel furniture and devoid of decoration. They were met by two senior FBI agents.

"Well?" asked Wallace.

The older agent, obviously in charge, said, "Hasn't said a word, sir. Demanded a lawyer on the way in, but not a peep since."

"Good. Let's get to it."

A brief discussion ensued about whether the president could be permitted to see former US Ambassador Oliver Crane alone. Wallace finally compromised on taking a single Secret Service agent into the room. He selected Randall Washington, a former Marine and a man he could trust completely.

Washington opened the door to the adjoining room. He entered, inspected the room and the prisoner, and then beckoned Wallace to enter. He took up a post near the door and the president strode in.

Oliver Crane was still wearing the suit he was arrested in, minus his belt and tie. He was handcuffed and the chain of the cuffs attached to a sturdy bolt in the tabletop. Crane's eyes were red, his features drawn. His usually perfect hair was a mess.

"Mr. President," Crane implored.

"Shut up, Oliver. I'll do the talking." Wallace pulled out a chair and sat down.

"First, let me outline just where things stand. There is incredibly strong evidence that you have committed espionage. Given that you have worked against a mission aimed at stopping a series of terrorist attacks, some might even call it treason."

Oliver Crane winced at the president's use of the word treason.

"We have known each other a long time, Oliver, and I first want you to know that means nothing to me right now. I'm here only because American citizens are dying from nerve-gas attacks and we don't have time to waste. I'm going to make you an offer. It's not negotiable. Are you ready to listen?"

Crane nodded weakly.

"Good. First, you will answer some questions for me. Then Frank Branigan and his people will have many more questions. You will answer them as well. All of them. Completely and honestly. If we are satisfied that you have been honest with us, I will arrange for the Attorney General to charge you with something along the lines of mishandling classified information, something other than espionage. You will plead guilty. Depending on how this all plays out, I will—at a time entirely of my own choosing—grant you a pardon. That's the deal. Take it or leave it. My advice is to take it."

Crane considered this for a moment. "Would this pardon be at the end of your current term or at the end of your second term? I assume you'll get re-elected."

Wallace laughed, something he rarely did, especially lately. "Oliver, you moron, don't you get that there are ongoing terrorist attacks happening out there? Attacks that you are supporting and that I have been able to do nothing about. If we don't get on top of this there will be no second term. I'll be lucky to finish this one. And you? What do you think a jury is going to say about your involvement in this? All I will do is give you my word that you will receive a pardon. Period."

Wallace slapped the table, which startled both Oliver Crane as well as the Secret Service agent. "Now give me a fucking answer!"

"Very well, Mr. President. I accept your offer."

Brendan Wallace leaned back in his chair for a moment, savoring this small victory. He then leaned forward and fixed Oliver Crane with a sharp glare. "All right, Oliver. Let's start with how you got to working for the Russians?"

"It all started in Afghanistan. You obviously know that Jonas Lanka, the RSO, is a Russian asset. I think he has a Lithuanian family connection that put him in touch. It's just about the money for him. When we were in Kabul and my son was studying at Cambridge, Lanka arranged to have some London Russians hook him up with a woman who took him on a weekend trip to Copenhagen. They filmed him injecting her with drugs...heroin, I think. She overdosed and died. They used that video to manipulate me into working for them. It was just a tiny bit of economic intel, but once I gave it to them, they had me on espionage."

"Christ Oliver, that's how they always work. Set you up small then nail you with evidence of your own treason. Why didn't you contact Kabul's Agency Chief of Station? CIA could have taken down Lanka and his handlers and found a way to protect your son."

Crane groaned and held his head in his hands. "By time I knew how bad it was, it was too late."

"What about this Korshkin? What were you told about him?"

"Whoever was Lanka's handler told him that Korshkin absolutely could not fall into US hands. They were really agitated about that, made a lot of threats. Exactly why was not clear to me and I don't think Lanka knew either."

"And the two officers you tried to turn over to the London Police?"

"That was poor judgement all around. Lanka's contacts in the Russian mob had tried to intimidate them with a couple of local punks, but instead they were with some big guy in a turban and those idiots were literally taken apart. Then they sent a pair of bigtime killers to take them out. Instead, they took down at least one of them in a back-alley ambush. The story was they're a couple of reserve officers, but we assumed they must be some kind of special ops people with deep cover. It couldn't have been a coincidence that a guy like Jose Barbosa, with his background, just happened to get involved."

The president smiled. "No, Oliver, they really are just a couple of reserve officers. The young woman received the Medal of Honor last year. Remind me to send you a copy of the citation. And Captain Barbosa's involvement actually was just good luck—or bad, from your perspective."

Wallace went on. "So what are the Russians planning for those two now?"

"Jonas knows more of the details, but apparently Moscow is willing to commit a lot of resources to keeping Korshkin from leaving the UK. They've hired just about everybody working for Russian organized crime and have them combing Scotland."

"Why Scotland?"

"Korshkin has property in Glasgow, and probably Edinburgh. They assume he's gone to ground somewhere familiar. They want to follow those two officers to him or, failing that, take them out and keep them from helping Korshkin. There was some mention of other resources, but I really don't know anything about that."

Oliver Crane took a deep breath and looked down at the table. "We also notified the British security services about our suspicion that they were involved in killing those two Russians. Last I heard they planned to pick them up for questioning."

Brendan Wallace smiled again. "Actually, they slipped away and are in the wind."

"Well, I'm not surprised. Captain Moore's grandfather is no ordinary banker. He has some very unusual connections and probably set the whole thing up."

"You could be right, that I don't know. I do have one other question, though. Who was your contact in the security services?"

"That, Mr. President, is one thing Jonas kept to himself. I have no idea. I only know this guy has been working with the Russians for a long time. To find out who he is, you'll have to get Jonas to talk. Good luck with that."

Wallace rose. "Very well, Oliver. I'm sending in Frank Branigan. Keep cooperating and someday you'll breathe free air. I hope to God we get hold of this Korshkin and that he tells us something important. For everyone's sake, but particularly yours and mine."

The president strode out of the room followed by his agent. In the next room, he said to the FBI director, "Frank, he's talking." He gave those around him a quick rundown on what he had learned. "Now I've got work to do. Go squeeze him dry."

Brendan Wallace headed for the door.

"I know Crane is an old friend. Just how hard can I push?"

"As hard as it takes." To Karen Hiller he said, "Let's get the hell out of here. And on the way back, I want to talk with Alex Clarkson."

CHAPTER 35

APRIL 7

CIA Headquarters, Langley, Virginia

J ENNIFER KIM RECEIVED a message to report immediately to a part of the building she had never been to before. It took her almost twenty minutes to walk there from her cubicle, and she had to ask directions more than once. Once she arrived she found only a room number, no identification. This seemed odd, but she noticed a card reader beside the door. If her card opened it, this must be the right place. She held up her Agency ID, there was a soft buzz, and the door clicked open.

She entered to find the room unoccupied. Looking around, she was surprised to see that, unlike most of the building's functional government furniture, this room was furnished with early American antiques. She took a seat in a heavy captain's chair that proved to be surprisingly comfortable.

Kim was startled when a door concealed in the far wall suddenly opened and Director Alexander Clarkson walked in. She shot to her feet but was too surprised to say anything.

"Officer Kim, I'm Alex Clarkson." The director stepped across the room and shook her hand. He stepped back and took a seat at a small antique desk, and Jennifer Kim sat back in the captain's chair.

"This desk was made by an ancestor of mine, Josiah Clarkson, in about 1820. Same with your chair. I believe things should be used as they were intended, not just displayed in a museum. Don't you agree?"

"Yes, sir, I do. And I must say, these are beautiful pieces. Being from Boston, I've seen quite a few."

Clarkson ignored the compliment. "Sorry about the vague invitation, but I sometimes find it useful to meet with people off the books. There's a stairway from this room up to my regular office. Bill Colby had it installed. Best thing he did for the Agency."

Jennifer fidgeted a bit. She had never been comfortable with small talk from superiors way above her pay grade.

Clarkson sensed her discomfort. "Well, let's get to business. This is obviously about Operation Pegasus. I've had all your reports sent directly to me. Strange situation over there."

Jennifer was surprised the director was personally involved, but there were rumors this op had originated at the White House, so perhaps it was not so strange. "Yes, there are some unusual developments, but I think our people are on the right track."

"What do you make of those two?"

"I was a bit uncertain at first—no intel experience, not much respect for procedure. But they have proven pretty resourceful and can play rough when required. They told us at The Farm that combat skills don't necessarily translate to the streets, but in this case, apparently they do. I think we could have done a lot worse."

"I would agree," said Clarkson. "You probably heard they were chosen by the President himself. He's read a number of your reports as well."

This revelation gave Jennifer Kim a slight knot in her abdomen, but she tried to conceal it. She did not even want to think about how the president regarded her work.

"So," Clarkson said, "they took down that Russian mobster in a back alley. Impressive. Anything more on who took out the other one?"

"Not a thing," replied Kim. "Captain Moore's grandfather employs some ex-military. I'm wondering if he set that up."

"Good thought. If anything more on that comes up, be sure to include it in your reports."

"Of course."

"It looks like our people are getting close to Korshkin. I need to let you know what's happening with regard to exfil. The British are still determined to keep Korshkin from leaving the country and now our people are officially fugitives. That complicates things. We're working that angle as best we can, but State is putting up roadblocks. To make matters worse, there seem to be differences among the Navy brass about their involvement. An Admiral Piotrowski has a ship, the *Makin Island*, that will be close to Scotland in a few days, and the skipper is on board with an exfil operation. The CNO and NavEur want no part of it, though, and are keeping our vessels in the North Atlantic out of British waters. This whole thing with our people being fugitives has spooked the president to the extent that he won't order NavEur to get involved. He's worried this will blow up and that we won't get Korshkin, or even worse, we get him and he has nothing worthwhile and at the same time we piss off the Brits enough for them to back out of our joint operations. See the problem?"

Jennifer had heard bits and pieces of what Clarkson just described, but now those pieces of upper level politics all fell into place. "Yes, sir, I think I do."

"Good. So here's the plan. As soon as we hear from McGregor what he needs medically, the Navy will put together whatever and whoever they need to help get Korshkin back here. They will take an Osprey out of Andrews, get refueled on the way, and land on *Makin Island*. You'll be going with them."

She was going into the middle of it? This was the first she had heard about it. She simply nodded, trying to seem unconcerned about being sent back to the field.

"You will have paperwork instructing the skipper of *Makin Island* to give you any and all assistance in exfiltrating Korshkin and our people and getting them back to the US," Clarkson said. "There won't be any way to know just how you can do that until we know more about Korshkin's condition. McGregor's last report mentioned a location in the Orkney Islands, so we will start with the assumption that Korshkin is still there. Clear?"

"Right. Is the Agency making any other preparations or is the *Makin Island* the whole plan?"

"Fair question. We tried to get a boat out of Norway into position to help, but they weren't permitted entry into British waters. Apparently the Brits knew the owner had some connection to us." Clarkson reached into his breast pocket and pulled out a small envelope. "Call this number and tell whoever answers approximately where you'll be and when you'll need to leave. They will probably be able to help."

"Who is it?" asked Kim.

"Sorry, need to know. In fact, I don't know much myself. This came to us via a third party. In the meantime, some of our exfil people in Europe are working up alternate plans. We will keep you informed."

Clarkson rose, signaling the meeting was over.

"You're doing a fine job," he said. "This could be a huge win for the Company and I'm relying on you to bring Korshkin in." He headed for the door but turned back.

"Jennifer, I understand you do triathlons."

"Yes, I do. Five so far."

"So you must do a lot of ocean swims."

"Every week, even in the winter," she replied with some satisfaction.

"Sea kayaking?"

"Yes, sir. Some of that on Chesapeake Bay."

"Good," said Clarkson. He handed her another card. "These people will set you up with some specialized training and get you a good dry suit."

Before she could reply, he was out the hidden door and she was left standing in the middle of all the antiques with a rapidly enlarging knot in her abdomen. Suddenly, this assignment was becoming a lot more than a desk job.

CHAPTER 36

T HE UZBEK HAD run across Caleb Carter a few weeks earlier while making his way east. He was at a truck stop and decided to have a quick dinner when the garrulous young man sat down next to him at the long counter. Carter was a short-haul trucker and fulfilled the stereotype of the typical American working man: burly, red faced, unkempt beard, and a baseball cap. An unambitious, unintelligent, uninteresting lump. That was until he started talking about his militia connections. At that point, the Uzbek began to take an interest.

Exploiting his training, he was able to get young Caleb to reveal that his father was some kind of big shot in a local militia. Caleb described to the understanding stranger how hard he had worked to be accepted by the others and how they had largely ignored his ideas for actions that would really shake things up in the Mississippi Delta. Despite having acquired more than a hundred AK-47s and tens of thousands of rounds of ammunition, the others refused to live up to their ideals. Caleb had been trying to move up in the ranks, but bad luck or government agents had always blocked his rise.

Then he brought up the sarin attacks. "Now those guys know really what they're doing," he said. "How in the hell do you suppose they got hold of sarin?"

The Uzbek had made a snap decision. He bought the kid a few drinks and then hinted he might be able to get hold of one of those sarin bombs. Caleb Carter was positively salivating at the idea. He began talking details right there at the truck stop, and the Uzbek thought he might have to take him out back and cut his throat just to shut him up. He was able to calm the kid down, though, and get him outside where they reached a tentative deal. Caleb would scrape together five thousand dollars in cash and call one of the Uzbek's throwaway cell numbers. They would then arrange a meet.

The Uzbek contacted a reliable operative who placed Caleb under surveillance. He wasn't worried that he would sell him out to the FBI, but he was worried the young hothead would blab to everyone in town about what a big man he was about to become. But Caleb showed at least enough self-restraint to keep his mouth shut.

The meeting was set for a back road near one of the oxbow lakes along the Mississippi–Arkansas border. The Uzbek didn't need the money, of course, but he did need a local chump to be connected to the sarin. Caleb and his father—Pappy, as the kid liked to say—were well-known militia figures. Linking Caleb to the explosion of a sarin bomb was the tricky part. He didn't really care if the idiot actually pulled off an attack, though that would be a bonus. He just needed Caleb to be undeniably associated with the sarin—not just a suspect.

The answer came to him one evening while he was driving. All he had to do was rig the bomb to go off the next time Caleb took it out of its case once an hour had passed from the sale. He knew the young agitator would not be able to resist showing his Pappy, or maybe all his militia friends.

Caleb was right on time. Contrary to the monster truck the Uzbek expected him to be driving, he pulled up in a rusted-out old Subaru. He handed over a bag with an assortment of greasy bills ranging from twenties to hundreds, bundled into thousand-dollar stacks held together with rubber bands. The Uzbek made a cursory show of counting the cash then retrieved a case from a hidden compartment in his RV, opened it to show his client, described how to arm it, and then he closed the case and handed it over.

The Uzbek worked his way back to the highway and an hour later was cruising north on I-55 headed for Memphis. He parked at a Walmart and prepared to settle down for the evening when he saw a breaking news story about another sarin attack. The device had exploded in Mississippi at a rural cabin belonging to one Jacob Carter. His son, Caleb, and two so-far unidentified men were all found dead at the scene. The senior Carter was known to be active in a small local militia, but it was unknown how or if there was any militia connection. Also unknown was whether the Carters had accidentally detonated the device or if some other group or person was responsible.

The Uzbek had not expected results so quickly, but he was pleased with the outcome and decided to use some of Caleb's five thousand to buy himself a good dinner. He made a reservation at the Capital Grille and used one of his burn phones to dial up an Uber.

CHAPTER 37

IT HAD BEEN a slow trip north from Edinburgh. By time they had stopped outside Inverness, the gateway to the Highlands, to purchase a few extra supplies it was well into the afternoon. Not wanting to arrive in the Orkneys at night and unsure of the ferry schedule, Mike and Kelli had worked their way up the northeast coast and stopped in the small coastal town of Lybster, a fishing port with a picturesque harbor and its own lighthouse. They found a comfortable nineteenth-century inn off the main street.

Their Canadian passports passed muster, and they were shown to a large room with two single beds. The landlord was apologetic and winked at McGregor, who had to suppress a smirk.

After a dinner of pan-seared scallops, the two officers sipped a local highland single malt, all the while keeping an eye on their vehicle and the window to their room. Fortunately, the Russian mob's reach didn't extend to Lybster.

Even so, for the second night, neither got much sleep. One of the two was always in an overstuffed chair by the window, aware of every movement on the quiet street. Mike had taken most of the watch so Kelli could try to rest the sprains and bruises she got when Igor had thrown her down the stone steps in Edinburgh the day before.

Recalling Dieter Wolff's warning about possession of a firearm used in a shooting, Mike had called the number Wolff had provided. They were given a time and location of an intersection north of Inverness where they were met by an elderly Scotsman who took possession of Mike's pistol and gave him a replacement. In a minute, the man was back on his ancient motorcycle, a grizzled border collie in the sidecar, and they disappeared down a tiny side road.

Now Mike held the weapon on his lap as he peered out into the night.

While Kelli slept, he recalled his own feelings when he saw Kelli against that wall, knife at her back. He had to acknowledge, if only to himself, that his decision to take that shot had been about more than just the mission. He thought about Danielle, the beautiful architect to whom he had once been engaged. She had died in an accident at work, and he could not deal with that kind of loss a second time.

But to move ahead, he had to take that chance.

Kelli woke early. She sat up, looked out the window and asked, "Do you think we'll run into more Russians?"

"Now that we know how much effort they're putting into finding us, we should probably expect that we will. This time there won't be just leg wounds. We're getting too close to Korshkin to let them walk away. Now it's hardball."

"Agreed." Kelli was quiet for a minute then added, "Mike, were you really going to stick that thing into Igor's eyeball? You don't need to answer—I just needed to ask."

"I'm not sure. Yeah, probably. I'm starting to think the Colonel might be right about Yemen. A year ago, I doubt I would have even considered it."

"I've been thinking the same thing about myself," Kelli said. "But we're too far down the rabbit hole now to back off. Next time, no interrogations."

Mike decided to change the subject. "I wonder what your grandfather is up to right now. I get the feeling that he and Ian have something more ambitious planned than just touring around in that beer truck."

"I'm sure they do. That remark he made about not knowing who they were dealing with made me a little nervous. Or maybe it was just the way he said it. He's getting too old for this kind of thing."

"Hell," said Mike, "I'm getting too old for this kind of thing. But I wouldn't worry too much about Sir Charles. I just have a feeling that beneath those Saville Row suits you'll find a pretty rough character."

"That's what worries me."

About then, the sun peeked above the horizon. They prepared for travel, though on this day it felt more like preparing for battle.

The landlord packed them some coffee, bread, and cheese, which they ate on the way north. It was not long before they arrived at the north coast port of Scrabster where they had no trouble getting passage on the Orkney ferry. There were only a few trucks, cars, and a single motorcycle. Hoy was actually visible in the distance, but that was not the ferry's destination. They passed around its west end and up to the town of Stromness on the major island of the Orkneys called Mainland, just to the north of Hoy.

As they passed, Hoy was an imposing sight with high granite cliffs and heavy surf. They could just make out the small bay where they hoped to find the elusive Korshkin, but a light fog hid any structures.

CHAPTER 38

AFTER THEY LEFT the ferry at Stromness, a small but bustling port at the west end of Scapa Flow, it was an easy drive along the south coast of Mainland, past green fields with grazing sheep, and a few abandoned farmhouses, their stacked stone walls still standing, but the thatch or wooden roofs long ago decayed in the harsh climate. In half an hour, they arrived at Houton, a sheltered bay with another ferry terminal. This route would take them down to Hoy, but to its north coast, far from their destination at the west end. It was the first available ferry, though, and the drive to their destination would allow them to check for surveillance.

They had not counted on the number of vehicles headed for Hoy. The deck was packed with trucks, cars, and motorcycles. There was even a large backhoe which seemed to take forever to get properly aboard. They were finally underway and despite a brisk wind, the brief crossing was relatively calm.

They stood out on the deck for a while, though the wind was cold and unrelenting.

"Grandfather and I sailed through here once when I was living in London," Kelli said. "Scapa Flow was a major fleet anchorage during the war and Lyness, the other end of this ferry route, was a big base."

"Wasn't there a battleship sunk near here?"

"The HMS *Royal Oak*. She was torpedoed by a German submarine that managed to get in through a narrow channel. There's a buoy marking the site of the wreck." She pointed towards the northeast. "It's too far from here to see, though."

"Must have been tough duty up here."

"The winters can be rough—heavy storms and constant cold wind. The RAF pilots had a particularly hard time of it. There are still some buildings from the war. We once toured a big communications station up on a hill south of Lyness. Too bad we don't have time to have a look. There's a Naval Cemetery, too—you would find it interesting. Grandfather showed me a memorial to a nurse, a medical officer, and a dentist from one of the hospital ships killed during the first war."

Mike scanned the horizon. "Let's hope we don't add to that list."

Kelli was about to admonish him for his pessimism but thought better of it. "Look, Lyness is coming up just ahead."

They docked at what could hardly be called a port. There was the pier, a couple of storage buildings, a few remnants from the war, a tiny museum, and a small hotel. Once their Land Rover was off the ferry, they headed west along the coast road until Mike shouted, "Stop!"

Kelli slammed on the brakes. "What?"

"Emily's Tea Room! Who knows when we'll have a chance to eat again and I could really use some coffee."

Kelli laughed at her partner's enthusiasm, but agreed. A cup of tea after the cold ferry crossing was a good idea.

The shop was a small, pale blue building perched on the north side of the road next to Scapa Flow. There nothing visible in either direction.

They walked in to be greeted by the smells of tea, coffee, and something absolutely wonderful baking.

The charming owner greeted them and they fell into their Canadian identities. Mike ordered a latte and Kelli a pot of tea. They each got a scone.

In a few minutes they were enjoying what Mike deemed the best scone he had ever eaten. Kelli had to agree. "This lemon scone is better than anything I ever had in London," she said. They purchased two more for lunch. The owner carefully wrapped each and they tucked them into their packs. They resumed their journey to west Hoy.

They drove along the coast road, passing only the occasional knot of sheep grazing on the heather that covered most of the island. Consulting a map they had found in Inverness, Mike directed Kelli to turn onto a side road that ended at Rackwick, a small collection of buildings near the sea. There was a parking lot for hikers—empty at this time of year—and a stone hut for those caught out in one of the frequent storms.

The nearby shore was covered by rocks, mostly the size of baseballs, but some a lot larger. A bit farther down the shore was a short stretch of sandy beach that ended at an impassable headwall. To the north were three large hills; the underlying granite having resisted the effect of the ice-age glaciers that shaved down the rest of the Orkneys, leaving a smoother terrain. There were hiking trails leading up into the hills.

To the south, leading to the southwest coast and—hopefully—to Maxim Korshkin, there was also high ground, but not quite so high as in the other direction. With Kelli on point, they left the trail and were immediately slowed down by the soft mounds of heather. They had to travel inland and cross a small stream before the grade became more easily passable on foot. An hour after leaving the car, Mike's GPS told them they had traveled just over a half-mile and less than that of actual progress towards their destination. Despite the work of crossing diffi-cult terrain, they had underestimated the effect of the constant cold wind. More concerned about rain, both wore light waterproof parkas over turtlenecks. They now stopped to don fleece pullovers they had stowed in their packs.

Kelli took advantage of the stop to scan the terrain behind them with the small Nikon binoculars she carried on all her deployments. The open terrain did not allow for the kind of countersurveillance possible in a city.

"We have company. Take a look."

Mike looked where she pointed.

"Do you see him?" she asked. "Guy in a tan coat. Looks like he's having more trouble than we are with this damn heather."

"I wonder if he's another city thug like that guy in Edinburgh. Prob-ably not used to being out in this kind of country."

"Well, whoever he is, he sure is no hiker. He has some kind of small shoulder bag and that's about it. My guess is that he's following us and probably has a satphone to report where we're going."

"Good bet," Mike said. "We can't just let him keep following us. We're going to have to take him out—and soon. But where?"

"Up there." Kelli pointed at a hilltop a few hundred yards away. "See that rock outcropping? We'll go around the side of the hill then circle back and get behind the rocks. We can take him as he passes."

"Infantry 101. Let's hope this guy hasn't read that Chapter."

"You think Igor would have anticipated that move?" asked Kelli.

"You're right, these guys are used to beating up addicts and hook-ers, not dealing with military skills."

They picked up their pace, and as they passed the rock, they saw that some quirk of weather or geology had split it vertically. There were actually two rocks about ten feet high and separated by enough space for a person to easily pass between them. Kelli lay down behind the rocks and Mike went around and into the gap between them. They waited for almost twenty minutes before they heard the man grunting with the effort of climbing the hill.

He was in his forties, overweight, and wearing a quilted jacket that was tight around his waist—he definitely spent all his time in the city. As he passed, both fired three shots from a distance of about forty feet. Five hit and the man went down immediately.

Mike approached the body and confirmed he was dead. "One in the head and two in the neck."

They dragged him between the rocks; more to escape the wind than for concealment. He carried a Model 96 Beretta in .40 caliber with one spare magazine, a folding knife, and a wallet containing two hundred pounds and ID for Constantine Lysek of Aberdeen. His bag contained a sausage, a roll, and a liter bottle of water.

And a satellite phone. The last call had been made less than two hours before. "Probably when he left the parking lot," said Mike. "We have to assume whoever he was calling knows more or less where we are."

Mike felt a peculiar prickly sensation on the back of his neck, like he was being watched. He tucked himself further between the rocks. At that moment there was a tremendous "crack" followed by fragments of rock showering both of them and inflicting several small cuts on Kelli's right cheek. An instant later came the sound of a rifle shot.

"Okay, I think they know exactly where we are," Kelli said. Both lay flat in the gap between the rocks.

Mike low-crawled to the far end of the gap and took a quick peek. "The bastard is about two hundred yards down the hill and just walking towards us out in the open. He must know we don't have long guns."

"It won't take long for him to get in position to start shooting into our little hideout. We need a plan—and quick."

"He probably saw us take out Constantine," Mike said, "so he knows we have suppressed small-caliber weapons. Not much of a threat."

Holding up the Russian's Beretta, Kelli replied, "He may not be thinking about this." She dropped the magazine. "Pretty much like what we carried in Yemen, but the magazine only holds twelve rounds. The .40 S&W does have a lot of velocity, though. A hit at a hundred yards is not out of the question."

"All right." Mike knew Moore's skill with handguns was extraordinary, so this plan could actually work. "I'll roll out my end and start shooting. That will get his attention and you can open up with that cannon. If this doesn't work, we're in deep trouble."

They waited a few minutes for the rifleman to get closer. Mike slipped out to the left and from a prone position aimed a foot above the Russian's head and opened fire. The silenced pistol did not attract his attention right away, but then the man stopped and began to swing the big sniper rifle off his shoulder.

Kelli opened fire with the Beretta. The blast from the .40 caliber rounds was deafening. It was difficult to tell, but her third or fourth shot hit the man on the upper left arm. He cried out and spun down to the ground, scrabbling behind the heather for concealment.

After a few minutes the man yelled in heavily accented English. "I had planned to let you live if you gave up Korshkin. Now I'm going to fucking kill both of you and find him myself." This was followed by another shot that struck the rock on Mike's side. A bullet fragment penetrated his jacket but was stopped by his body armor.

"We can't put up with this for too long," said Mike. "Even if he can't get a direct shot, he can chop us up with fragments. Thank God for Mr. Wolff, but he can still hurt us. I'm thinking we just take off down the far side of hill and hope one of us makes it. That arm wound is bound to slow him down."

"Michael," she said quietly, "think this through. At this point, you're the mission. I can't tell Officer Kim what's wrong with Korshkin, that's on you. You take off and I'll use the Beretta to cover you. I should be able to buy enough time for you to get away from his line of sight."

"Not happening. I've been left behind, and I didn't like it. Besides, if I'm running downhill he can probably take me at over four hundred yards. He's obviously pretty good with that rifle. Maybe we can hold out until dark."

"And how do we travel over this ground in the dark? And besides, what are the odds he has night vision?" Kelli was feeling frustrated by their lack of options. As a Marine, her instinct was to confront the enemy and have it out then and there.

Mike thought for a minute. "All right. Maybe we can bring him in closer. One more hit from that Beretta might immobilize him."

"And how do you propose to do that?" asked Moore.

"Watch and learn. Igor," Mike shouted. "we've been killing Russians for a week. Did you hear about Belov? He was pretty good, and we took him in London. And how about that little guy? Story was nobody had ever touched him. Now he's history. You're next."

Moore put the spare magazine into the Beretta and watched as the Russian began to carefully work his way closer. He fired two shots and with the second she felt a sharp sting on the back of her right calf. "Well, you obviously succeeded in pissing him off."

"Not Igor," the Russian yelled. "I am Vasily. I'll leave a note on your corpses so they know who killed you." He fired another shot. A small piece of rock nicked McGregor's ear. Moore fired one round, deliberately missing wide. The Russian moved a little closer, moving around the rock formation so they could not escape to a safe distance before he got them in his sights.

After ten minutes, Vasily had fired five times into the rocks and both Americans had suffered one additional wound, both to the thigh. Kelli had fired three more rounds with one hit to the body. After less than a minute the Russian was back on his feet.

So, he had body armor too.

"Well, that sucks," said Moore. "Best bet is to try for a shot to the leg. Then we can bolt."

The Russian was finally in a position in which he could fire directly down the gap between the rocks and at an angle where a direct hit would be possible. "We can move to the far end," said Mike. "We'll have better cover there."

"But we can't return fire from there. He'll just go back to chopping us up." Kelli took careful aim and began to squeeze the trigger. She had obviously decided that it was time to end the standoff, one way or the other. McGregor prepared to join her. He steadied his aim to bring his short-range weapon to bear. Time to give Vasily everything they had.

The Russian began to raise his rifle. The sniper's head suddenly jerked back, and a spray of blood erupted from his neck. Neither had fired a shot yet.

Somebody was out there—but who?

Moore stood and stepped out from between the rocks, and after a moment, McGregor joined her. She was surprised to see a big man in camouflage fatigues about two hundred yards down the hill. He wore the green beret of the Royal Marines and had a suppressed sniper rifle over his shoulder. He walked uphill towards them. She did not recognize the big man, but there was something familiar about him.

In a few minutes the man approached the two American officers, smiled broadly, and said, "Sergeant David Campbell, Her Majesty's Royal Marines. Pleased to meet you."

"Not as pleased as we are." Kelli still did not recognize him, but she stepped forward and took his hand. "So, Sergeant, what brings you to Hoy?"

"You may remember my Uncle William? Sergeant Major Campbell?" he added.

It was Kelli's turn to smile. Of course, Sergeant Major Campbell had served with them in Yemen alongside Major—then Captain—Singh. Moore and McGregor both knew they would have probably been buried in that desert country without the two Royal Marines. "Yes, I seem to recall that big Scot. You look a lot like him."

"Everyone says that. Well, Major Singh rang up Uncle William and asked him to keep an eye on you two. The Sergeant Major is still down in Oman, but he knew I was on leave at home in Inveraray, so he suggested I head up here to see if you needed a hand. Looks like I arrived just in time. Who, by the way, was the late gentleman with the rifle?"

"He called himself Vasily," answered McGregor. "Let's find out."

They walked back to the Russian's body. There was a fist-sized hole in his neck and a large pool of blood. There was also a fair amount of blood on a hasty dressing he had applied to the wound Kelli had given him on this upper left arm. She made a quick search.

"No ID, but his pack has gear for several days out here, a satphone, plus sixty more rounds of ammo. And a night-vision monocular." She gave McGregor a 'told you so' look. "Of the two, he was obviously the pro."

"Take a look at this rifle," said Campbell. "Custom M-14 with a German scope and a light nylon stock. Don't get one of these at the local gun shop. And a lot of his ammo is armor-piercing. Must have been expecting your body armor."

McGregor opened the man's jacket and with some difficulty removed his custom body armor, which still bore the flattened .40 caliber bullet that has impacted the ceramic insert over his sternum. He then tore open his shirt. "Have a look at that. You ever seen tattoos like these?"

"Spetznaz probably," Sergeant Campbell said. "Not like the Russian prison tattoos I've seen. Fits with the custom weaponry."

"If that's true, then this guy may have been sent to augment the local thugs. Makes me wonder what else they have on the way. I think we have to assume he reported in at some point. Let's have a look at that phone." McGregor picked up the Russian's phone, turned it on, and scrolled through the menus. "Last call about three hours ago—that was before the other Russian's last call. At a minimum, whoever sent them knows we're in Orkney, though they may not know more than that."

"Last Russian? Fat guy in a tan jacket?"

Kelli nodded. "His body's between those rocks."

"I wonder if our Officer Kim can track down that number he called" Mike said. "Let's take the phone, but remove the battery first. They might be able to track us with it."

"Better to write down the number and destroy it," said Campbell.

Kelli jotted the number in a notebook, then Campbell smashed the device with the butt of his rifle.

The trio returned to the shelter of the rocks. Campbell pulled a small stove from his ruck and began to brew tea. McGregor and Moore were happy to share it.

"I'm curious, Sergeant, just how you happened to show up when you did?" asked Kelli.

"I made a guess that you would come up to Stromness on the ferry. The overnight boat from Aberdeen would have left you too exposed, and the timing wasn't right. At Stromness I picked up that fellow," he nodded at Constantine, "who was obviously on the lookout for you. He took off after you in an old flatbed truck and met up with that chap"—he pointed at the man he had shot—"at the Houton ferry. I convinced a young lad in a fishing boat to run me and my motorcycle over to Lyness and I got there about fifteen minutes ahead of you. They watched you at the tea shop then followed you down to Rackwick. I held back a bit and then followed them up into the hills."

At the mention of the tea shop, McGregor and Moore both pulled their scones from their packs and shared them with the Sergeant.

"Wonderful," he said.

After they were fortified, the two Americans agreed they must get on to locating Korshkin.

"I'll tuck Vasily between the rocks," Campbell said. "They won't be visible from the ground unless you're right beside them and they will be hidden from air or satellite surveillance. And the next rain will wash away the blood. I'll spend the next few days patrolling, just to be sure there are no more visitors."

As they started out towards the coast, Sergeant Campbell handed the Russian's rifle and extra magazines to McGregor. "Might prove useful."

"Sound idea, Sergeant; wish we'd had it half an hour ago. And please give our regards to your uncle and the Major."

"Commander, you're never on your own. Remember that." With a wave, the big Scot hefted his own rifle and pack and began to patrol, very much as he had on countless days from Oman to Afghanistan.

CHAPTER 39

BRENDAN WALLACE WAS tired. He had been bombarded all day with reports of demonstrations resulting from the discovery that a Mississippi militia was in possession of a nerve-gas bomb. There had also been a few smaller demonstrations by heavily-armed militia groups claiming that the Carters had been assassinated by a sarin bomb in an attempt to divert blame from the radical immigrant groups who were actually responsible. And now Frank Branigan, Sonny Baker, and Alex Clarkson stood in front of the Resolute Desk after calling for an urgent meeting. Karen Hiller was off calming down the Mississippi Congressional delegation.

The president looked closely at each man. They all looked as tired as he felt. "Sit down, for God's sake. You look like pallbearers." They moved to a cluster of wing-back chairs.

"Mr. President," began the FBI Director, "we've succeeded in getting Jonas Lanka to talk. He couldn't give us the name of the Russian mole in the British security services, but he did give us enough information that, combined with leads the CIA developed in Britain, we might be able to identify him."

"And?" Wallace hated drama.

"Nothing yet. We do know that until recently, the Russians haven't shown much interest in Korshkin, or at least they weren't working very hard at finding him. When these attacks started, Lanka began to get a lot of heat about locating Korshkin, and particularly about keeping him out of our hands. We originally assumed it was just British internal politics—embarrassment at being fooled by the guy. But now it appears likely that effort was, from the beginning, directed out of Moscow."

Wallace broke in. "Alex, what do your people know about this?"

"Not much, I'm afraid. We knew the SVR has been looking for the people who actually stole those warheads, but they haven't made much progress. Until things blew up in London, we didn't really have anything to connect the Russians with these attacks. We're now starting to think this could be an SVR op from the start. Create chaos with nerve gas attacks and, more important, make it look like different groups were responsible. It's what the Russians call a maskirovka—a deception. They've been doing it since the Czars."

"The pieces all fit," Wallace said. "Why the hell didn't we see it earlier?"

Branigan winced. "Well, sir, we looked where they wanted us to look: at the usual suspects. Arabs, immigrants, Central American gangs, known criminals, and now, right-wing militias. We've been behind every step of the way."

"So how do we get ahead of it? We obviously need to get our hands on the guy who's running the op, and hopefully Korshkin can do that. Alex, where are we on that?"

"Our people should be in the Orkney Islands right now. We hope to hear they've contacted Korshkin any time. We are concerned, though, about the pushback we're getting from the Navy regarding exfil. NavEur and the CNO are putting a lot of emphasis on their future relations with the British."

"Alex, I don't see how I can just overrule them without more to go on. From what Sonny tells me, you have a skipper who's ready to support the mission. Can you make it work or not?"

"Depends on what we need and what other assets we can mobilize, but probably. In the meantime, we need to find some way to discredit the misinformation the British are getting. If we just tell them it's coming from a Russian asset in their ranks, they are going to want proof—or at least some convincing evidence. Right now all we have are conjectures."

"Do you have any assets in the security services? People who can start shining some light on who might be helping the Russians keep us away from Korshkin? And how about this Cathcart? He is obviously after Korshkin for personal reasons, but maybe if he understood that what he's doing is actually working against British interests, he might back off."

"Mr. President," said Sonny Baker, "you may recall that you issued an executive order about not developing sources in friendly security agencies."

"Yes, Sonny, I remember and you don't have to remind me that you were opposed. That was Karen's idea, if I recall, and it made good sense at the time. It was a judgement call." Turning away from his National Security Advisor, he looked to Alex Clarkson. "Do we have any assets or not?"

"Nobody with access at the upper levels, and nobody who can get to Cathcart without blowing our op. But we may be able to get some people looking in the right direction."

"All right, then. Get on it. And keep me informed about developments in the Orkneys. If we have no choice other than giving CNO a direct order, I'll do it, but by God, if I do, this guy Korshkin better be gold."

Everyone rose, and with the usual chorus of "Yes, Mr. President," headed for the door.

Wallace walked towards his desk, paused, and made a decision. "Just a moment."

They all stopped and turned to face him.

"I think it is very clear that an op like this, nerve gas on US soil, had to be approved at the very top, and you know who I mean. Once we get a handle on the current mess, I want every brain cell in this room working on the same thing: how do we make this painful, and I mean excruciatingly painful, for Putin and the SVR."

There were nods all around, but only Alex Clarkson spoke. "Mr. President, that is the best damn order I have ever received."

Everyone left the oval office and Brendan Wallace returned to the Resolute Desk, no longer feeling tired. By nature, he was a planner, and now there were plans to be made.

CHAPTER 40

THE RELENTLESS COLD wind off the North Atlantic was taking its toll. Mike and Kelli both had the hoods on their parkas up but wished they had packed hats. McGregor's hands were stiff. Each time they began to make progress, they had to detour around another impassable terrain feature. To conserve their dwindling energy, they took more frequent rest breaks, but each time their inactivity led to further loss of body heat.

Finally, they decided to just keep moving until they reached their destination. After two more hours of hard hiking, McGregor and Moore were peering over the steep cliffs of the southwest shore of Hoy. They were at the north end of the small bay. On the south side, there was an aging concrete pier on the back of which was perched a small building, also of old cracked concrete. Not exactly homey, but they knew it must be the home to Marta's uncle and now, Korshkin. There was a storage shed beside the building, but no other structures. A small satellite dish was mounted on the steep sheet-metal roof, and a large cable of some kind ran out into the ocean. A breakwater of rock and large concrete blocks blocked the south end of the bay, but a large defect in the head-wall and gaps in the breakwater confirmed the story about why the station had been abandoned.

They moved along the rocks until they came to what seemed to be the best way down. First, they lowered their packs using a length of rope Kelli had bought near Inverness. They secured the rope to a rock outcropping and McGregor, the more experienced rock climber, worked his way down to the rocky beach, a process made all the more difficult by the ocean wind and his cold, stiff hands. Moore, less affected by the cold, followed.

As they turned to get their packs a rough voice asked, "And who might you be?"

They turned to see a large bear of a man in well-worn oilskins walking towards them over the rocks and holding an equally worn AK-47. It looked like it still worked.

"Lieutenant Commander McGregor and Captain Moore. We're here for Mr. Korshkin." McGregor hoped this was the right answer. At least the man did not have a Russian accent. "Are you Vegard?"

"That I am. And happy to see you." He extended a huge hand that felt rough as shark skin. "I was wondering when you would come for my Russian friend."

He stepped closer, picked up their packs with one arm and led them towards the building. "I assume from your arrival here on Hoy that you met my niece."

"Yes, we did. We hope we didn't put her at risk."

"Marta is a smart woman. Smart enough that she didn't call me."

They entered the building and were surprised to find that, unlike the crumbling wind-swept exterior, the interior was cozy and inviting. It was one large room with a kitchen at one end overlooking the sea and two beds at the other end. In between was a sitting area with a small table and mismatched chairs. The floor was warm from electric heat, and the eclectic furniture was worn, but appeared comfortable.

"What's your source of electricity?" asked Mike. "Heating this place must use a ton of power."

"The tides. I have a unit anchored to the seabed about four hundred meters out. The tides and currents here are strong enough that even at slack tide it puts out about twelve kilowatts. Peak is around forty. There's a battery bank in the shed that can keep me going for a day if there's trouble."

Vegard stepped around a large leather sofa and said, "And here's my guest."

Korshkin lay resting on the sofa, propped up on pillows and covered with a quilt. His skin was a pasty grey, his breathing rapid, and when Mike took his hand it was cold and clammy.

The Russian woke. "Are you the doctor?"

Mike confirmed that he was and began a brief examination. In less than a minute he said, "I think I've found the problem. Your pulse is only thirty-two, Mr. Korshkin. Is that new?"

"I have had spells of slow heart, but it has only become constant since I arrived here. Now I'm too weak to do much of anything."

"Your blood pressure is also low, 86/45. You look dehydrated. Have you been taking fluids?"

"Not much," he replied. "It takes too much effort. And then I must use the WC, and I have no strength for that."

"Is there anything you can do for him?" asked Kelli.

"Let me check one more thing." Mike pulled a small heart monitor from his medical pack and attached the leads to Korshkin's chest.

"Complete heart block. That pretty much explains everything. The upper chamber of the heart has the pacemaker that sets the rate. Right now it's going at eighty-eight. The system that conducts the beat down to the lower heart—the ventricles—that do the actual pumping has stopped working, so the ventricles set their own rate, which is usually very slow. I suspect the problem was intermittent at first, which explains his spells. Now it's permanent. Mr. Korshkin needs a pacemaker, and that I can't do. I've put in a few temporary pacemakers in the ER, but even that would be impossible here. Perhaps if Officer Kim can get me some medication that speeds the heart we could get him fit to travel. Mr. Korshkin, do you take any medications?"

"Aspirin to protect my heart." He gave a bitter laugh. "I guess it isn't working. Also a blood pressure pill, but I ran out."

"For right now I'm going to try a little IV fluid and see if that helps. Then I'll send a report with what I've found."

"This might be a good time to bring up how they're getting us out of here," added Kelli.

Mike started an IV and then hooked up a liter of fluid. After that, he opened the comm device and prepared their report.

From: Keystone
To: Dover

1. Have located Granite. He is currently unfit for travel. Diagnosis is complete heart block. Will ultimately require a pacemaker insertion. Suggest you investigate arranging for placement of temporary pacemaker during exfil.

2. Request delivery of the following to this location:

   a. Dopamine for infusion, sufficient for three days.

   b. Infusion pump.

   c. Portable cardiac monitor; the unit included in medical pack has limited battery life.

   d. Collapsible litter.

3. Note that Empire and Keystone were intercepted en route in west Hoy by two Russians. One was probably local organized crime, but the second believed to be Spetznaz. Both KIA. Bodies unlikely to be discovered prior to exfil.

4. Urgently request update on exfil plan.

5. Current location will be encrypted by the GPS in this unit.

CHAPTER 41

CIA OFFICER JENNIFER Kim was startled when the comm device on her desk began to beep. She read and re-read McGregor's message, then forwarded it to her supervisor and, as ordered, to Director Clarkson. She called her contact in Navy Medicine on a secure line and read the relevant parts of McGregor's message. He told her that he would have what she needed available within three hours.

Within five minutes, Alexander Clarkson was on the phone.

"Be at Andrews in four hours. Have whatever medical support McGregor needs with you. You'll be traveling by Marine Corps Osprey to the USS *Makin Island*. The skipper will know you're coming, and my assistant is on her way to you now with White House-level orders directing him to assist you any way he can. I am also sending a Lieutenant Courtney Klein, who is a liaison officer with us from Naval Intelligence, to assist you. Assist—not replace. This is your op, Kim: do whatever it takes to get Korshkin out. I'm also sending one of our Russian-speaking analysts along with someone from the FBI to begin interrogation. They are traveling separately. Once Korshkin's aboard *Makin Island*, your mission is complete and they take over. Clear?"

Jennifer was scribbling notes and trying to digest the barrage of information. "Clear, sir." Clarkson hung up. Kim immediately called back her contact at Navy Medicine and relayed the travel plans. So far, the mission was making progress despite Russian interference. Kim was pleased with her own performance and the support from Clarkson; though she couldn't ignore the tightness in her chest. She had failed once before, and that mission was a lot less critical than this one.

Thirty seconds later, Clarkson's matronly assistant appeared with a sealed envelope stamped TOP SECRET. Kim signed for it. The woman, one of those career Agency employees married to her job, smiled at her and said, "The director really is impressed by your work, Miss Kim. I will tell you that happens very rarely. Best of luck." She turned on her heels and left as quickly as she had come.

Jennifer headed home to pick up a duffel bag she had already packed. She opened a well-concealed safe and took out her passport, a few hundred British pounds as well as some Euros, plus off-the-books cell and satphones. She selected a customized Sig P320 RXP and slipped it into a nylon holster.

Jennifer called to arrange for an Agency driver to take her down to Andrews, and then laid down for a few minutes to clear her head. She dared not sleep however, lest she find herself back in the Carpathians.

Two hours later, Kim arrived at Joint Base Andrews. Her driver, who had said nothing once he confirmed her identity, seemed to know exactly where they were going. They stopped at a hanger where an Osprey, the peculiar Marine Corps aircraft capable of normal flight as well as hovering like a helicopter, was being towed out to the tarmac.

Standing near the hanger was a gaggle of three Navy officers in khaki uniforms and black windbreakers. Standing a little apart was one enlisted man in utilities. Courtney Klein was short and studious looking with dark curly hair, which had become unmanageable in the wind. She wore an academy ring. The senior of the three was a Commander Patel, a medical officer who she discovered was a cardiologist. The other was a lieutenant commander who was a critical care nurse. The enlisted man, a corpsman and second-class petty officer, was apparently there primarily to carry several large packs of equipment, including the gear requested by McGregor.

Klein stepped closer to Kim and said without introduction, "I hear the people in the field are a couple of reservists. Is that really true?"

"Yes, it's true. Is that some kind of problem?"

"Do you really think they're the best people for something this sensitive? What kind of experience have they had?"

"Captain Moore is a fellow Academy grad, so you have that in common." She paused. "And after an operation last year she was awarded the Medal of Honor."

"I'm sorry," she said after a moment, "if an academy grad had received the MOH, I would know about it."

"Apparently not," replied Kim. "Presented to her by the Commandant himself. There's a nice photograph in her file. You would be impressed by the citation, but it's classified."

Klein said nothing.

"And the doctor received a Navy Cross. Actually, I think it was his second. Don't worry, though, I'm sure they don't know how you used the influence of Rear Admiral Klein—who happens to be the Pac Fleet G2 as well as your uncle—to get you out of that crappy billet in Bahrain and into the nice assignment in Hawaii you just came from. They probably won't be questioning your qualifications. Maybe you could offer them the same courtesy."

The young lieutenant turned to walk away when Kim stopped her. "Listen up Lieutenant! The choice of these people was made way above your paygrade; I mean way above. And remember this: you are here to assist me. So far, you aren't doing a very good job of it."

Klein began to speak, but Jennifer Kim put a finger in her face. "One more thing, for the remainder of this mission, for communication purposes, you will be designated Sparrow.

"Lieutenant Klein, you are dismissed."

Kim actually hated it when the men in the Agency did something like this—wagging their dicks, she called it. But damn, it was satisfying.

A Marine sergeant rounded them up, and got everyone and their gear loaded onto the Osprey. The cargo area was equipped for passengers, but in the minimalist way of all military aircraft. Klein seemed nervous about the strange contraption that was going to get them there. The medical personnel kept to themselves, but appeared energized about being part of a high-profile mission.

Kim put in earplugs, then noise-cancelling headphones over them. Even so, the roar of the turbines was fierce. Once airborne though, the stress of the mission finally caught up with her, and she nodded off.

CHAPTER 42

THE UZBEK ENJOYED stopping at out-of-the-way American state parks. They all had good road access, plenty of parking, and he could use them to rest, have a meal, or just get some exercise without arousing the slightest suspicion.

He sat in a folding chair outside his RV reading his latest decrypted email. More bad news. His handlers had lost contact with the Spetsnaz operator they had inserted into the Orkneys. They assumed he had been lost to enemy action. How the hell had these two amateurs succeeded in taking out multiple operatives, in some cases very capable ones, sent to stop them? They had to be trained agents or special warfare types with a very deep cover. The message said there was no other option to stop the Americans from making contact with Korshkin. The last hope, and it was regarded as a longshot, was on its way, but it would not arrive until after they were with Korshkin. Because of the risk he would expose his real identity and thus link the nerve-gas attacks to the SVR, the Uzbek was instructed to shut down his operation and get out of the country within forty-eight hours.

He had been expecting this, and he had been preparing several options for the finale of his operation, as well as for his departure. He looked over his map program, took inventory of what he had available in the RV, and then began sending emails. Once this was done, things would happen automatically.

After finishing a piece of salami—he had to admit the Americans could make a decent sausage—the Uzbek left the park and headed west towards Seattle.

CHAPTER 43

JENNIFER KIM ACHED all over. The Osprey had been in the air for almost six hours, most of the time fighting heavy turbulence. They had landed, not on *Makin Island*, but on the aircraft carrier USS *Abraham Lincoln*, outbound towards the Mediterranean. She didn't know it, but this stop had required direct intervention by Sonny Baker to arrange.

It took almost two hours to refuel and have technicians check a warning light. They seemed satisfied that whatever it was, it wasn't serious. Kim wondered why the aircraft manufacturer decided to give warnings about something that wasn't important.

They did get a good meal in one of the wardrooms and, mercifully, had access to the heads. They boarded the Osprey and endured five more hours before they settled onto the deck of *Makin Island*, which was cruising at sixteen knots, heading northeast, about one hundred eighty miles southwest of Scotland.

Kim had never been assigned to a Navy vessel before. *Makin Island* was a slightly smaller version of the *Abraham Lincoln*, and her flight deck held both helicopters and several of the new F-35 fighters. She knew the ship's primary mission was to deliver an embarked Marine battalion by air or by landing craft. Before she could pull her gear from under the cargo net, an enlisted Marine hefted both her duffel bags. "I'll be sure these get to your quarters, Ma'am." She was quite sure she had never been referred to as Ma'am before. She wasn't sure she liked it.

Kim reported immediately to the skipper, Maxwell Pauley, who was on the bridge. "Max Pauley," he said and extended his hand.

"Jennifer Kim. Is there someplace we can talk privately?"

He turned over the conn and they adjourned to his quarters. After a minimum of pleasantries, Pauley got down to business. First, he reviewed the documents Kim had brought with her.

"This is pretty unusual, as I'm sure you know. I get the importance of your mission, and I've already told Vince Piotrowski that I'll help as much as I can. I have to tell you, though, that I got a call from NavEur himself, ordering all vessels, aircraft, and personnel under his command to stay out of UK airspace and territorial waters without specific permission from the British, as well as the NavEur chain of command."

"Yes, but I'm not under NavEur's command."

"And that does give us a bit wiggle room. Now that I know your destination, we'll alter course to get us within small-craft range of Hoy. Our original thought was to drop you by helo about a mile out and have you take a swim board in to your target. Now we can't get within three miles and that's too far to swim. Even our special-ops guys would have a hard time in these conditions. I've had some people from our embarked MARSOC, the Marine Corps special ops group, set you up with a kayak they use for infiltration. We can put you in the water as the tide starts in, and at a location that won't have you fighting the current. Best we can do."

Kim nodded. The number the Director had given her was for a special-services officer who gave her a crash course on open ocean swims and the use of sea kayaks. Given her previous experience, she was sure she could handle it—assuming there were no surprises.

"Do you have exfil arranged from Hoy?" Pauley asked.

"I was given a deep cover contact. He's been notified and said that he could be there the morning of the eleventh. Can you put me in tomorrow?"

"Definitely. But you may want to wait to see how the weather develops."

"I need to be there tomorrow. We have to get our man ready to travel, then get him out as soon as our exfil plan is in place."

"Can do. I'll have someone take you down to help get your gear stowed in the kayak, and then we'll set up a quick meet with the helo crew that's going to put you in. I took the liberty of having the medical personnel you brought taken down to our sickbay. Our people will help them any way they can. How about that Lieutenant that came with you? What do you want us to do with her?"

"She's my liaison with you and with Langley while I'm off the ship. I'll brief her myself and let you know her specific duties before I leave."

"Give my operations officer a briefing before you go, too. I'm going to give Admiral Piotrowski a quick update, but for the moment I don't think NavEur really needs to know much of what we're up to."

"Agreed." Kim was beginning to like this man.

The skipper picked up a phone and a minute later a Marine corporal appeared and escorted her deep into the lower level of the ship.

She was introduced to three members of the MARSOC unit. They were professional, but clearly not enthusiastic about being involved in an Agency operation. They gathered around an eighteen-foot sea kayak. Unlike most that Kim had seen, this was not a high-visibility color like orange or yellow. Instead, it was the flat grey of a Navy warship. There were two paddles secured to the sides, and the two cargo holds—fore and aft of the cockpit—were accessible through round, waterproof hatches. The cockpit had a small display screen that was programmed to show a GPS position updated every thirty seconds, course and speed, projected time and direction to destination, and water temperature. With the help of the Marines, she stowed her gear and the medical supplies McGregor had requested. Kim was surprised at how much cargo this sleek little boat held.

The MARSOC team took charge of the kayak and told her they would bring it up to the hanger deck and have it fixed to the helicopter. The same corporal then brought her to the ready room for HMLA-269, where she met the pilot and crew chief.

The pilot, a compact young man wearing Captain's bars on his flight suit, did not try to hide his surprise that his mission was to drop a kayak and a civilian into the ocean off the island of Hoy. "No offense," he said, "but do you have experience with this kind of mission? It's trickier than it seems."

"I guess it's your job to make it not tricky. Is there anything in particular I need to know?" No need to mention this was her first time.

The crew chief, a staff sergeant, spoke up. "Well, Ma'am we can't drop you in the kayak so the way it works is we drop the boat then move a few meters away and in you go. We'll move to a stand-off position until you board. We should be able to put you in downwind from the kayak to make it easier. Have you boarded a sea kayak in open water?"

"It won't be a problem."

The pilot smirked at the crew chief.

"We were told you have your own dry suit and that all your gear is already stowed," the crew chief said, "so I guess all you need to do is meet us on the hanger deck at 0600."

"What about weather?"

"You can get an up-to-date weather brief yourself before the mission," answered the pilot. "Last I heard there's a moderate low-pressure system moving up from the southwest. You should start with a light offshore wind, but that's going to change at some point and you'll have increasing wind in your face. We were told to time your insertion for daylight and favorable tide. Not much we can do about the wind."

"I'll just have to deal with it. Corporal, can you show me to my quarters?" Kim followed the Marine down two decks to a berthing area for female officers. The cabin was for a senior officer and had only one bunk. Kim derived some small satisfaction from the fact that the obstreperous Lieutenant Klein was bunking with the nurse they had brought aboard with them. As she walked by their room, she could already hear them arguing about something.

Knowing that she would be up at 0400 to be ready to launch at 0600, Kim sent an encrypted message reporting their arrival, set her alarm, and, without even getting undressed, was asleep in less than a minute.

CHAPTER 44

APRIL 9

Lerwick, Shetland Islands

THE SKIPPER OF the MV *Western Isle* inspected the damage to his vessel. A one-hundred-fifty-foot general cargo vessel, the *Western Isle,* ran a regular route from the west coast ports of Britain, usually Liverpool, up to the Hebrides, Orkneys, and Shetland Islands. The day before, while passing west of Hoy in the Orkneys, a rogue wave had broken loose some deck cargo and washed it overboard. It looked like a bundle of construction lumber had been poorly secured, and when washed over the starboard side, it had caused minor damage to one of the davits. He was confident he could find a replacement part in Lerwick and that the delay would be minimal.

According to the cargo manifest, they had lost only a dozen twelve-foot four-by-fours destined for a contractor in Lerwick. This was a regular customer, so the captain would offer to pick up a new bundle on their next trip and deliver it without cost. He expected that delivering a few bottles of spirits today might help smooth things over until the problem could be made right. He intended to find out who had secured the deck cargo and have the man accompany him on his visit to their customer.

The skipper gave no further thought to the lumber, which now joined the thousands of tons of cargo lost overboard every year on every ocean.

CHAPTER 45

JENNIFER KIM WAS strapped into a seat on the UH-1Y Super Huey, the latest iteration of that venerable Viet Nam-era helicopter. They were traveling light, with only the flight crew, the crew chief, and a Navy rescue swimmer in addition to herself. The kayak was attached to the right skid.

Kim had been up since 0400. She had briefed the operations officer, gotten a weather report, had a spirited discussion with Lieutenant Klein, gulped down some coffee, and then geared up for the mission.

The helo skimmed the wave tops, which showed small patches of froth as the wind picked up. Toward the horizon, the featureless grey of the ocean transitioned into the monotonous grey of the clouds. She wondered if this is what Homer had meant by the wine-dark sea.

After about an hour, the aircraft slowed, and the pilot announced they were five minutes from the drop. The crew chief opened the door and Kim was surprised at how cold the air felt.

Soon, they were hovering less than ten feet above the swells. Kim was seated at the edge of the door, her helmet off and the hood of her dry suit pulled up. The kayak was released and dropped onto the water, rolled a bit, and then stabilized.

The helicopter side slipped, and Kim felt the chief give her a slap on the back. She braced her feet on the skid and pushed off.

The cold water came as a shock. She was submerged momentarily, but in the buoyant dry suit she popped like a cork back to the surface. Kim was alarmed when the swells obscured the kayak, but when she looked up and saw the crew chief pointing, she assumed it was towards her boat, and after swimming a few strokes, the grey shape became visible. She scrambled aboard without embarrassing herself too much, gave the chief a thumbs up, and the helo turned and headed southwest back towards the *Makin Island*.

Kim located the pedals for the boat's little rudder, activated the navigation system, and pulled loose one of the paddles. She looked in the direction where Hoy should be, but saw only a dim mist. The wind was picking up, and there were moderate swells already. She was comfortable in her dry suit, however, and as soon as the nav system displayed an arrow pointing her way, she began to paddle.

The wind, which had been from the southeast at first, slowly shifted to the east and increased in intensity. After an hour of hard paddling into the wind, she was less than halfway to where she was headed. Her shoulders and back were starting to ache. As increasingly large swells washed over the bow, she was pummeled with cold water and—despite the work of paddling—began to chill.

Kim's spirits were buoyed when she spotted the small bay on Hoy from just over a mile out. The swells kept increasing in size, but she felt confident she could reach the shore before the tide peaked.

She had learned not to fight the swells as they washed over the bow. She simply held the paddle at waist level and let it pass. The next swell hit her off the starboard bow.

Just as it peaked, Kim felt a heavy blow to her chest followed by a searing pain. She released the paddle with her right hand, but had the presence of mind to keep a grip with her left.

She thought for a moment that she might pass out, but she fought through the pain and took stock of her situation. Her craft seemed undamaged by what she could now see was a floating piece of lumber. She, on the other hand, had been struck just below the right shoulder. Her dry suit and the lightweight silk underwear beneath it had been torn open. She could see blood, but it didn't seem like a lot. Kim could barely move her right shoulder, though, and even minor movement resulted in a horrible tearing sensation in her upper chest.

The wind and swells were pushing her out more than the tide was pulling her in, so whatever she did, she had to do it quickly. Using her left arm and shoulder for most of the propulsion, and compensating with the rudder, she was able to make headway, but much more slowly than before.

After about thirty more minutes, Kim looked at the nav display and was discouraged to see her progress had slowed dramatically. She found a canteen and the small medical kit and, hoping that some pain relief would allow her to paddle harder, she took a tablet of hydrocodone.

It didn't take long for Kim to notice at least some improvement in the pain, but now another problem was becoming a worry. The tear in her dry suit was allowing the frigid ocean water to pour in, and she could feel her suit slowly filling with water. She knew she had to be developing hypothermia. Was this going to be Romania all over? A failed mission, only this time even she wouldn't even survive.

No, she was too damn close to just die out on the ocean.

With renewed vigor, Jennifer Kim pulled at the paddle with all her strength. Like a pilot flying an instrument approach, she hardly looked at the island but instead peered at the nav screen as the distance slowly ticked down.

Kim knew she was getting weaker–her paddling irregular, her muscles tight, and her thinking unclear. The nav screen arrow still pointed straight ahead, and when she looked up, the island seemed to be right in front of her.

A few last pulls, then she heard a scraping sound. The paddle hit something and she stopped moving.

Was this it? Had she made it? She could see rocks large and small right in front of her and in her clouded mind realized the kayak was up against the shore. If she could just get out and pull the kayak onto the rocks, she would have succeeded in her mission.

But she couldn't. Maybe if she rested for just a minute. It would be awhile before the tide changed and pulled her out to sea. She could rest for just a minute and then pull her boat up onto the shore.

CIA Officer Jennifer Kim lost consciousness, let go of her paddle, and slumped forward, her right hand in the cold water.

CHAPTER 46

"**M**R. PRESIDENT, DIRECTOR** Clarkson on the secure line."

Brendan Wallace picked up the blinking red phone, waited for a moment while the secure connection went through, then said, "All right Alex. I hope you have good news."

"Well, Sir, progress at least. Our officer was put into the ocean about four miles west Hoy just over an hour ago. Conditions look good, and the Navy reports she was in her boat and heading for shore. I'm hopeful that we'll hear from her in another hour."

"I suppose that's what passes for good news these days. How confident are you that we can actually get this guy out?"

"We have to rely on the doctor's diagnosis. He says Korshkin has some kind of heart block and that he needs a pacemaker. He's requested a medication to get him fit for travel, and that's going in with our operator. Our officer has been in touch with an exceptionally capable deep-cover contact who is arranging to get Korshkin out to the *Makin Island*. The Navy has also sent a team to the *Makin Island* that's equipped to place a temporary pacemaker, and the ship has a well-equipped medical department to support them. There's also a team there to begin interrogation immediately."

"That all sounds good. What else do you have, Alex? You didn't call just to tell me you had a boat in the water and some doctors on the ship, did you?"

"There is one other thing." Clarkson paused for a moment to see if Wallace would say anything. When there was no response, he went on.

"You may recall that a senior member of the British security services has been carrying out some kind of personal vendetta against Korshkin."

"Right, right," said Wallace. "A fellow called Neville Cathcart. So what's happened? Does he want to help us now?"

"Not quite. He's disappeared. I know you were reluctant to do any kind of surveillance on the British, but we have had some people keeping a discrete eye on him and they now have no idea where he is. He has a long history in the field so he could easily go underground. Some of our people are starting to think this may have been more than just personal for Cathcart."

"Meaning what?" asked Wallace.

"We're concerned he might be defecting to the Russians."

"For God's sake, Alex, are you telling me Cathcart is the mole?"

"Well, he might just have run off with his mistress, but we have found some other connections that suggest the Russians are involved. His disappearance could complicate things in London."

"How so?"

"If he doesn't turn up, we have no way to convince the British that he's been manipulating them with regard to Korshkin. That will make it even harder to re-establish good relations; especially if they find out we've taken Korshkin despite their wishes."

"First, Alex, keep in mind we don't actually have him yet. And once we do, it's your job to see that they damn well don't find out that we do."

"Yes, sir. Absolutely. We just have to cover all contingencies. What I wanted to ask you was how aggressive you think we should be in tracking this Cathcart down. If he gets over to the Russians, its trouble. But if the British find us looking for one of their own people, the shit is really going to hit the fan. I mean, we don't exactly have hard evidence against this guy."

"You're right about that, Alex. We absolutely cannot have Agency involvement in this. Do you have any local resources who are deniable?"

"Not many. Not in Britain. Let me talk to my people and see what we can come up with. How far can we go if we do locate him?"

"Alex, must I do all the goddamn thinking? Bring him in, if you can, but you sure as hell cannot kill him. Are we at least clear on that?"

"Yes, Mr. President. I'll get right on it."

Brendan Wallace hung up the secure phone, sat back in his chair, and closed his eyes. The next twenty-four hours would probably resolve this, one way or another.

CHAPTER 47

"OFFICER KIM? JENNIFER?"

Jennifer Kim thought she was dreaming. Did dying people dream? Did they know they were dreaming? She just couldn't work it out.

Suddenly though, her injured shoulder exploded into a balloon of pain as something pulled her out of the kayak. She woke with a start and realized a large man had thrown her, like a sack of grain, over his shoulder. She looked up and saw someone else pulling her kayak onto the rocks. It was a woman, and when she looked at Kim, there was no mistaking the dramatic green eyes. Was it Kelli Moore? But the hair was wrong—it was blonde hair that peeked out beneath her watch cap.

Before Kim could understand what she was seeing, she passed out once more.

When she woke again, she was lying on something soft. A bed. And she was covered by several blankets and a heavy comforter. She could see her dry suit and other clothing lying beside the bed and she realized she was naked. Captain Kelli Moore sat next to her in a chair. Across the room she heard the voice of Lieutenant Commander McGregor.

"Officer Kim," said Moore, "good to have you back. We kept looking for you and were getting very worried when we found you in that kayak up against the rocks."

"Am I on Hoy? Did I make it?"

"You did. We unpacked your kayak and the doc is working on Mr. Korshkin. Looks like he is feeling better already. Can I ask what happened to you?"

"There was a piece of lumber floating in the sea. A big swell threw it up and it hit me in the chest."

"That explains it," said Moore. "Your dry suit was torn open and the lower half filled with sea water. You were hypothermic, but luckily not so bad we couldn't warm you up. Can you swallow? I have some tea."

Moore held up a large spoon and Kim sipped from it. She was reminded of the times her mother had given her tea in a spoon when she a little girl. She sipped the warm liquid and it was rejuvenating.

"Doc," Moore said, "Officer Kim seems to be feeling better. Maybe you can check her over now."

Mike McGregor stepped over and smiled at her. "I'm going to check your shoulder, okay?"

Kim nodded. He pulled down the blankets a bit to reveal a large purple bruise developing below her swollen right shoulder, as well as an oozing cut that started just below her collarbone and extended below the edge of the blankets.

McGregor, who had surprisingly warm hands, gently pressed several spots around the shoulder and upper chest. Several areas were painful, one exceptionally so.

"Looks like you've fractured some ribs." He pointed at the worst spot, "This is where one of your biceps tendons attaches. The shoulder joint seems all right, though." He took her wrist and elbow and gently moved the shoulder a bit. The pain was mild. "Try moving your shoulder yourself."

That was intensely painful and she stopped.

"Looks to me like the tendon's been injured and your pectoral muscle torn for sure. I think an MRI will be in order once we get back. Let's have a look at this laceration." McGregor pulled down the blankets to reveal a laceration that extended from her collar bone all the way down to her upper breast. Her dark nipple was very erect, and, despite her near-death experience, she felt embarrassed.

Her embarrassment faded, though, when McGregor put on gloves and very carefully began to clean her wound, apparently oblivious to her anatomy.

"Okay, this isn't very deep," he said, "so I think we can close it with tissue glue. Kelli, can you give me a hand?"

Moore also donned gloves and held the wound edges together as McGregor applied a liquid that hardened almost immediately, holding a small part of the wound to together. They worked their way down and finished in a few minutes.

"The glue acts as a dressing so nothing more is needed. Gravity is going to pull all that blood in the bruise down into your breast and it's really going to ache. I see Captain Moore cut off your underwear. Did you bring anything else?"

"Don't worry," said Moore. "I found your bag of clothes in the kayak. You'll feel better if I help you into that sports bra. Doc, I think your work here is done. I'll help Officer Kim into her clothes, and then we can get off a report."

Moore bent over and spoke softly to Kim, "This is the reality of being a woman in the field. You'll get over being embarrassed pretty quickly. Trust me." Kim raised her eyebrows and nodded.

McGregor returned to monitoring Korshkin. It took another twenty minutes for Kim, with Moore's help, to carefully get into her clothes. There was another moment of potential embarrassment when the big man who had carried her in came through the door while she was less than half dressed. But he simply smiled, announced the kayak had been concealed from view, and then stepped over to his home's small kitchen and began working on lunch.

Finally, dressed in a warm fleece pullover and khaki cargo pants, Kim walked, a bit unsteadily, to the couch where she was introduced to Maxim Korshkin, the entire reason she was here. She was surprised that he was actually a rather charming old man who thanked her profusely for her part in his rescue.

"You aren't rescued yet," Kim told him. "But things are looking up."

Kim hesitated, but decided to push ahead. "Mr. Korshkin, it would certainly make us feel better if you could share some information. A show of good faith, so to speak."

"I'm sure it would," replied Korshkin. "You must be the CIA officer Dr. McGregor mentioned. It sounds like you had a harrowing journey, so I must thank you for delivering the medication which has me feeling better than I have in weeks. I owe you much, and you can be sure that I will repay you and your government many times over."

"But..."

"I'm sure you can understand that I will feel much better if you retain the highest degree of motivation to complete your mission. Therefore, I will share everything once I am on US soil, or at least aboard an

American warship. Forgive an old man for being so demanding, but this is all I have to exchange for my safety."

"No offense, Mr. Korshkin, but we've gone to quite a lot of trouble to get you this far. Can you not share anything?" Kim wanted to include some morsel of useful intel in her first report and thought that with Korshkin looking at salvation, he might at least throw her a small bone.

"Very well. You are a delightful young woman who has suffered on my behalf. The Russians are behind the whole thing. How about that?"

McGregor laughed. "We've been killing Russians all week. Can you tell us anything we don't already know?"

Korshkin looked alarmed. "Russians have been trying to stop you? Not the British?"

"Yes, Russians." said Kelli Moore, "And they came pretty fucking close."

"Then you have already confirmed my veracity." The old Russian had apparently recovered from this nasty surprise. He smiled at Kim and said, "One additional detail. That is all for now." He motioned for her to come closer and then he whispered softly so only Kim could hear.

Korshkin turned to the big man. "Vegard, my friend, now that I'm feeling better I could use a small taste of the marvelous whiskey they make here."

Vegard, who had been silent up to now, pulled a bottle from a cabinet. "Five glasses?"

As they sipped the local Highland Park Scotch, Kim conferred with Moore and McGregor on her report. They sent the message directly to Director Clarkson—"Kestrel" for this mission—with a copy to Lieutenant Klein, "Sparrow," via the *Makin Island*.

From: Dover
To: Kestrel
Copy: Sparrow
        Commanding Officer USS *Makin Island*

1. Dover arrived at destination.

2. Condition of Granite improved and fit for travel.

3. Anticipate exfil first high tide tomorrow. Will advise Sparrow by secure satphone.

CHAPTER 48

THE UZBEK OPENED the door of the storage unit located in Moses Lake—for some reason the Washington city had an unusual number of such facilities. He rented it more than a year ago and had placed a device that took wide-angle digital photographs through a tiny hole he drilled in the door. The photographs were taken every minute, twenty-four hours a day, and once a day they were emailed to a secure address. He reviewed them periodically to see if anyone had been snooping around his unit. After six months of no activity, he had purchased an over-the-hill old Ford Focus from a drunk who had lost his license enough times that he had finally decided to give up driving. He drove it to the unit with the owner's plates, which he'd promised to replace, but never had. The trunk contained some clothes, passports, and cash. He made a point of passing through the northwest on his journeys, and when he did, he stopped by and started the car and checked the tires and battery.

Today he removed the Ford and backed his RV in. He worked for about an hour activating several electronic devices, then he locked the unit and drove to I-90 where he took the long drive across Washington to where he had rented a room—with a previously unused name and credit card—at a small bed and breakfast in Port Townsend, west of Seattle.

He arrived in time for dinner, after which he began to make calls on his many burner phones and one on an encrypted satphone. The latter was brief, but critically important—a single word.

CHAPTER 49

MCGREGOR STOOD OUT on the pier as the eastern sky turned bright. The sea was calm—the low-pressure cell that Kim had struggled against had moved out. He watched as a pod of orcas cruised north in search of harbor seals. He was getting concerned because the tide had been coming in for a while, and according to the tidal chart Vegard had, would peak in less than an hour. There was no sign of a boat coming to take them out to the *Makin Island*.

At that moment, a peculiar craft rounded the headwall about two hundred yards offshore, then turned, heading directly towards the opening at the north end of the seawall. About fifty feet long and with a lot of beam, it looked like a cross between a tugboat and a yacht. As it passed, he could see the name *Puffin* on the stern, along with the "Port of Stornoway" written below it. In the wheelhouse was a tall man in a peacoat and watch cap who waved to McGregor.

He was surprised to see the odd vessel make an impossibly sharp turn into their small harbor, head straight for the dock, make a ninety degree turn to face seaward, and then approach the dock sideways. The fenders kissed the dock, and a young man appeared from below and threw McGregor the bow line while he headed aft and took up the stern line.

The boat was secured to the dock, the engine was shut down, and the tall man emerged from the wheelhouse. It was Sir Charles. Of course it was.

He again waved at McGregor, then he turned to the other man. "Ian, would you check below and be sure we're ready to get underway? The tide will start to ebb in half an hour." Ian nodded and went below. Sir Charles jumped onto the dock.

"Michael," he said, while shaking his hand, "so good to see you. How was your trip up to Hoy?"

McGregor never thought it would be Sir Charles here to pick them up, but now he found he wasn't really surprised. "Delighted to see you, Sir Charles. We had to shoot a Russian in Edinburgh, and a couple more here on Hoy. There's a Royal Marine on patrol up there,"—he pointed to the top of the cliff—"so we should be all right for the moment."

"You have been busy," said the older man with a twinkle in those green eyes. "You both came through unharmed, I take it?" This was said with more concern as he eyed several cuts on McGregor's face caused by rock fragments during their encounter with the Spetsnaz operator.

"Yes, sir. Just some minor wear and tear."

"Well, let's get on with it. Is everyone in there?"

Without waiting for an answer, Sir Charles headed for the small building.

McGregor was still wondering just how Sir Charles knew where they were and what they needed, but he assumed it must be the part of his life that wasn't banking. They both entered to see Vegard cleaning up the kitchen, Kelli and Jennifer Kim stuffing a backpack, and Korshkin lying on the couch hooked up to an IV pump.

Kelli raced across the room and threw her arms around her grandfather. "Why am I not surprised?" She looked out the small window. "Is that ungainly thing yours?"

"It is. Bought it from an old acquaintance on the Isle of Harris two days ago. It's actually more gainly than it looks. Two MAN diesels, steady as a rock in heavy seas, all the latest electronics, bow and stern thrusters, and even a little wine cellar. It is a bit slow, though. We coaxed eighteen knots out of her on the way up, but that was with a very light load. Ian and I were going to cruise up to Norway until the heat was off—so to speak—but then a Miss Kim called." He turned to Jennifer. "That would be you I presume?"

"Yes," she said. "CIA Officer Jennifer Kim." She extended her left hand. "Sorry. Bit of an injury on the way here. And you must be our deep-cover operative."

"Very deep, indeed," he said. "Sir Charles Moore, but please just call me Charles. The last time I did anything for the Agency was lifting ... you, it was you wasn't it? Out of Romania. I don't think we were introduced at the time."

"I may have been unconscious. Thank you, Sir Charles. That flight has become a legend in the company. And I never had a chance to thank you."

"Ian did most of the work. I just paid the bills. He's out on the boat. I'm sure he would be delighted to meet you."

Kim headed for the door.

"And Kelli, I think the new blonde look really suits you."

"Just part of my disguise," she replied, but with a smile of satisfaction at her grandfather's approval.

"Not much of one." He laughed and turned to Mike. "Have you a camera?"

McGregor rummaged in his pack and produced his phone.

Sir Charles put an arm around Kelli and said, "Go ahead, Michael. I'm putting this one in the study next to my photo with the Queen."

"You will not!" said Kelli just as Mike snapped the photo.

"So back to business," he said. "Time to go." To Vegard, he added, "I hope this was not too much trouble. You should be safe once we're out of here."

"Aye, nobody after me." Vegard was a quiet man, who was sure once this gaggle left, he would once again have his solitude with only calls from Marta, and the occasional trip up to the market. Just the way he liked it.

Korshkin stepped over to Vegard and put a hand on his shoulder. "Vegard, my friend, I know I cannot repay you, but be sure that I will try. The same for Marta." Before the big man could reply, Korshkin turned away.

They gathered up their gear and headed for the boat. Korshkin leaned on McGregor for support but was able to walk and even step onto the boat. They moved him below and found a place for him to lie down, and secured his IV pump beside him.

Vegard and Ian cast off the lines, one of the big diesels turned over, and the thrusters pushed the *Puffin* away from the dock. Several quick maneuvers and they were heading out into the Atlantic.

Kim used her secure satphone to call Lieutenant Klein, who was on the bridge with the Captain. It was Pauley who took the phone. "We know where you started. What's your estimated speed and what kind of vessel do you have?"

Kim climbed, with difficulty, up to the wheelhouse and handed the phone to Sir Charles. "He wants to know what we are and how fast we're moving."

"We're in a Krogen 52 upgraded with two MAN diesels. I can give you a sustained fifteen knots."

They heard Pauley speak to his navigator, then a moment later, "Steer a course of 285. You should intercept us in just under five hours. Call us back every hour with a course and position update. Our medical team would like an update on the condition of your passenger."

"Commander McGregor tells me he is stable," Kim said. "The drug I brought is being given IV and seems to be helping."

"Very well. What? Wait one." They heard Pauley and someone else speaking in the background.

"There's a problem. The last satellite pass picked up a Russian ship, the *Sergei Andreyev*, on a course that will come pretty close to intercepting you. She's making about twenty-five knots—you should have her in sight in less than two hours. My intel officer tells me she is an oceanographic research vessel just over one hundred fifty feet. Probably not heavily armed, but certainly will have small arms. Another problem is an order from NavEur—we're in his AOR now—to avoid taking any action with regard to this vessel that can be attributed to the US Navy, unless, of course they fire on us. I'm going to divert one of our destroyers, the *Gravely*, to monitor the situation and assist, if they can. Keep us informed of any developments. *Makin Island* out."

"That is...disagreeable," Sir Charles said.

"Unless you have something I don't know about, all we have are a few handguns," Kelli said. "Oh, and Michael took that Russian's sniper rifle. That might make an impression."

"My dear, you should know me by now. Ian! Looks like it's time to prepare for guests."

In less than a minute, Ian climbed to the wheelhouse carrying three new M-27 rifles, the Marine Corp's replacement for the squad automatic weapon. "Ten thirty-round mags per weapon," he said.

Kelli hefted one. "And where did you get these?" asked Kelli.

"Dieter arranged for his contacts at Heckler & Koch to deliver them in Stornoway when we took possession of the boat. Best he could do on short notice. Haven't really had a chance to sight them in, but we should be able put up a good scrap. More dead Russians, I suppose."

Mike appeared with the custom M-14. "A new friend of ours thought this might be useful. Seems he was right."

Ian looked it over with a professional eye. "Nice piece."

"Should we change course?" Kelli asked.

"I don't think so. They'll be getting satellite updates and have a speed advantage. Whatever we do, they can still intercept us before we can rendezvous with *Makin Island*. Also, they may not know we're aware of them. Our best bet will be to let them get close, thinking we have no idea what they're up to."

"And then the hunter becomes the hunted," said Ian.

"Precisely," replied Sir Charles. "Let's use our time productively."

"Agreed," Kelli sighed. "Guess I'll have to get back into that damned corset."

CHAPTER 50

APRIL 11

Makin Island

CAPTAIN MAX PAULEY sat in his sea cabin pondering how best to deal with this new threat. He had no doubt that the Russians were making one last attempt to stop Maxim Korshkin from getting into American hands. The fact that they were dispatching a valuable research vessel showed just how desperate they were. The problem was that any communication with *Gravely* would be known to NavEur and the CNO, who could easily countermand anything they didn't like.

And then there was that annoying Lieutenant who had come aboard with the CIA officer. She clearly wanted to be part of the decision making, but somehow Pauley didn't trust her. No, this one was on him.

He told his messenger to ask the XO to report on the double. In five minutes, Commander Michelle Lebec knocked on the door.

They sat at his tiny table, sipping coffee. "Michelle, there's no way around the fact that we're going to be playing pretty close to the edge on this. If the Russians can blame us for anything that happens to their ship, NavEur and the CNO will be sure you and I go down for it. On the other hand, if they succeed in preventing Korshkin from getting to us, the president and National Security Advisor aren't going to be happy. And then there's the unknown number of additional Americans who will die as a result."

233

Lebec was from an old French-Canadian seagoing family and third-generation US Navy. She knew the phrase "things went wrong, and you were there" all too well. It tended to dominate Navy thinking. She shook her thick black hair, something she did when stressed, and answered, "Then we should probably do what's right for the country and hope we get lucky."

"My thought as well," said the skipper. "I'm going to order a course change for *Gravely* that will have them intercept the Russian. They have at least a ten-knot speed advantage so they should arrive not long after the Russian intercepts our people."

"And what are your instructions to *Gravely*?"

"Just the course change. I'll advise Commander Gonzalez I'm dispatching an officer by helo with further orders. That will be you. They're going to launch in twenty minutes."

"And just to satisfy my curiosity, why is it that a helo can't just pick up the people on that boat and fly them back here? I'm sure there's a reason, I just can't think of it."

"I suppose I need to show you this." He handed her a sheet of message paper. It read:

From: NavEur
To: Commanding Officers USS *Makin Island*, USS *Gravely*, USS *Truxtun*
             EYES ONLY
SUBJ: AIR OPERATIONS

1. Due to complex international developments, the above vessels are forbidden to utilize air assets to remove persons from any UK flagged vessel while operating in NavEur AOR without prior approval from NavEur.

2. You POC is NavEur Chief of Staff, Captain Roger Chaplain.

3. Comments or questions are neither solicited nor desired.

R Chaplain
By Direction

"Well, that's clear enough. Any idea why NavEur has such a bug up his butt about this operation?"

Pauley sighed. "Admiral Piotrowski seems to think he has totally committed to this joint operation plan with the Royal Navy and is afraid that pissing them off would deep six the whole thing. Personally, I think the whole NavEur command structure is way too cozy with the British. I hear Chaplain's up fishing in Scotland with some Lord practically every weekend and NavEur's daughter is a student at Oxford."

"Can you at least tell me what my orders are for *Gravely*?" she asked.

"To do whatever they possibly can to protect our people and their mission without an act that can't later be denied."

"A missile launch would be out of the question, then?"

Pauley could not quite tell if his XO was being facetious.

"Assume that you're under satellite observation unless those clear skies suddenly get very cloudy. Can you believe this weather? How often is the North Atlantic clear with five knot winds?"

"On the average, skipper, more or less never. I'll try to think of some ideas on the way. I haven't looked at the chart recently. How far is *Gravely*?"

"With their new course, about forty minutes by helo. I told them best possible speed."

"Very well, sir. I'll be on the flight deck in ten. I'll try not to let you down."

"Michelle, I know I'm putting you in a tough spot. It was only six months ago that they relieved Joe Castelli on *Bataan* basically for doing the right thing. I can live with that happening to me, but I don't want to bring you down with me. But this is a vital mission and you're the best person I have."

"Skipper, six months ago I was on the SurfLant staff and knew all the details surrounding Captain Castelli's relief. He rescued wounded sailors and Marines and was shown the door for it. Story was Admiral Piotrowski had to fight to even get him his retirement. If we pull this off and the CNO wants my hide, I'll be proud to give it to him."

CHAPTER 51

APRIL 11

MV *Puffin*

IAN STOOD AT the window of the wheelhouse and watched the horizon to the north. They'd picked up a vessel on radar a few minutes before and now it was visible with binoculars. The bearing was constant and the range closing.

"Looks like the Russian. About the right size and the bow wave is consistent with the twenty-five knots they reported."

"Have Officer Kim call *Makin Island* and tell them we have radar and visual contact," Sir Charles said, "then get everyone ready for action. Given Officer Kim's shoulder injury, I think you, Kelli, and Commander McGregor will have to handle the rifles. I'll handle the helm, and Officer Kim can stay with our guest."

"Right. And you'll probably want these too." Ian handed Sir Charles one of the M-27s and his own Wolff Waffenfabrik body armor.

"I took a quick look online at the specs for the *Sergei Andreyev*. They have better speed than we do, but they only have bow thrusters—not stern—and they have a small rudder. We can't outrun them, but we can outmaneuver them. They shouldn't be able to ram or board us. They are a genuine research vessel, hydrologic mostly. I doubt the scientists or technicians will have any taste for battle. They do have a Russian Navy crew of twelve, so figuring a few on the bridge and at least one in engineering; they shouldn't be able to put more than nine up against us."

"Still, that's three to one. We need surprise to cut those odds down to size." Sir Charles outlined his thoughts then Ian went below to prepare for the coming battle. On the way he motioned to Kelli to join him.

"I need to ask you something," he said. "I have no doubt that Commander McGregor is a first-rate physician, but should I be worried about him if it comes to a fight?"

Kelli Moore smiled. "The Doc is a complex guy for sure. But here's the thing. In Yemen last year we were outnumbered three to one, with mostly wounded, medical personnel, and a few Marines against an infantry company. McGregor was in command, and you know what told us: 'we're going to kill every fucking one of them.' And we did. In London we ambushed Belov in an alley. He stabbed the Russian in the chest with that gadget Grandfather gave us, then jammed it into his neck. If it comes to a fight, we want him on our side."

Ian nodded and said not a word.

In the main space below deck, Ian gave Kelli an M-27 and kept one for himself. He then distributed the spare magazines. "Commander," he said, "I think I have a mission for you and your new M-14."

Kim's shoulder was in no shape to hold the third M-27, but she had her SIG in a hip holster. She was visibly unhappy that her injury relegated her to watching Korshkin. She knew it was the right decision, but this would have been a chance to redeem herself for Romania.

Ian outlined his plan for the coming engagement, and it became clear that he was much more than Sir Charles's driver.

In just under ten minutes the *Sergei Andreyev* was easily visible off the starboard quarter. They showed no sign of slowing down, and it was becoming apparent they planned to ram *Puffin*. As if it wasn't already obvious, this was no research mission.

As *Andreyev* got closer, they slowed somewhat, the captain obviously concerned about minimizing damage to his own vessel. Despite the Andreyev's light steel hull and size advantage, a collision at over twenty knots involved a lot of energy.

The two vessels were less than fifty yards apart, and sailors were visible on the open stern — all of them holding AK-47 automatic rifles. Seconds before the inevitable collision, Sir Charles cut the Puffin's throttles and engaged the starboard bow and port stern thrusters. The *Puffin* spun ninety degrees and the Russian glided by.

As it did, Ian and Kelli stepped onto the stern and opened fire. Kelli emptied an entire thirty-round magazine of 5.56 mm rounds into the bridge. Ian, obviously highly skilled, began to fire three-round bursts that took down at least four of the Russians, perhaps five. McGregor meanwhile propped the bipod of the M-14 on a table and fired single armor-piercing 7.62 mm rounds at the hull just forward of the stern and above the waterline into what he hoped was the guts of Andreyev's engineering plant.

The surviving Russians did not dive for cover as they had hoped, but instead stood fast and raked the *Puffin* with more than fifty rounds from their own AK-47s. Research vessel or not, these guys meant business.

Kelli was hit by a ricochet that struck her left shoulder blade. The body armor did its job, though, and she was stunned for just a moment before putting in a fresh magazine and pouring more fire into the fleeing Russian. Mike and Ian's body armor absorbed several fragments, but they seemed otherwise unhurt. Ian added to Kelli's fire and

Mike was about to do the same when they heard someone shouting in Russian. It had to be Korshkin.

Mike raced below, expecting to see a wounded Korshkin.

But it was Jennifer Kim, lying on the deck, bright red blood pumping from her left groin area.

"What happened?" shouted Mike as he tore open his medical kit.

"Someone was aiming a rifle from amidships. She drew her pistol and got off a shot through that little window"—he pointed to the small porthole with broken glass. "Then a bullet came through the side and hit her."

Mike turned to see the bullet hole in the hull about a foot below the porthole.

He put a wad of gauze on the wound and pushed hard. He placed his thumb a few inches above the wound and pushed there was well. The flow of blood diminished. "Kelli," he yelled, "need a hand here."

Moore ran in and was stunned for a moment by the sight of Jennifer Kim, soaked with blood. McGregor, now in ER mode, said "Open the surgical kit in my pack."

She did so.

"Now show me what we have."

Moore held the surgical instruments in front of him.

"Here's what I need you to do. Open one of the scalpels with a number ten blade. When you're ready, I'm going to take the scalpel and that vascular clamp, and you're going to do just what I'm doing: put pressure on the wound and on the artery above it. I have to open her up and put the clamp on the iliac artery."

"Open me up?" cried Kim.

McGregor was startled. He thought she was unconscious.

"I'm really sorry," he said as calmly as he could. "I don't have anesthesia, but if I don't do this you'll bleed out before I can get you to a surgeon."

"I'm going lose my leg, aren't I?"

"No, your leg can go without blood for a surprisingly long time. Just take a deep breath. I'll work as fast as I can. Kelli, remove your hand from above the wound, but keep up pressure on the gauze until I can apply the clamp."

As soon as Kelli released the pressure, fresh blood began to flow through her fingers. She flinched when McGregor put the knife only inches from her fingers. "Don't worry," he said. "I'll try really hard not to cut you." Moore was not amused.

McGregor cut through Kim's cargo pants, then made a second incision through the skin and into the tissue below. Kim gave a short gasp and squeezed her eyes closed but said nothing. He cut deeper and was through the subcutaneous tissue and down to the fascia, the thick membrane that covered the muscles and surrounding structures. Kim cried out, but only for a second. McGregor knew this had to be agonizing, but he was fixated on the task at hand. He very gently cut the fascia, then picked up a small forceps and spread the fascia. They could then see the pulsating iliac artery.

McGregor had some difficulty getting around the back of the artery, but when he finally did, and closed the clamp, the flow of blood diminished, though it did not stop entirely. He packed some gauze around the clamp and put a loose dressing over both wounds.

"Jennifer, you still with us?"

Her eyes were still closed, but she was able to say, "Did it work?"

"It did. I think I have some morphine. Are you allergic?"

"I've only had it once—the last time I was shot. I don't remember any problem."

McGregor started an IV and gave her four milligrams. He had only two bags of fluid, but Kim's pulse was faster than he would like, and she was sweating—early evidence of shock. He ran the first bag wide open.

Then he turned to Kelli. "Thank you. That's a hard thing to watch. Those big amphibious ships usually have a surgical team, so if we can get there on time, they should be able to handle at least a temporary arterial repair. Could you check with your grandfather and see what our status is?"

Kelli Moore used her non-bloody hand to squeeze the hand of Jennifer Kim, and then she climbed up to the wheelhouse.

In about five minutes she returned. "Some good news, but mostly bad. Grandfather and Ian are fine. We're taking some water from a bunch of bullet holes, and the pumps are barely keeping up. Looks like the oil pump to the number one diesel was hit, so we're on one engine, which limits us to nine, or at most, ten knots. The Russian seemed to be heading away, but now it's making a broad circle. Grandfather thinks they're dealing with damage themselves and treating their wounded before making another run at us. He said there was a little smoke coming up through an open hatch on the stern, and before they turned away he could see what was probably a damage control party heading that way. Maybe you hit something important in their engineering spaces."

"Not too bad, I suppose. We need to get a report off to *Makin Island*. Maybe after a direct attack in international waters, the Navy will think about giving us some help."

CHAPTER 52

COMMANDER MICHELLE LEBEC sat beside *Gravely's* CO in the Combat Information Center. They both watched the brief battle between the *Puffin* and *Andreyev* unfold in real time courtesy of the Harris X8 Octocopter that had been modified for extra range by the Naval Research Lab. This was off-the-shelf technology that was aboard for trials during the upcoming exercise. *Gravely* had two and both were fitted with long-range, real-time video capability.

"That was a beautiful maneuver to avoid the collision," Tony Gonzalez, Gravely's skipper said. "I thought they were done for sure."

"And when three of them appeared with automatic weapons and hosed down those Russians?" added Lebec. "Who the hell are these guys? My briefing said there were a couple of reservists and a CIA analyst on board, and that the guy who owns the boat was probably an old banker and maybe his driver. Something here doesn't fit."

"They were obviously better prepared than we—and the Russians— thought. Problem is that they took quite a bit of fire themselves, and their speed is down to just under ten knots. The Russian is making a broad circle to starboard. Probably doing some damage control themselves—see the smoke coming up from that hatch in the fantail? A couple of guys in breathing masks went down with firefighting equipment a minute ago."

"And there are four dead men up on the superstructure," Lebec said. "The way they hammered the wheelhouse, the bridge crew must all be dead or wounded too. Their skipper is probably one of them, so whoever is second in command may be calling Moscow for instructions."

Gonzalez stared at the live feed. "They don't look to be breaking off. If I were them I would come up from behind and use the cover of the bow to put fire on their stern. That would give them a big advantage, since to return fire, our people will have to be out in the open."

"Captain Pauley was pretty clear he wants this vessel to get to *Makin Island*. Is there anything we can do to help, short of violating direct orders?"

"I'm open to ideas," said Gonzalez to the crew members in the CIC.

Lebec had known Gonzalez back at the academy and expected this kind of openness. Gonzalez was a big man with a broad smile who was known for getting things done—but not always in the way the brass might have preferred. It was universally believed Gonzalez would never make flag rank and would likely retire when he hit the twenty-year mark. He was just the kind of guy who had pushed the envelope a bit too far a bit too often.

The young operations specialist spoke up. "Begging your pardon, sir. I heard you describing our orders and they seemed rather carefully worded."

"I'm all ears," said Gonzalez. Lebec nodded in agreement.

"Well, Skipper, I'm thinking about not taking any action that can be identified as coming from a US vessel. Those drones are small and painted grey, so they won't be visible to satellite surveillance. They're also civilian technology, no Navy markings or DOD part numbers. So I think we're covered."

"And what can a drone do to that vessel? The skipper said. "It's not a Predator; it can't launch missiles."

"No sir, but some of us have been, you know, talking about how we could arm a drone and came up with the idea of attaching a few pounds of C4 to the camera mount, landing it on the target, then using the camera circuit to detonate it. One of the Chief Gunners Mates had EOD training. I'll bet he could make a shaped charge. We could land it on their fantail and the blast would go right down into their engineering space. It looks like they already have some damage there. Maybe we could add to it."

Gonzalez looked at Lebec. "Talk about improvising weapons on the fly. I'm game. If we don't do something quick, we're going to lose those people. Petty Officer Gibson, make this happen—and now."

The young man made two quick calls to other parts of the ship. "Chief says it will only take a few minutes to shape a charge and insert a detonator. The guys in the hanger can remove the camera from the second drone and mount the charge as soon as they get it. They'll wire the detonator to the camera circuit so when we turn it on—boom." He grinned.

"How can you fly it without the camera?" asked Lebec.

I'll use the second drone. Keep it right behind the first one to tell us where it is. I will need someone to fly it, though."

"Get whoever you need," said Gonzalez.

In just under six minutes the armed drone was aloft.

CHAPTER 53

KELLI MOORE WATCHED the *Sergei Andreyev* turn in a broad circle until, finally, it was directly astern and about a mile away. There would be a second attack, and the Russian's plan was starting to become clear. They were going to attack from astern.

They moved Kim and Korshkin as far forward as possible while McGregor tried to gather as much of the boat's furnishings as he could move to protect them from the inevitable automatic weapons fire. Ian and Kelli, meanwhile, found sniper positions and waited for the *Andreyev* to get within range. Ian now had the sniper rifle and fired an occasional shot just to suppress return fire. Sir Charles watched through binoculars and developed a plan of maneuver.

Then they waited.

CHAPTER 54

MAX PAULEY AND Courtney Klein leaned toward the monitor showing the remote feed from *Gravely's* drone. Just ahead of it was a second drone with a grey, formless lump where the camera should be.

"Captain," Klein said. "Can I have a word in private?"

The Captain nodded toward his sea cabin, and she followed him in. "What's on your mind Lieutenant?"

"I've been hearing rumors from some of the bridge crew that *Gravely* has somehow armed one of its drones and is using it to attack the Russian. Is that true?"

"Possibly," said Pauley. "Do you have a point, or are you simply curious?"

"Sir, with respect, *Gravely* is about to violate one or more orders from NavEur, and they are under your direct command. Are you comfortable with that?"

"Remind me, Lieutenant, precisely where you fit into the command structure of this vessel."

"I'm aware I'm a guest here, but I'm also a Naval officer and feel it's my duty to point out that orders are about to be violated."

"Fair enough. You have done your duty. And, what, by the way is your mission here?"

"I'm here to support CIA Officer Kim."

"And does supporting her include allowing the Russians to kill her and everyone else aboard that vessel they're on?"

The conversation was taking on an unpleasant senior-Captain-to-junior-Lieutenant character.

Unfazed, Klein stood fast. "Of course not, sir. But we have to work within the constraints of our orders."

"I'm confident Commander Gonzalez and my XO have come up with a way to deal with this situation that falls within those constraints. It's a judgement call, and it's my judgement. You may return to your state-room. I will make a log entry that you expressed your concerns."

"But, Captain, I didn't mean..."

"Dismissed."

He returned to the bridge where he wrote out a quick message and handed it to his Communications Officer, "Send the following to *Gravely*."

From: *Makin Island*
To: *Gravely*

Your intent is apparent. Execute.
Pauley

CHAPTER 55

HE ANDREYEV WAS just over two hundred yards away when the first sailor popped up at the bow and fired a burst at *Puffin*. He ducked down, and a few seconds later a second man did the same, but from a different position. Only a few rounds hit from each burst, but given time there would inevitably be damage, or injuries.

Kelli maintained a disciplined fire, hitting different parts of the bow at random, in hopes of keeping heads down. This inhibited their attackers, but not enough. Ian remained quiet, until one figure stayed up just a fraction of a second too long and was rewarded with a bullet in the neck that nearly removed his head.

After about ten minutes of this, all the windows in the Puffin's pilot house had been shattered, and Sir Charles was steering from a seated position behind an improvised bunker.

Mike appeared behind Kelli—she briefly looked back at her partner, but quickly returned her focus forward. His face was bleeding. "Piece of wood got me. Not bad," he said, "but we are getting some rounds up forward. Sooner or later Kim or Korshkin are going to get hit. I don't think either of them could survive even a minor wound."

"Doing the best we can, Doc. Ian got one, maybe wounded a second. But they're hitting us faster than we can hit them. Looks like the Navy has decided to sit this one out."

"We've been there before. I'm going to try Jennifer's cell. Maybe someone on the ship will answer."

Kelli fired another burst and Mike returned to his patients.

CHAPTER 56

APRIL 11

Sergei Andreyev

PIOTR SIDIROV WAS in the after steering room of the *Andreyev*, the bridge having been destroyed and Captain Pushkin killed. Until an hour ago, Sidirov had been the starpom, what the Americans would call the executive officer.

It was incomprehensible to him that their oceanographic research vessel had been called upon to attack this little UK flagged boat. But their orders could not have been clearer. Take any action necessary to prevent the *Puffin* from making its rendezvous with the Americans. Even after the captain had been killed along with three members of the bridge crew, plus four more crewmen manning weapons, Moscow had demanded a second attack.

Sidirov was manning the tiny auxiliary bridge himself. The four remaining crew members, including their cook, were up at the bow firing at the *Puffin*. Actually, it was now three, since one had already been killed. He had been replaced by one of the civilian technicians whose patriotism was more admirable than his marksmanship.

The Andreyev's new captain quickly scanned the horizon to see if the American destroyer they had seen on radar—before that had been destroyed—was getting any closer. Moscow had assured him that diplomatic pressure and a clever maskirovka—a favorite Russian deception

251

tactic since the days of the Czars—would prevent the American vessel from getting involved. They would be observers, nothing more.

He saw the destroyer, at least three miles away and not approaching. Perhaps Moscow had been right. Behind him, Sidirov saw two small drones approaching. So, the Americans were content to simply observe the action, and that was fine with him.

He was perplexed, however, when one of the drones flew closer and closer, and finally hovered over the fantail. It settled gently, about ten feet forward of the stern.

No!

He shouted to the sailors whose station was aft of his position, but there was no answer. The sailors who normally manned those stations were now dead.

The explosion was not as loud as he expected, more like a sharp crack. Pieces of the drone smashed into the superstructure, but caused little damage. There was a hole in the deck, about a foot in diameter. Some smoke rose through the hole, but nothing more. Perhaps they had avoided major damage.

Sidirov called for one of the technicians to come up and man the bridge while he went below to inspect the damage. One they way, he continued to hear bursts of automatic fire from the bow and the distinctive impacts of return fire against the hull.

When he arrived in the area below the explosion, he found one of the auxiliary generators—already damaged in the previous exchange of fire—was now destroyed. The case for the gearbox that controlled steering was distorted, several welds had ruptured, and hydraulic fluid oozed out. Most concerning was an oil fire, the origin of which was unclear, but smoke was rapidly filling the compartment. Apparently the fire suppression system had been damaged as well.

He made a decision.

Returning to his station, he saw the *Puffin* was now about twenty degrees to port. He quickly determined that steering had indeed been compromised. As soon as *Puffin* realized that, they could maneuver away and out of range. He found a bullhorn and called for the men on the bow to cease fire and report below for damage control. Perhaps they could at least survive.

And, unfortunately, so would the little *Puffin*.

CHAPTER 57

APRIL 11

MV *Puffin*

SIR CHARLES SAW the *Andreyev* drifting off course. There was increasing black smoke rising from the stern, though he didn't know why.

Whatever the cause, the Russian was having trouble steering, so he turned to port and quickly opened the range between the two ships. He then called down to Kelli and Ian to cease fire and to check for damage.

In a few minutes, Kelli joined him in the wheelhouse.

"Korshkin and the Doc are fine," said Kelli. "Officer Kim looks rough, but the bleeding is still pretty slow. Doc thinks she can make it to the ship, but she's close to being in shock."

"Damage?"

"Plenty of bullet holes aft. Water is beginning to accumulate in the bilge, and if we go down even a few more inches at the stern, more bullet holes will be below the waterline. There's also a hole in the starboard fuel tank that Ian is trying to find a way to plug. I think we need all hands, so I'm joining Ian and will see if the Doc can help. It's going to be close unless we can get ahead of this water."

"Go ahead, do what you can. There are tools below. I'm going to assume that destroyer has notified *Makin Island* of our position and course, so it's probably wise for us to stay off the radio and satphone for the moment." He paused and then broke into a broad smile that crinkled his eyes. "Fine work by all of you. We're going to make it, I'm sure of it. By God, a sea battle! I feel twenty years younger!"

"You were right, Grandfather. They had no idea who they were dealing with."

Kelli asked McGregor to join the damage-control party. Korshkin looked the same, but Kim was sweating profusely and in obvious pain.

"I'll be right there, said McGregor. "I still have a little morphine that I'm giving to Jennifer. I think the pain is causing her more trouble than the blood loss."

In a minute, he joined them below. Alarmed by what he saw, McGregor began foraging for repair materials.

He returned a few minutes later to find Ian and Kelli in water above their ankles despite the pumps running at full speed. "Look at these." He held a double handful of used corks from wine bottles. "Maybe we can use them as plugs."

All three began to trim the corks and then tap them into bullet holes with a mallet from the tool kit. It seemed to help, especially after Ian wedged a tabletop against them and held it tight with a mop handle.

Kelli reported their patchwork to her grandfather up in the wheelhouse. The American destroyer had called *Puffin* on the radio, informing them that they were staying with the Andreyev due to its onboard fire. "I told their skipper we're having some flooding. He said they would advise *Makin Island* to increase speed and that in a worst case he would violate orders and send a helicopter to evacuate us. That would be a tricky maneuver though, moving our patients."

"Better than having them aboard when we sink," Kelli said.

Sir Charles grinned. "We are not going to sink."

CHAPTER 58

LIEUTENANT COMMANDER ALEX Trent–Jones read and re-read the priority message from Commander, Surface Flotilla. As skipper of HMS *Mersey*, a River Class patrol vessel, he had done fisheries protection, chased smugglers and illegals away from Gibraltar, and had performed more than a few rescue missions. But he had never received orders like these.

"Security services, satellite data, and communications intercepts all suggest fugitive Maxim Korshkin, suspected in sale of stolen nuclear weapons, may be attempting to escape from island of Hoy on private vessel, MV *Puffin*. Proceed course 325 degrees, best possible speed. Intercept and board *Puffin*, currently heading 275 degrees 102 kilometers west of Hoy. Take all aboard into custody. Emphasize need for caution as individuals on this vessel are armed fugitives. Report immediately once these persons are in custody."

Erin Wilke, the First Lieutenant and his second in command, read over his shoulder.

"What do you make of it, Number One?" asked the skipper.

"I've heard about this Korshkin before," she said, "but it's odd we haven't heard anything about him being in Scotland until now. Too bad we had to give that tug a tow into Stornoway, or we would be right on top of them. Do we have anything on this *Puffin*?"

"It's a seventeen-meter cruising tug. Registry shows home port of Stornoway—we must have just missed her—and it's owned by some kind of holding company. Top speed listed as eighteen knots, which is a lot for that kind of vessel."

"We can muster twenty, maybe twenty-one, and with her current position and course we should overtake her in an hour. I'll go see if we have her on radar," added Wilke.

"And give me an update on those Americans. Last I looked there was a destroyer to the north and another northwest of us, as well as one of their big amphibious ships."

Wilke spoke to a petty officer watching the radar repeater on the bridge. "Radar no longer holds that Russian contact, Captain. No matter what their course, we should still be able to track them."

"I don't like this," said Trent–Jones, a third-generation Royal Navy officer. "We get orders to intercept a British flagged vessel, and three American warships show up far from an exercise they should be part of. And now a Russian also closing on them has just disappeared. I bloody well do not like it."

"Do you think the Americans will try to interfere with us?" asked the First Lieutenant.

"Normally I would say no, but this situation is anything but normal. The security services seem very keen about getting their hands on this fellow Korshkin, but I'm hearing the same thing about the Americans. And now Korshkin is in international waters, the Americans have arrived, and so have the Russians. We need to stay sharp, Number One. And assume nothing."

MV *Puffin*

SIR CHARLES CALLED Kelli up to the pilot house. Conning the *Puffin* was getting harder, not only because of the single engine and the ton of water in the bilge, but also because of the constant cold wind coming through the shattered windows. Fortunately, most of their instruments still functioned.

"Take a look at the radar. There's a contact approaching from the south at about twenty knots. I used the satphone to call *Makin Island* and they identified it as HMS *Mersey*, a patrol boat. About two-hundred-fifty feet in length, lightly armed. They do have rigid inflatables and probably some Royal Marines. My best estimate is that they will intercept us before we can reach *Makin Island*. Those Royal Marines will be much more formidable than the Russians. And to be honest, I don't feel like firing on my own countrymen."

"Did *Makin Island* say they would help?"

"About what you would expect, they're looking into it."

USS *Truxtun* DDG-103

COMMANDER THOMAS KRUGER did not like the British. Indeed, his entire South African family had not liked the British. A descendent of the Boer farmers who fought several wars with the empire more than a century ago, Kruger was a third-generation rancher from Wyoming, but he retained an aversion to all things British. When Captain Pauley had signaled him to rendezvous with the *Puffin* and take whatever measures necessary to protect her from British interference, he took his orders both seriously and literally.

His first step was to contact his Chief Engineer, Andy Brubeck. "I want flank speed and I mean right now."

"Flank, Captain? We're running on turbines one and two right now, and we're about to open number four to begin some static testing on those software upgrades. You signed off on it yesterday."

"Delay it. We have a mission and need every knot you can give me. How quickly can you give me three and four?"

"I can cut a few corners and have both up and running in two minutes. Flank maybe a minute or two after that.

"Do it."

With *Truxtun* at general quarters and her four GE turbines now turning out just over thirty-two knots, his orders to the crew had been unambiguous. They were closing on the *Puffin*, but more important to Kruger, the British.

HMS *Mersey*

"CAPTAIN," WILKE SAID, "one of the American destroyers, the *Truxtun*, has changed course and is closing on the *Puffin* at high speed."

"Just how high, Number One?" Trent–Jones asked.

She took a moment to respond. "Pushing thirty-two knots."

"What are those bloody Americans up to? That's close to their top speed. Any other explanation for their hurry?"

"None that I can see, Captain. Apparently they want to get involved."

"Report this development to Surface Flotilla and request instructions."

"Aye, Captain. And you should know that a Russian freighter southwest of our position has just changed course and increased speed in the direction that research ship went off our radar." Wilke then headed for the Communications room.

In three minutes, Wilke was back on the bridge, and obviously flustered. "Proceed with your mission."

"And?"

"That's their entire response."

"Bloody hell. That American is four times our size, has half again our speed, a five-inch gun, and even their secondary battery outranges us. Could they be bluffing?"

"Probably, sir, but you know Americans. They put just enough cowboys in command to make these kinds of situations unpredictable."

Trent–Jones paused to consider the tactical situation, which was very much not in his favor.

"Do we have any potential support nearby?"

"None close enough to matter, sir."

"Very well, have our Marines prepare both inflatables and let's see how it develops."

HMS *Mersey*

THINGS DEVELOPED QUICKLY. "We have the American in sight, Captain," said Wilke. "Lookout says she's got a big bow wave, so likely still at flank speed. My guess is they plan to swing around astern of *Puffin* and come up between us."

"Any chance we can board before they get into position?" asked Trent–Jones.

"None, sir."

It did not take long for Wilke's prediction to prove correct. *Truxtun* passed about a half mile outboard of *Puffin*, made a high-speed turn, and positioned herself between *Puffin* and the oncoming *Mersey*.

Mersey slowed and turned parallel with *Truxtun*. The larger ship completely obscured the smaller *Puffin*.

"Captain," said the lookout on the starboard bridge wing. "Message from the American by blinker."

"What the devil?" said Trent–Jones. "Something wrong with their radio?"

"I suspect they want to keep the message private, Captain."

Trent–Jones had long ago forgotten most of the Morse code he learned as a midshipman. "Get a CIS up here right away." Their senior Communications Specialist, once known as a signalman or radioman, appeared in less than a minute and took up her position at Mersey's signal lamp on the bridge wing.

"They're repeating the message, Captain. *Puffin*...under protection...US Navy...break off...do not attempt to board or interfere... message ends."

"Cheeky bastards. Send the following: "We have our orders."

After a minute, Truxtun's light began flashing. "Reply sir. So...do... we...message ends."

"And, Captain, they have trained out their five-inch mount. Looks like they mean business."

One of the bridge petty officers said, "Captain, we're picking up fire-control radar from the American. Not that they need it at this range."

Trent–Jones grunted an unintelligible reply.

After exchanging several more messages of escalating hostility, Trent–Jones said to his Number One, "There's no way we can actually board with the Americans where they are. And we wouldn't have a prayer if their skipper decides to take his orders a bit too literally and opens fire. No, I am not about to lose the first British warship since the Falklands." To the young woman at the signal light who had her eyes fixed on the barrel of Truxtun's five-inch gun, he said, "Send the following: 'You have violated international law, NATO agreements, and US/UK treaties. Her Majesty's Government will lodge the strongest possible protest.'" She did.

"Reply, sir," said the CIS. "Knock...yourselves...out...message ends. What does that mean, sir?"

"What it means, Petty Officer Miller, is that they're laughing at us."

The First Lieutenant stared out at the American. "The Admiralty will not be amused."

CHAPTER 59

APRIL 11

MV *Puffin*

I N HALF AN hour, the enormous bulk of *Makin Island* was visible ahead. When they made visual contact, *Makin Island* made a slow turn and was now heading away from them at about four knots. The stern door was down, there was water in the well deck, and Sir Charles could soon see a sailor extend a green flag, indicating he could enter. *Truxtun* had taken up a position two miles ahead of *Makin Island*, but only after the *Mersey* had given up and headed north on her scheduled mission. *Gravely* had been tasked with following her on radar.

The *Puffin*, now making barely six knots, approached the huge well deck. Once inside they were thrown two mooring lines that Ian and Kelli made fast.

Mike appeared and climbed a ladder to the surrounding walkway. There he met with the medical officer who was waiting to assume care for Korshkin. "We have a more urgent case to evacuate first. The CIA officer took a bullet to the left groin. I had to clamp her iliac artery. Is there an embarked surgical team?"

"You're in luck," Commander Patel said. "There are a couple of reservists from the Fourth Medical Battalion on board for the exercise. One of them is a trauma surgeon from St. Paul, and the other does vascular work someplace out West."

"Not Bill Carlyle? I've met him."

"Right," said Patel. "Seems very solid. I brought a stretcher team down for Mr. Korshkin. Let's have them take your casualty up first. You can call the surgical team with this." He handed McGregor a small radio used for communication within the huge ship.

He was able to connect with Captain Bill Carlyle in only a few minutes. He briefed him on Kim's condition and was told the Captain would evaluate her as soon as she arrived and that they would prepare an OR. He also sent a messenger to find Commander Elizabeth Knox, the vascular surgeon.

As soon as Kim was on her way up to the medical department, they went down to evaluate Maxim Korshkin. The Russian was still receiving dopamine from the IV pump, but was well into the last bag. Patel took a quick history and looked at several ECG tracings McGregor had done. Agreeing with McGregor's assessment, Patel called for another stretcher team.

"He seems stable. It's incredible that the Russians would actually attack you to keep us from getting our hands on this guy. And then the British? He obviously knows something pretty important. A couple of guys came aboard this morning—one FBI and the other, I assume, is Agency, but they aren't talking. They do seem eager as hell to talk with our patient, though."

"That's why we got him out. He's yours now."

To Korshkin, he said, "A good person almost died getting you this far. Please make it worth her while."

"I think your government will believe that I have. Thank you, young man for all your help." He turned to Patel. "Shall we go?"

Four hours later, McGregor and Moore—out of their bloody clothes, showered, and wearing borrowed utilities—were sipping coffee in the wardroom near the medical department. Both had several small dressings on cuts they received during the battles. They had already met with the skipper and briefed him on events on the *Puffin*. He told them that the fire on *Andreyev* had gotten rapidly out of control, and that they had abandoned ship. *Gravely* had offered assistance, which was declined. They were told a Russian flagged cargo ship was less than an hour away and would take on survivors. *Gravely* would remain on station until then. He also told them about the incident with the British ship.

Max Pauley had also mentioned the situation with Lieutenant Klein. They decided to forward their report to Kim's superiors without Klein's input. Kelli said she would have a chat with the young Lieutenant later, "officer to officer."

Doctors Patel and Carlyle came in. Patel reported that he had placed a temporary pacing wire and that Korshkin's heart rate was now seventy, and his blood pressure normal. Carlyle said, "You did a nice job on that artery. The wound was from a bullet fragment, probably part of the jacket. The damage to the artery was a tear—like a small divot. We were able to do a primary repair, and it looks like blood flow is enough to save her leg. Beth is getting some ultrasound measurements right now. We'll have to leave it open, though. Too dirty to close without risk of infection. She's going to need a more elegant repair once we get her to Walter Reed, so no point in closing it anyway."

"Any other damage?" McGregor asked.

"Some fragments in the muscle. Those wounds are oozing a fair amount, so I packed the area and placed a couple of drains. We decided against giving her any blood right now. Her pressure is holding up with just some fluid replacement. You didn't mention her shoulder. I took the liberty of evacuating a big hematoma forming just below her clavicle."

"Oh, right. She was hit bit a piece of flotsam as she was paddling in to the meet. You've seen the damage."

"Nothing we can't take care of once we get the arterial injury under control."

"I just got word that the president wants Korshkin back in the states ASAP." Patel said. "They're sending us by Osprey to a military airfield in Norway tomorrow morning where an Air Force C-17 equipped for medevac will take us to Andrews. We'll move him up to Walter Reed where I can place a permanent pacemaker. The Captain said he was sending a couple of his F-35s as an escort. Do you know why the British are so spun up about this?"

McGregor shrugged. "No idea."

"Commander Knox will travel with Officer Kim," Patel said. "I think for security they will take her to up to Walter Reed as well. And you two, plus the two gentlemen with you, are also on the manifest."

"They're taking two UK citizens on the aircraft?" Moore said. "I hope our British friends don't hear about that."

"I just do what I'm told."

"And I left all my uniforms back in London," she said.

That night *Makin Island* slowed briefly and flooded the well deck. The little *Puffin*, her mission complete, was pushed out, several strategic holes opened in her hull.

Sir Charles had turned the M-27s and the Russian's M-14 over to the Marines and the remaining diesel had been pumped out. He had also agreed to allow a couple of electronics technicians to pull the radar and other electronics which were now destined for one of their personal boats. He then watched as the *Puffin* slipped beneath the waves to rest in eight thousand feet of water.

The following morning, Mike and Kelli were waiting just off the flight deck while Korshkin, a heavily sedated Kim, and their new medical teams were loaded on to the Osprey. Ian and Sir Charles, escorted by two Marines, were next. One of the sailors was about to escort Mike and Kelli out when a young nurse corps lieutenant arrived and spoke to Mike. "Miss Kim told me this just before they put her under for surgery." She handed him a note that read: Tell McGregor. Lewis. Moses Lake.

"Do you know what that means?" she asked.

He did not.

CHAPTER 60

PRESIDENT BRENDAN WALLACE beamed as he greeted Alex Clarkson and Frank Branigan. Along with Karen Hiller, they all sat in the Oval Office and sipped drinks while reviewing the reports which had streamed in all day.

"Alex, how's your agent? I heard she was badly wounded in the escape from the Orkney Islands."

"She is doing very well, Mr. President. Dr. McGregor was able to control the bleeding and fortunately there were a couple of reserve surgeons on board the *Makin Island* with the right skills to repair her artery."

"Make sure she gets whatever she needs. We owe her a tremendous debt."

"I will, sir."

"And Frank, I understand we're already getting some intel from this Korshkin."

"Oh, yes, sir." For the first time in weeks, the FBI Director seemed relaxed and confident. "He has identified our terrorist as a Russian SVR agent, Alexi Ulanov. Korshkin had a memory chip with him that contained photographs and a full dossier. We have his photograph out

268

and already have one hit from a surveillance camera at the airport in Salt Lake City about six months ago. We're expecting a lot more."

Sonny Baker walked in. "Sorry, just got off the phone with the CNO."

"Okay Sonny," Wallace said, "what about that Russian survey ship? I cannot believe they would use a science vessel to attack a foreign ship on the open sea."

"They were obviously desperate to conceal the identity of their agent. As for the ship, the fire could not be controlled, and they had to abandon ship. They refused our help, but the sea was calm, and they were picked up by a Russian freighter within an hour. The *Sergei Andreyev* sank within a few minutes of being abandoned. Our destroyer reported what was probably a fuel explosion."

"So as soon as the Andreyev's skipper gets on the horn with Moscow, they'll know we sank their ship with a drone. Exactly what kind of hell are we going to catch for that?"

"They'll make noise, but it's all deniable," said the National Security Advisor. "They have no video and I'm told the drone was too small to be identified by satellite."

"Sonny's right," Alex Clarkson added. "I understand they didn't have their best imaging birds in range, and with that ship burned to the waterline they could never identify the cause. We know they took hits from our people on the *Puffin*. Our position is, that's what sank *Andreyev*."

"All right, so a small pleasure craft and a few reservists sank a Russian research vessel. Fine. How about that destroyer skipper? Did he violate orders?"

"Sounds like it to me, Mr. President." Karen Hiller had strong feelings about personnel violating orders. "Good results, sure, but like your

Navy doctor, just another officer playing fast and loose with the chain of command."

"Now wait a minute, Karen." Sonny Baker was showing his irritation with the Chief of Staff more than usual. "His orders were to take no action identifiable as originating with a US vessel. We all just agreed it wasn't. And, frankly, I'm wondering just what the hell is going on with NavEur and the CNO. They've been bucking this mission from the start."

"Probably my fault, Sonny," Wallace said. "I wanted to maintain good relations with the British and the CNO and his people have been big advocates for that joint-operations agreement. On the other hand, they probably got played by Cathcart and the Russians. I need to think about this."

"Speaking of the British," Karen Hiller said, "how about that other skipper who trained his guns on a British ship?" She was on a roll.

"Karen," said Wallace, "admittedly we did play a bit loose with maritime law, but the British were about to seize an asset we had gone to tremendous trouble to get our hands on. Not to mention they would have interfered with medical care for a critically injured CIA officer. No, tell State to stonewall their protest. This will resolve itself once they know what's really going on. Now let's move on to something more productive."

Frank Branigan, who'd had no involvement with the Russians or the British thus far, spoke up. "Mr. President, let's assume we can get our hands on Ulanov. We may want to keep him under wraps, at least at first."

"Go on," said Wallace.

"Well, sir, the Russians took a lot of chances to keep a lid on this guy's identity. We could easily rub their faces in it and create an outpouring of anti-Russian sentiment, but I'm wondering if we can't take him quietly and use him to squeeze Moscow for some concessions."

"Frank," said Alex Clarkson, "I think you're working for the wrong agency. What an opportunity for a trade. They have several of our people we desperately want back, and Ulanov may be exactly the leverage we need."

Wallace put his elbows on his knees and tented his fingers. "Good thinking, both of you. Let's keep this guy under wraps, get whatever information we can, then at the right time make some discrete inquiries."

"And the two reserve officers who pulled this off?" asked the CIA Director. "Do we want to think about some recognition for them? Sounds like they did most of the heavy lifting on this op. After all, you did select them, sir."

Before Wallace could answer, Karen Hiller stood. "Absolutely not, Mr. President. I mean they got a chest full of medals last year for violating orders. Now they leave a trail of dead Russians across the UK and we reward them again. I don't think so."

"Steady, Karen," said Wallace, smiling. "I know those two really get under your skin, but you may have a point. They did a helluva job, but they also left quite a body count in a friendly country. Sonny, just have DOD cut orders sending them home. Thank them privately, and maybe we can do something later."

Before Sonny could answer, Hiller cut in, "And Alex, they were technically working for you so be sure they understand they need to keep their fucking mouths shut." She sat back down and turned to the president. "Sorry, sir, if I overstepped."

"Candor is what I pay you for, Karen."

Alex Clarkson, said, "Don't worry, Karen. I think the top-secret part of the mission made that point. But we will give them a reminder." Hiller scowled at his sarcasm, but apparently decided to let it go.

"All right. Is there anything else?"

The FBI Director seemed reluctant.

"Out with it, Frank," Wallace said.

"Mr. President, I know this is a touchy subject, but we are holding Ambassador Crane and the London RSO incommunicado at Quantico. We really can't continue that. His family has lawyers making inquiries, and they've mentioned the media and getting several Senators involved. Have you decided how you'd like to proceed?"

"For God's sake, Frank, can't you and the Attorney General handle this? I can't be connected to any kind of deal, you know that. Cut them a deal that will lock them both up until after I'm out of office, and beyond that I don't give a damn. Just do it, and then I can release a statement denying any involvement in the deal and saying they should have been treated much more harshly."

"And the pardon for Ambassador Crane?" Branigan asked.

"I suppose I'll have to do it, won't I? Last hour of my last day in office—no sooner. I certainly hope you got plenty from those traitors."

"Actually, we did. My people and those from the Agency will be sorting things out for quite a while. Lanka had a lot of connections. For one thing, some of those connections have allowed us to put together a pretty solid case against Neville Cathcart. By the way, I heard he was heading for the continent in a small boat when his engine failed, and he was brought back by the volunteer lifeboat service. There's a rumor his engine had been sabotaged."

"We're leaking information to the British through channels," Clarkson added. "Once they figure out they were being used to protect a

Russian terrorist op on US soil, they're going to be embarrassed. We can use that to smooth over things for the Navy as well as for McGregor and Moore."

"Good, good. Tell your people I appreciate their work on this. Too bad about Oliver, but he was dirty and now he's got to pay for it. And speaking of the Navy, I think this needs to be the end for CNO. Sonny, tell him he's not getting a second term in that job. We need someone who can think outside his own wheelhouse."

"I'll take care of it, Mr. President."

"Are we done here? I have a dinner with..."

"The new Secretary of Commerce," Karen Hiller said. "And yes, sir. I think we're done."

Brendan Wallace returned to the Resolute Desk and did not look up as his guests departed.

CHAPTER 61

MIKE AND KELLI had landed hours before at Joint Base Andrews on a huge New York ANG C-17 Globemaster III that had been dispatched to Norway to retrieve them, the medical teams, and their patients. Just getting back in the country had taken hours, as they had no formal orders and were traveling with civilian passports. Mike was able to use their comm device to connect with Kim's supervisor at CIA, who apparently pushed their problem high enough to get Agency transportation dispatched and paperwork backed by enough authority to get them out the front gate. Kelli had asked about Ian and her grandfather, both of whom had been whisked away immediately after landing by a couple of anonymous suits, but she received only shrugs from their new minders.

They were first greeted by Kim's supervisor who, after retrieving the classified gear, demanded a detailed report on his officer's condition. He then debriefed them in some detail with particular attention to their encounter with the Russians on Hoy and the battle at sea. He pushed for the identity of the individual who happened to be on Hoy with a sniper rifle just when he was needed, but both doggedly refused to say.

They were served what tasted like convenience store sandwiches and truly awful coffee while they waited alone in a nondescript room.

They both assumed the door was locked so they didn't bother to find out.

After an hour, a middle-aged woman in a grey Armani suit arrived and introduced herself as Doreen, the director's assistant. She asked for more information about Jennifer Kim in a way that made them think she was genuinely concerned. She also brought copies of military orders detaching them from their embassy duties and terminating their mobilization. They were both amused that their packets contained the usual accounting information, including a blank travel claim. Doreen gave an odd look when Kelli said, "Good thing that damn corset was free. I'm guessing the Marine Corps would not cover that expense."

Doreen went on to say that the director had authorized Agency transportation for them back to Ann Arbor. They both smiled at the thought of being whisked home in an Agency jet. She then escorted them through a maze of hallways to what looked like an underground parking structure. They were met by a man in a black utility uniform. Doreen handed him a sheaf of papers.

He looked through them. "This is very unusual. I've never heard of anything like it. And on the approval line it just says, 'VOD'. What the hell does that mean?"

Doreen pursed her lips. "Verbal Order of the Director."

It was then that he looked closer at Doreen's ID badge which identified her as 'Executive Assistant to the Director.'

She added, "Yes, that Director."

Suddenly more cooperative, he asked, "And what about those weapons we confiscated? Those things are illegal in every state, you know."

"The Director said to return them." The man opened a locked room and returned with a yellow plastic case which he opened to reveal the two suppressed handguns Dieter Wolff had given them. He then picked up a phone and said, "They're cleared and ready to go. Yeah, that's right. Director's assistant is standing right in front of me."

In a minute, another man in a black uniform drove up in one of the big black SUVs used by many federal agencies. He got out, handed McGregor a clipboard and said, "Sign here."

Perplexed, Mike looked at Doreen, who laughed. "Did you think we were flying you home? You're driving, but the Director was kind enough to loan you one of our vehicles. You can leave it at the parking lot of your Reserve Center. We'll arrange to have it picked up."

She turned to the two men in black. "Would one of you gentlemen show them where they can stow those weapons where they won't be found? It really wouldn't do to have you two busted on a weapons charge while driving an Agency vehicle. Safe travels."

She turned to go, but Mike suddenly remembered the note he had received aboard the *Makin Island*. He handed it to Doreen. "Officer Kim said this to one of the Navy nurses right before surgery. She wrote it down and gave it to me. I don't know if Korshkin told it to your people or not."

"Our people are with Mr. Korshkin in Bethesda. He's had some trouble with the anesthesia they gave him for his pacemaker. It might be awhile before he can confirm this. I'll pass it along, though. "

She walked away, heels clicking on the concrete floor.

Mike and Kelli loaded their vehicle and exited CIA Headquarters into the afternoon traffic. Nine hours later, they were in Ann Arbor.

CHAPTER 62

MCGREGOR'S INFORMATION WAS passed straight to the director. Alex Clarkson, eager to deal with a piece of raw intel on his own, did a bit of digging and found the only intersection between Moses Lake and the name Lewis was a Carson Lewis who owned Lewis Mini-Storage in Moses Lake, Washington. This tidbit of information was passed to Frank Branigan, who had one of his people give Lewis a call.

Carson Lewis was not a man to talk freely with Feds, but as this might involve terrorists, he admitted that he had seen something rather suspicious recently and that yes, he would consider talking with the FBI, if they were willing to make the trip out to Moses Lake.

An entirely different line of investigation began with the small computer drive which Korshkin had turned over when he arrived aboard the *Makin Island*. Two low-res images of the suspect Korshkin identified were included. These had been disseminated to the vast federal databases and some hits, and possible hits, began to trickle into the sarin task force. An enterprising programmer had structured their database to cross reference image hits with other information already received. One place of particular interest popped up: Moses Lake, Washington. The suspect had been spotted on a security camera eight miles from Lewis Mini-Storage.

FBI Agents Olivia Foster and Carlos Ortega were halfway from Spokane to Seattle, returning from grand jury testimony, when they were diverted to Moses Lake. They were less than twenty minutes away, and it was just off I-90, so they thought they could probably wrap up the stop and still be back in Seattle for dinner.

It sounded like just another tip among the thousands already received in the sarin bomb investigation, but this one had something most others did not: reference to a CIA source.

Agents Foster and Ortega arrived at the self-storage unit where they were met by the owner, a jumpy little man in a Washington State ball cap, wearing a large revolver openly in a holster on his right hip.

Foster eyed the weapon, an old Ruger Blackhawk in what she judged to be .45 Colt, but she decided not to mention it. This was an area where starting a conversation by asking the witness to disarm would pretty much end any chance of cooperation. "So, Mr. Lewis, what do you have for the FBI?"

"I want you to know that this is a place that respects our customer's privacy. I don't just talk to the FBI for any little thing."

"We understand, Mr. Lewis," said Ortega. "You obviously saw something important."

"Well, I think I did. You remember that terrorist attack in Georgia?" Both agents nodded. "The news said there was a beat-up old RV seen nearby. I tucked that bit of information away up here." He tapped his forehead.

"And you think you saw it?" asked Foster.

"You bet I did. Yesterday afternoon, a guy pulls in driving this beat-to-shit RV. Drives it over to unit 108, pulls out an old beat-to-shit Ford Focus with Montana plates, and puts the RV into the unit. He closes the door for almost an hour, then opens it, and drives away in the Ford. So,

I'm wondering, what was he doing in that unit for an hour? Gets hotter than hell in there after a while. Well, I get curious and climb up on the roof. I opened the ventilation hatch and looked inside. There's the RV, but inside the door, there's some kind of electronic gadget. Now isn't that kind of suspicious?"

"I'd say it is, Mr. Lewis. Let's have a look." Foster thought for a moment about the business suit and heels she was wearing and said, "Carlos, I don't think I'm dressed to climb up on the roof. Would you mind checking it out?"

"Sure thing." He followed the owner up the ladder attached to the six-unit building and walked across the roof to unit 108, where Lewis pulled the cover off the vent. Ortega pulled out a Maglite and peered inside.

"There's something mounted on the inside of the door alright. Looks like some kind of camera."

Foster looked carefully at the door where she discovered the tiny hole. "I think you're right. There's a hole about a quarter inch in diameter on the right side of the door, more or less at eye-level."

"That's where this thing is mounted." Ortega and Lewis climbed down.

The two agents accompanied Lewis to the office, where they looked over the records for unit 108. Ortega called their office, and in five minutes they discovered that the unit had been rented with cash by a man dead for three years.

A call to the Seattle Special Agent in Charge got the request for a federal warrant in motion. This was followed by a flurry of calls to and from the US Attorney and the FBI chain of command.

Two hours later—warp speed by Federal standards—the warrant was issued.

CHAPTER 63

THE UZBEK WAS tired and frustrated. He had planned to be out of little Port Townsend the day after he arrived, and by now be hundreds of miles away at sea.

Knowing he would be using the boat just once, he instructed his agent to find something sturdy but inexpensive. Now, sitting in the engine room of the Bruce Roberts 44, he cursed himself for his poor judgment. He would look forward to dealing with that bastard agent sometime later.

The boat's steel hull was pitted with rust, but that was cosmetic. His agent had delivered it to Port Townsend and had disappeared without telling him that the radar wasn't functioning, the water tank leaked, and the fuel pump for the miserable little diesel was on its last legs. He could hardly have professionals work on it, not with his bosses having failed to stop that goddamned Maxim Korshkin from getting to the Americans.

Fortunately, installing a new Garmin Phantom radar was not complex. It took a day for the local marina to acquire a suitable fuel pump, but that was also not difficult to swap out, though it required three trips to get tools and gaskets he didn't have. The water tank he patched with epoxy putty. Finally, he was ready to get going.

He decided to check once more to see if the buyers from the Central American cartel had moved the RV. They were coming up from Texas, so he knew it would take a while. The GPS in the RV showed its location unchanged.

Then he looked at the download from the surveillance camera.

First, there was the old geezer who owned the storage facility standing in front of his unit with two suits whose appearance screamed "feds." Another frame showed the female agent not three feet from the hole where the wide-angle lens was mounted, looking straight at it. He skipped through a series of images with nobody in them until he arrived at the most recent, taken two minutes ago. There was a Washington State Police car, a trooper, and two local cops. The door to the unit had not been opened and the feds were absent.

The police must be guarding the unit pending arrival of a warrant. He felt a sharp pain in his gut and knew that he had very little time to act. He took out a satellite phone that had never been used and which he had been saving for this purpose. He entered a number and hit send. The phone went into the water and the Uzbek started the diesel engine. He pulled in the mooring lines and backed slowly from the slip. His Ford—wiped clean of prints—was still in the parking lot.

CHAPTER 64

THE MEETING IN the Situation Room had been put together fast. The President, Directors Clarkson and Branigan, Sonny Baker, and Karen Hiller sat at the conference table surrounded by staff.

"Mr. President," Frank Branigan said, "several hours ago two of our agents from the Seattle Field Office were in Moses Lake, Washington investigating a tip about a suspicious RV left in a storage unit. We gave this priority because a security camera less than ten miles away had shown a man with medium probability of being Alexi Ulanov. They discovered the storage unit had a surveillance device on the door and contained an old RV matching the description of one seen near the attack in Georgia. That was enough for them to get a federal warrant. Our agents were in the office of the facility's owner waiting for the warrant to be faxed while state and local police guarded the unit, when the RV exploded, destroying the vehicle, most of the other units in the same building, and killing the three police officers guarding it. Two people accessing their units in nearby buildings were killed by what was almost certainly sarin. Fortunately, there was a brisk wind that dispersed the gas into a sparsely populated area near the lake. Emergency services do report several more deaths in the area, and there will be at least a dozen more hospitalized."

"How about your people?" asked Wallace.

"Upwind and unaffected. They are coordinating decontamination right now. Once that's done, we can get forensics teams into place, but from what I hear, the explosion was powerful enough to obliterate most forensic evidence."

"So, what about Ulanov?" asked Karen Hiller.

"Nothing right now. The photographs we have are out to all law enforcement, and we're stepping up review of security camera footage we have access to. We'll find him."

Wallace wanted some good news. "At least with him on the run, these attacks should be over. And it sounds like the remaining bombs were destroyed, so hopefully nobody else will turn up with one."

"Very likely, Mr. President." Branigan said. "Alex, have your people turned up anything new?"

"Not much. We're developing some information on Ulanov. Looks like he's been involved in several deep-cover ops, and it would be nice to take him off the board. We aren't hearing anything that suggests he made it back to Mother Russia yet, so he's probably still in the wind."

"So far as dealing with the Russians," Sonny Baker said, "I'd suggest we wait until we either lay hands on this guy or know he's back home before bringing this up. Let them sweat a bit."

"Agreed," said Wallace. "Karen, we need to schedule a press conference within the hour, and I'll need opening remarks. Have them on my desk in thirty minutes." As usual, the president stood and left with no acknowledgement of those still getting out of their chairs.

CHAPTER 65

THE VOYAGE FROM Port Townsend to Seward, Alaska had been arduous. The Uzbek had avoided Canadian waters, so he had to pass west of Vancouver Island in an open ocean passage that itself had taken five days. Finally, overcome with fatigue from sailing solo, he had to seek refuge. He dropped anchor in one of the deep inlets on the west side of Moresby Island, where he slept for twenty hours straight. Fortunately, recreational boat traffic was light this time of year, and he was able to continue unobserved north to Alaska's Inside Passage. And he was well protected. His boat was registered in the name Roger Owens, an identity for which he had near perfect documentation, including a genuine Washington driver's license, employment history, and social security number. When it came to identities, nobody could match the SVR.

He stopped once at the small town of Thorne Bay on Prince of Wales Island, where he purchased a hundred gallons of diesel, refilled his water tank, and picked up some provisions. A few locals asked questions, but more out of curiosity than suspicion. For the remainder of his voyage through the Inside Passage, he conserved fuel by using sail as much as possible and he anchored at night in deserted inlets. He supplemented his provisions with the occasional salmon, and once, a small halibut.

Finally, he hugged the shoreline while transiting the Gulf of Alaska and was blessed with clear skies, except for one small storm which he rode out in a bay on Hinchinbrook Island. He arrived in the Port of Seward, where he was met by a deep-cover operative from Anchorage. The Uzbek paid for a week of dockage and left.

His contact, Pavel Bukharin, had entered the US ten years before using the passport of a real American citizen killed in a motor accident in the Philippines. On entering the states, Bukharin moved to Anchorage where he purchased a vintage Twin Otter aircraft, which he modified and used in a marginally successful charter service, mostly serving hunters, fishermen, and tourists, and in lean times, delivering light cargo to remote villages. His mission in the US was to make occasional off-the-books flights into Canada and across the Bering Straits to Siberia, carrying cargo for his real employers.

Unknown to Bukharin—or the Uzbek—the pilot had aroused the suspicion of the FBI when an Air Force F-15 had picked him up leaving Russian airspace the year before. Instead of confronting him, they decided to place him under loose surveillance. After almost six months of no apparent illegal activity, the Anchorage Field Office had downgraded him to occasional spot checks. The last had happened only a week ago.

Bukharin drove him to a private gravel airstrip owned by a fishing lodge on the nearby Kenai River. They took on fuel in the small city of Dillingham and spent the night at Bethel, a salmon fishing center in the Yukon-Kuskokwim Delta. There, as a result of one of the spot checks, the local police sent a message to the FBI in Anchorage. The message was not seen until the following morning, about an hour after the Uzbek and his pilot had taken off with a flight plan for Anchorage. They decided to dispatch a pair of agents to the small airport just north of Anchorage from which the Otter usually operated. It did not arrive.

CHAPTER 66

THE ATMOSPHERE IN the situation room was electric. "After the Otter failed to arrive in Anchorage," Branigan said, "alert messages went out to all airfields in Alaska that could supply jet fuel—fortunately the Otter's a turboprop, which limits its fueling options. A manager at Nome notified our Anchorage Field Office that it had landed the previous evening and had taken on a full load of fuel.

"Having no agents in Nome, we notified the local police to detain the aircraft, pilot, and passenger. When a police officer approached the Otter, however, the pilot shot him twice in the chest, and the aircraft immediately took off without permission."

"For God's sake, do not tell me we came this close to nailing the bastard and he slipped through our fingers." Wallace was as close to shouting as he ever got.

"We may have caught a break, sir. Sonny, fill us in."

"The USS *Nimitz* is conducting Arctic training just east of St. Lawrence Island and has one of its E-2 radar planes out keeping an eye on the Russians. The Anchorage Field Office contacted the Air Force up at Elmendorf to see if they had eyes out as far as Nome. They put them in touch with the Navy."

"And?"

"The E-2 picked up the Otter departing Nome. It's heading straight west towards Russian airspace. Give me a second, I think we can speak directly to the controller on that E-2." One of the military aides, an Air Force Captain, tapped a few keys and a Navy officer appeared on one of the screens.

"Lieutenant Commander Benton Lee, Mr. President." This was said with the soft Charleston accent familiar to Wallace.

"What's the current situation, Commander?"

"That Otter's getting pretty close to Russian airspace, sir. We did vector two F-18s in their direction, but the target will be in Russia before they can get within visual range."

"So there's nothing we can do?"

"Those F-18s do have the latest AAMRAM missiles and can easily engage the target from beyond sixty miles."

"Any chance of Russian interference?"

"They have surveillance aircraft up, so they'll know if we launch. Their only combat aircraft are a couple of SU-35s, but they're a few hundred miles west of us and in no position to cause any kind of dust-up."

Lee added, "But to destroy a civilian aircraft without visual confirmation, we would need NCA authorization."

Wallace did not look at his advisors and did not pause. "Take the shot."

"Aye, sir." Lee activated a comm link. "Arrow leader, weapons free. Repeat weapons free."

"Archer, please confirm," came a voice almost obscured by static, "are you telling us to launch on a civilian aircraft without visual ID?"

"Roger, Arrow, confirmed. I am in direct communication with the White House. I can patch the president through to your frequency."

After a second, "Ah, no, Archer. Not necessary. Target is locked."

After a few more seconds, "Two missiles away."

For almost a minute, there was silence. Then, the controller spoke. "Target destroyed, Mr. President. No question, it's a kill."

"Good work, Commander." Wallace signaled to the aide to break the connection.

"Well, that changes everything. We need to give careful thought as to how we deal with the Russians and what we tell the public. Meet back here in thirty minutes."

Wallace strode from the room, a broad smile on his face. Got the bastard.

CHAPTER 67

THE WHITE HOUSE

May 10

BRENDAN WALLACE ENTERED the Situation Room wearing a new shirt and sipping a fresh cup of coffee.

Everyone stood, but no one shared the president's good mood.

"What?" Wallace asked.

"This came in about two minutes ago," replied Sonny Baker. "It's from the Russian Embassy. It's going out to the news services in"—he looked at his watch—"three minutes."

"Go ahead and read it."

"The Ministry of Defense of the Russian Republic has announced that the individual responsible for the regrettable terrorist attacks against the American people has been identified as Lieutenant Colonel Alexi Ulanov, an army officer known to be suffering serious mental health issues following heroic service in Syria. Colonel Ulanov was seriously injured in an attack by a Predator drone that may have also caused a traumatic brain injury.

Once identified, Ulanov attempted to flee in a stolen aircraft, but was overtaken by military forces of the Russian Federation and killed. The Russian Federation expresses its shock at the behavior of this deranged individual and extends its deepest condolences to the American people.

No further information is available at this time."

"Goddamn it," Wallace said. "They must have prepared this as soon as we got our hands on Korshkin. So how do we deal with this, and how do we deal with the press?"

"The Russians probably don't know just how much we got from Korshkin. For example, that zip drive he gave us has a photograph of Ulanov in an SVR uniform. And my people have already checked the Russian's own records. No Lieutenant Colonel Ulanov has served in Syria—though they're probably backfilling this as we speak."

"So, how should we play it?" Wallace asked.

"I'd say we hit them hard with evidence showing their story is bull-shit," Alex Clarkson said, "then counter with an offer that works to our advantage."

"Such as?" Sonny asked.

"Hang on, Sonny," Wallace said. "I think I see where Alex is going with this. For starters, we already have two big wins. Ulanov is off the table and we know there won't be more sarin attacks. Second, the Russians have admitted he's one of theirs. That gets us out from under the conspiracy theories about immigrants, Arabs, militias, and drug gangs."

"Exactly," added the CIA man. "We pile on Ulanov being Russian and at the same time go back channel with the information we have and push hard for a few concessions."

"Once again, such as?" Sonny replied.

"For starters, have them start cracking down on those ransomware attacks being run by their organized crime groups. They're becoming both a drag on the economy as well as a national security hazard."

"I like it," Wallace said. "That's big enough that it's probably all we can get. But it will be worth it. Sonny, I want you to have that fucking Russian ambassador in your office in an hour. Sweat him hard. You have my OK to show him all we've got. On Ulanov at least. "

"I'm on it, Mr. President." Sonny Baker did not like deferring to the CIA, but this was a plan that could yield big benefits with very little down side.

Wallace stood, but before heading for the door, he added. "Remember that order about coming up with something that will hammer the Russians? Still applies. It may take more time and more patience, but while I'm still in office, I want to see Putin squeal." He looked at Clarkson, Baker, and Branigan each in turn.

"Got it, sir," replied Alex Clarkson.

Then Wallace left the Situation Room—Karen Hiller, as always, right behind.

EPILOGUE

MAJOR RANDEEP SINGH answered the door of his flat near the Regent's Canal in a quiet neighborhood known as Little Venice for its network of historic canals. He saw a blonde woman he recognized as Angela Wolff.

She presented him with a box, handmade from rich walnut. He opened it to find what looked at first like the vintage Browning pistol he had carried during his entire career, nestled in a blue velvet lining. On closer inspection, however, it bore the hallmarks of Dieter Wolff's work, such as a reflex sight and lightweight construction.

"Father made this himself, specially for you," Angela said. "In addition to the reflex sight, it has a locking breech, high-strength Swedish steel, and some titanium to lighten it. It will last a lifetime."

She handed him a card. On one side was printed WOLFF WAFFEN-FABRIK. On the other, in precise script, was written, "With gratitude. DW"

He looked up, but Angela Wolff was already walking away. He smiled and said to himself, "He knows."

VICTOR NOVAK, FORMERLY known as Maxim Korshkin, sat on the upper deck of the houseboat owned by the recently widowed Beverly Katz. Her unfortunate husband, Bernie, had ignored her pleas to have a stress test and had succumbed to a massive heart attack while in the arms of his mistress. Beverly's mourning was eased when she inherited Bernie's real estate empire, but she had only the most basic understanding of how to manage it.

Enter Victor Novak, who was still trying to get his hands on what was left of his own London real estate. The combination of an attractive widow and an intriguing foreigner who knew real estate seemed like karma. By this point, the American intelligence agencies had squeezed every drop of useful information from Victor and despite their desire to tuck him away in a federal prison, the man had a bullet-proof immunity agreement. And he had, in fact, been both completely cooperative and immensely helpful. Some of the agents he dealt with had started to like him, and, even worse, they were taking investment advice from him. The Department of Justice decided it was time to put him into witness protection.

Novak heard through old contacts that since their op was blown and the odious Neville Cathcart was in custody, the SVR had given much less priority to finding him. He had thus decided to strike out on his own. With Beverly's money, his knowledge, and a bit of luck, all things were possible. Besides, hurricane season was almost upon them, so tomorrow they would pack up her Escalade and head for her condo in Santa Fe. In a month she would be Mrs. Victor Novak.

IN THE WEEKS since their escape from Hoy, Mike and Kelli had seen each other only a few times. They ran together occasionally, saw each other in the ER, and one evening they met downtown for drinks. Both thought more than once about bringing up London, but neither did. Then they received orders for a brief trip to DC. They were given few details other than to pack alphas and dress blues and to take a civilian flight out of nearby Detroit Metro Airport. When they arrived at Reagan National, they were met at the gate by a Marine officer and a civilian, who were courteous, but uninformative.

Having just been involved in a CIA mission, McGregor and Moore were more amused than surprised. They were again not surprised when they arrived at a mid-scale Arlington hotel not far from the Key Bridge, and were told they had an hour to change into uniforms.

They were met in the lobby by the same pair who had collected them at the airport. McGregor had the impression they had simply been sitting there waiting for them. Their car delivered them to the nearby CIA Headquarters at Langley, not far upriver from their hotel. They were shown to what seemed like a sitting room incongruously furnished with fine antiques.

What did surprise them was the presence of Ian and Sir Charles, seated in captain's chairs and sipping coffee. Everyone shook hands and Sir Charles gave Kelli a warm embrace.

Kelli had heard little from her grandfather since they were all flown off *Makin Island*. She knew they were both technically fugitives and that the State Department was working to resolve that. For that matter she and Mike were fugitives as well, and unlike her grandfather, they had actually killed people in the UK. Oddly, they had heard nothing about that either since returning home.

"Grandfather, what have you two been up to?" she asked.

"We took the precaution of dispatching the Gulfstream to the US the day before we departed London. I have plenty of assets here, so once our CIA friends cut us loose, Ian and I traveled about, checking in on some of my properties. I've been keeping in touch with the right people, and it looks like things are finally resolved with the British authorities. I suspect the same is true for you and Michael. Perhaps the people we're seeing here can tell us."

Just then, a door opened, and they were invited to ascend a flight of stairs into a large office suite. Jennifer Kim was there—no surprise—wearing a dark blue suit and white linen shirt and looking far better than when they last saw her. McGregor knew she had required additional surgery to fully repair her artery and had a procedure on her shoulder as well. He was pleased—personally and professionally—to see her looking so well.

In addition to Kim, there was also Colonel Mark, their commanding officer, Major Randeep Singh, and CIA Director Alex Clarkson.

Clarkson stepped forward, introduced himself, and shook hands all around.

To Mike and Kelli, he said, "First of all, I want to thank you both for bringing Officer Kim back to us. Exceptional work."

"There were exactly the right people available on board the *Makin Island*," McGregor said. "Sometimes you get lucky."

Clarkson smiled. "Napoleon always said he wanted lucky generals. At any rate, your mission was a tremendous success. Korshkin has been a fountain of information and has helped us identify and neutralize the man responsible for the terrorist attacks. I'm sure you heard about the explosion out in Washington." Everyone nodded.

"The explosion was his vehicle going up with the last of the sarin. Unfortunately, he escaped. The FBI tracked him to a charter service in Anchorage. They had the guy running the charter service under surveillance. No question he's been running a deep-cover op for some time. They made it as far as Nome, but went down over the Bering Sea. You probably heard the story that the Russians discovered he'd gone rogue and took him out trying to escape."

Moore laughed. ""And that story in the *Navy Times* about two F-18s returning to the *Nimitz* each short a missile. How does that tie in?"

Clarkson chuckled. "You should be working for me, Captain. But I think the president would prefer I said no more."

"On another subject: has Mr. Korshkin provided you with anything unrelated to the terrorist attacks?" asked Singh.

"Yes, he has," replied Clarkson. "A lot of it deep background, some current, and a few bits of information that have proven vital to ongoing operations. If you're wondering whether we have shared anything with your people, the answer is, not yet. Once they clean house after the Cathcart business, we probably will."

"And speaking of housecleaning," said Sir Charles, "have you cleaned up the mess involving your ambassador and RSO?"

"Touché, Sir Charles. Yes, that's been pretty well resolved and two excellent people have replaced them. Sorry I can't share the details."

"I'll know soon enough. And what of the naval officers who helped pull us out? I understand the brass may have had some problem with them."

"Not really. The CNO just retired, as did NavEur. An Admiral Piotrowski is the new NavEur and Captain Pauley is his Chief of Staff.

The skipper of the destroyer that sank the *Andreyev* has decided to retire. I think he may find a home here at Langley. The other destroyer skipper, the one that ran interference with the Royal Navy, seems to have come out clean."

An aide ducked into the room and Clarkson asked her to step forward. She carried several boxes and folders.

"The primary reason you're here today is to participate in the awarding of the Intelligence Star to three outstanding people, CIA Officer Jennifer Kim, Captain Kelli Moore, and Lieutenant Commander Michael McGregor. Captain Moore, please step forward."

Moore stepped forward and stood at attention. The Director's gaze was momentarily drawn to the pale blue ribbon she wore above all others, the Medal of Honor. He took a folder from his aide and read:

CENTRAL INTELLIGENCE AGENCY CITATION

Captain Kelli Bridget Moore

is hereby awarded the

INTELLIGENCE STAR

In recognition of her courageous and heroic performance during a vital intelligence undertaking to rescue and exfiltrate a critical asset. Her actions were carried out under conditions of repeated hazard and great personal danger. Captain Moore's courage and resolution, devotion to her mission, and disregard for her own safety resulted in success of a vital mission and upheld the best traditions of the Nation, the Central Intelligence Agency, the Marine Corps, and the Naval Service.

Clarkson handed her the citation and an ornate box containing the medal. He repeated the process two more times for McGregor and then for Kim. In keeping with the nature of the CIA, all the citations were vague. Only those in the room really knew the details.

"Remember," he said, "only a few dozen of these have been awarded, and most of them have been posthumous."

Jennifer Kim's face became tight when he said this. She knew that without McGregor and the surgeons on *Makin Island*, she would likely have been one of those posthumous recipients and would now be represented by another anonymous star on the wall of the lobby. She looked at McGregor, who looked back and gave an almost imperceptible nod of understanding.

"The very best part of this job," the director said, "is to direct and to honor people such as yourselves. Regrettably, your mission remains classified, so there will be no mention of this in your service records, and you'll have to turn in your medals and citations when we finish. The Agency will store them, and if this is ever declassified, we will deliver them to you."

They all expected this, and they each returned their medal and citation to the aide.

Clarkson then asked Major Singh to step forward. "I want to personally thank you for the assistance you rendered during this operation. In particular, when our people were being led into an ambush by a contract assassin—a former Stasi operative."

Singh was about to object when Clarkson handed him a photograph. "This was recently brought to my attention."

It was a poor-quality photo, obviously taken from orbit, of a tall man in a turban walking out of a London alley. The time stamp identified it as having been taken about three minutes after a CCTV image had shown Ernst Grosse being yanked off the street.

"This is the only print and the original no longer exists. And don't look so surprised. We are the CIA."

Singh smiled at the Director. "I told the Commander that he was never on his own."

Next, Clarkson stepped over to Colonel Aaron Mark. "You told us not to underestimate these people. If we did, I apologize. I don't think we have anyone who could have brought this off any better."

Mark, like many military officers, was not fond of the intelligence agencies. He was gracious, nonetheless, and accepted the compliment. "And would you mind if I added something to the ceremony?"

"Go ahead," Clarkson said.

Mark withdrew an envelope from his uniform pocket.

"Captain Moore, as the Director said, the best part of command is being able to recognize and reward extraordinary people. The promotion board for Captain to Major published its results yesterday and coincidentally, I received a call from the White House authorizing me to advance you immediately."

Colonel Mark removed two gold oak leaf insignia from the envelope. "Traditionally, your commanding officer pins on one and a family member the other. Sir Charles?"

Sir Charles Moore positively beamed as he took the insignia. They removed the captain's bars from her tunic and replaced them with the oak leaves. He hugged Kelli and kissed her cheek, a small tear glistening in his eye. The Colonel shook her hand.

Director Clarkson said, "I hate to break up your promotion, Major, but I'll be needing my office."

Everyone turned to leave.

"Officer Kim, just a moment."

He waited for the rest of the group to leave his office and then said, "Jennifer, you've succeeded in a mission far more challenging than anyone expected and nearly died in the process. I'm told you should be fit for full duty in a few months. Until then I'd like you to work on something very important to me. I think you'll find it's very important to you as well." He handed her a card with the name, Otto Benninger, and an office number. "Otto has been around the Agency for quite some time. I regard him as the single best mind we have, and he's expecting you in"—he looked at his watch—"half an hour."

Kim felt gratified by her assignment, and very curious. When Clarkson glanced at the door, she sensed she was being dismissed. "Thank you director, I'll do my best."

In the parking lot, Colonel Mark excused himself. "I'm expected at Quantico. I'll see the two of you," he looked at McGregor and Moore, "in September."

Mark stopped and turned. "I don't know what it is, Doc, but you seem to be a magnet for gunfire. Remember what I told you back in Ann Arbor?" He looked from McGregor to Kelli Moore. "Both of you." Then he was gone.

The rest of the group got into a Lincoln Town Car, which Ian drove to the Four Seasons in Georgetown where, to the surprise of no one, Sir Charles had a suite.

After a lunch of crab and champagne, Sir Charles announced that he had decided to cut short his stay and to fly on to Bermuda, where Ian had a sister and Sir Charles enjoyed visiting their casino. He asked Major Singh if he would like to join them on the trip back to London.

"The Royal Marines never turn down free flights," he said.

They arranged to pick up Singh's bags at his hotel and on the way out, Sir Charles told Mike and Kelli, "The suite is paid for the next four nights. I happen to know your Colonel Mark wrote you orders for five days so why don't you take a few days of vacation? God knows, you've earned it."

Kelli looked at Mike for a moment. "Grandfather, you are a schemer. And I love you for it."

Ian whisked his and Sir Charles's luggage out of their suite, and then returned to open a large closet, which contained both of their bags. "I took a chance."

To the astonishment of her grandfather, Kelli threw her arms around Ian and said, "You are the brother I always wanted."

Embarrassed, Ian stepped into the hallway followed by Sir Charles, who said, "I have dinner reservations at seven thirty. You might as well use them. Oh, and the Gulfstream is getting an upgrade. I'll have the crew pick you up in four days and drop you in Ann Arbor on the way."

Then he was gone.

Kelli strolled into the Four Seasons Bar about seven. She found a seat and studied herself in the mirror. She liked what she saw. That afternoon she had bought an angled-hem sundress—white with splash of multicolored wildflowers. With it she wore the jade choker her grandfather had bought for her years ago from a Covent Garden antique dealer. The brilliant green matched her eyes.

While waiting for Mike, she sipped scotch—McCallan's, of course—and observed the Washington glitterati. Several times one of the well-dressed, would-be captains of the universe tried sitting down next to her, but she dismissed each with a withering glare.

She spotted Mike, fussed a moment with her hair, and took a deep breath. No more games. She ordered him a Bookers, neat, just the way he liked it.

Kelli turned in her chair to face him. She positively sizzled with energy as she gave him that electric smile that few people ever saw.

McGregor looked at her and barely had time to say, "Uh, wow," before Kelli put her hands on his shoulders, pulled him close, and kissed him—hard.

She looked into those mysterious grey eyes and said, "Evening, sailor. You and I have some unfinished business."

THE END